Irfan Virk

Irfan Virk is a writer and artist living in Leicestershire, England. You can find out more about him by visiting his website at www.irfanvirk.com.

Other books by Irfan Virk

My Mate's as 'Ard as Nails (My Obdurate Companion)
My Mate Could Talk for England (My Voluble Companion)
The BBC Micro:bit and the Moon Dust Aliens

The Fine Artist in Me

Irfan Virk

Daisy-i

The Fine Artist in Me
Published in Great Britain by Daisy-i 2021

Copyright © 2021 Irfan Virk
Cover illustration Copyright © 2021 Irfan Virk
Frontispiece photo Copyright © 2021 Irfan Virk

A CIP catalogue record for this book is available
from the British Library.

ISBN: 978-1-9163290-3-4

This is a work of fiction. With the exception of public historical
figures, names and characters are the products of the author's
imagination. Any resemblance to real individuals, living or dead, is
entirely coincidental. The opinions expressed in the text are those
of the characters and should not be confused with the author's.

Daisy-i Limited
Pera Buisness Park
Nottingham Road
Melton Mowbray
LE13 0PB

For my mother

Acknowledgements

For their encouragement, their helpful suggestions and for the loan of their keen eyes, my thanks go to Christopher Ryland, Terry Shrehane and Thomas Wills-Virk.

Chapter 0

He bought the Norton with the savings from his paper round. The motorbike was paid for with two ten-pound notes freshly squeezed from an ATM. A bargain for doing up. Or so he had let himself be persuaded to believe. He wheeled the big bike home from the other side of town with the help of his friend, Olly. It took them two hours to get the bike home. A laboured journey, but full of kudos.

There had been only one incident. It occurred as they attempted to cross a road at the head of a T-junction. In negotiating a passage between two cars, Olly had been obliged to go first. Frank had been unable to control the heavy bike single handed. Consequently, the bike's offside pedal scraped against the rear of a vintage Ford Consul. Frank had glimpsed an irate driver out of the corner of his eye, and had been prompted by fear to signal Olly to get a move on. It looked briefly as if they would escape. However, the driver scrambled out of his car and caught up with them a moment later.

He dragged them back to his car to inspect the damage to his precious restoration. Fortunately, it hadn't been as bad as the scraping had suggested, and they had continued to deny responsibility. Eventually, an exasperated driver was pressured by tooting horns to get back in his car and move on. He had driven off in a huff of smoke, cursing their youth and obvious lack of insurance. They had giggled nervously at the narrow escape and had, thereafter, taken extreme care with their heavy steed.

Back home, Frank repeated the same line about doing the bike up to his bemused father. He conveniently glossed over the fact that he was under age for riding motorbikes. After all, it was bound to take some time to do the thing up. By the time it was ready for the road, he would obviously be old enough to ride it legally.

In the meantime, he took to riding the bike down the passage alongside his house. This ran down the side of each pair of houses and then branched off, at right angles, to the left and to the right. It couldn't have been more than twenty-five metres long. It was certainly no more than a metre wide. The passage was just wide enough to avoid scraping the handle bars against the dark brickwork as the bike freewheeled down the incline towards the communal brick wall at the bottom.

Frank had lost several layers of skin before he'd stumbled on the idea of tying his father's spirit level across the handlebars to help him keep the bike on a level course. With the level lashed into place, it had required an act of faith to avoid looking head on. But once he'd made the leap, it had worked brilliantly. From then on, he never bothered looking forward. The spirit level was a much better guide for keeping the bike straight.

It was harmless enough fun and would undoubtedly have continued to give him a lot of pleasure, except for the fact that he began to try to bump-start the engine as he rolled down the incline. Given the state of the machine and the ordinary laws of thermodynamics, the engine should never have fired.

It must have been the case, therefore, that some misguided joker of a guardian angel – having tired of hearing Frank making *vrooming* noises out of the side of his mouth – must have decided to give him a little encouragement.

In the event, on a hot summer's day, with the air heavy with the smell of petrol, the big engine suddenly fired, and the bike took off like a frightened foal. An astonished Frank froze as he sighted the wall at the end of the passage speeding towards him. There was no time for him to react; time stood still for some other part of him. And then he felt himself slowly dividing from that other self as he realised the inevitability of his predicament. A moment before the impact, an ethereal part of him was airborne, and watching in horror as somewhere below him a hapless Frank smacked into the unforgiving brickwork.

– Frank, he whispered after what seemed like a lost eternity. Frank. Wake up. Wake up, Frank. And then imploringly, Please wake up, Frank. Please. Come on. It's not time to go yet. And then with anger and desperation, Wake up, you muppet!

– Who're you calling a muppet? grumbled an awakening somnambulist, as Frank heaved himself into a most peculiar focus.

Autumn

Chapter 1

He arrived in London a day early, and since he didn't know anyone, he spent the day wandering around the public art galleries, feeling rather self-conscious. Late that night, tired but also relieved to find that the day had finally ended, he found a secluded spot on the embankment overlooking Tower Bridge. He curled up in his sleeping bag under the soft light of the river's glow and dreamt fitfully of the morning and of other bright beginnings that had gone astray.

Contrary to expectations, he woke to find a lack of misgiving anywhere within himself. Thus, in a buoyant mood and with his soul in search of a clearer vision, he packed his things. It was his intention to present himself at his new college that morning as Britain's obvious answer to Pablo Picasso.

– Don't want to be late today, *Frank*, said Frank to his inner self with a sense of purpose in his voice.

– You can say that again, Frank, replied *Frank* equally enthusiastically.

– Don't want to be late today, *Frank*, said an obliging Frank.

– Oh, stop it, Frank, said *Frank* in playful mood.

It would have warmed his psychiatrist's heart to hear him like this since it was rare for him to be on such good terms with himself; it was much more common to see him in a confused humour, with his personality oscillating between two very different characters. If taken to their extremes, it would be hard to imagine two more dissimilar personalities. For whereas Frank was shy, *Frank* was a regular exhibitionist. Where Frank was hard working and studious, *Frank* was a thorough wastrel. And where Frank was thoroughly clued up about his subject, *Frank* was, visually speaking, practically illiterate. However, although *Frank* may not have known much about art, he knew his way around art schools. After all, he had spent the best part of five years in various artistic institutions. He could more than hold his own against any piss artist.

Notwithstanding their differences, they shared one thing in common – apart from their homonymic name. Namely, a passion for the female form. This was the one subject that could be guaranteed to unite them. It was the one thing that had prevented them from completely falling apart these past few years.

Frank finished packing his things and swinging his knapsack around on to his back, made his way jauntily towards the tube station.

– A word in your ear, *Frank*, said Frank casually.

– I'm all ears, Frank.

– I don't want to put a dampener on your mood, *Frank*—

– But?

– But this is the third time, *Frank*.

– It's no big deal, Frank.

– You don't think so?

– No. It'll be different this time.

– Oh?

– Yea. There's only a year left, Frank. By this time next year, you'll be able to call yourself a BA Hons (Fine Art).

– Listen, *Frank*, said Frank, while looking *Frank* straight in the eye. If you screw it for me this time, I swear I'll swing for you.

– Ah, don't be so melodramatic, Frank, said *Frank* cheerily.

– I mean it, *Frank*.

– Listen, you, said *Frank*, getting rather tetchy with Frank. I don't much care for this attitude of yours. And I resent you implying that I'm to blame for something.

– Don't act so bloody innocent, *Frank*, said Frank, almost spitting the words at him. I know you.

– And I don't know you?

– No.

– No?

– No.

– No?

– No.

Coming out of the tube station some twenty minutes later, he was immediately struck by the noise and bustle of the traffic. It reminded him of a manic set of dodgem cars he'd seen at a fairground in Skeggy the summer before last. Those cars did at least stop periodically; this tide of traffic seemed never-ending.

Frank eventually crossed, but then discovered that the approach to the college was guarded by a vicious one-way system. While he was wondering if he'd dare try his luck again, he was upstaged by an old man who slipped out of his house and began to stride across the road. He held his walking stick out high in front of him like a totemic shield. It was clearly a well-rehearsed act; it forced the traffic to come to a dead stop. Those drivers who could see what was happening, and who might normally have turned apoplectic at a minor traffic hold-up, could only sit and admire the style of the old man. It was a moment of pure theatre. Frank shook himself out of his surprise and grabbed the opportunity to scamper across in the old man's wake. Once across, he quickly passed through the college's gates.

In marked contrast to the scene outside, here was relative calm. He paused just inside the quad and quickly became quite emotional as he took in the scene that confronted him.

– Jesus, Frank, said *Frank* to himself, trembling with quiet excitement. Will you look at that? Did you ever see so much rump, Frank? And hardly a feller among them.

Without further ado, he dropped his knapsack to the floor and pulled out a small spirit level from his pocket. Like a photographer desperately trying to capture the fleeting moment, he responded to the feminine rhythm all around him. He jerked to the left, and to the right; this way and that way, hastening to align his level to catch the deflection of receding posteriors.

It was the start of a brand-new year at St Sigeberht's College, and as was customary on these occasions, the Dean of the Art School and the College Warden were taking morning coffee on the balcony overlooking the quad. Gazing at the scene below, they could see the students making their way towards the college registry:

the freshers uncertainly; the returning students with discernible urgency. There was good reason for the haste of this latter group: they knew that ahead of them lay a lengthening queue to register. That particular formality was the trigger for loan payments to be cleared into student bank accounts. Not that the college was inherently slow in processing students. It was just that the registry struggled to cope with the sheer numbers on the first day back after the summer break. Invariably, the queue of students would stretch around the college.

St Sigeberht's was one of several colleges which together made up the University of East Hamling. The college catered to about eight thousand students across a wide range of courses. Its chief strength, however, lay in teacher training, especially in initial teacher training. St Sigeberht's was also unique in the federation, in that it had attached to it an art school, and moreover, an art school with an international reputation in fine art.

The college was situated in London's East End – just off the Commercial Road. The main building was set back about fifty yards from the main road. It was fronted by a quad lined on three sides by trees. The academic staff used this space as a privileged car park.

There were two entrances to the building: a formal entrance used for official functions and by visiting pop groups (it was the quickest way of getting their kit into the main hall) and a side entrance which was guarded by a porter's lodge. A balcony was cantilevered out above this entrance. The Dean and Warden often used this balcony for their morning coffee. They were sitting there now, absorbed in watching the arrival of students after the summer holidays.

"A good crop this year, Dean," said the Warden, meaning that numbers had risen on last year's intake.

"Yes, it certainly looks that way," replied a cheerful Dean. Meaning that at least four and a half of the new Art School intake had expressed an interest in cricket – three and a half up on the previous year. The Dean recalled that this summer past had been a constant trial. Surely the labours of Hercules must have been child's play compared to finding a full eleven from the Art School. He often had to scour the neighbouring public houses to persuade some of the local talent to turn out.

This year, however, things looked decidedly better. Indeed, one student at his interview had actually expressed an interest in scoring. This was the half. Apparently, this student had a background in collecting numbers of one sort or another. He was judged ideal and had been offered a place on the spot.

The fact that his drawing had been rather weak was unimportant. The Dean's argument at the interview had been that the Art School had plenty of idiots who could draw (or at least claimed they could) but not one of them appeared capable of keeping an accurate score book. It occurred to the Dean that he ought to get this student to start on last year's averages. What was his name now?

Down in the quad, Frank was getting an eyeful – several eyefuls, in fact. No matter which way he turned, his eyes were assaulted by yet another magnificent image. It all proved too much, however, and he began to feel quite dizzy. He was about to fall when he reached out and found something to grab. Unfortunately for him, the *something* was a rather well-developed breast belonging to a Ms Zoe Trope.

Now, another person might have brushed aside such familiarity from a complete stranger. Especially one that appeared to be trying to use a spirit level as an aid to better vision. Zoe, however, instinctively true to her vocation, seized the opportunity and, having secured an interested audience by forcibly venting her lungs, launched into an impromptu performance of her *Pfaff piece* – the one in which she is said to be making love to an angst-ridden sewing machine, but which looks rather like what all in tag wrestlers do to opponents when they think the referee isn't looking.

The Dean and the Warden, having the balcony seats, were obviously best placed to comment on the merits of this spirited performance.

"Ah," said the Warden, helping himself to his third Jaffa cake, "I see Ms Trope is with us again, Dean."

The Dean was busy rummaging around for digestives in the biscuit box and sort of hummed in reply.

"Incidentally, Dean," continued the Warden, "What happened to that chap? What was his name now? He used to partner her last year."

"I believe he's still in traction at the London."

"This chap might go the same way," ventured the Warden.

The Dean had managed to locate the last digestive and could therefore give his full attention to the performance down below.

"Mmm, yes. Possibly," he said. "Zoe looks to be in excellent form." Then, by way of justification, added, "Ars longa, vita brevis." A pertinent remark in the circumstances, since Frank and Zoe were at a critical point in the performance: Frank, in the name of art, was about to be suffocated; Zoe was about to climax.

The Dean helped himself to another biscuit and was about to dunk it into his coffee, when the Warden drew his attention to the spirit level that Frank was using to prise open Zoe's thighs from around his neck.

"What do you suppose that young man has in his hand, Dean?" Then, noticing Frank's desperate efforts to free himself said, "Dear me, I hope he's not going to become violent."

The Dean peered quizzically at the duo and caught sight of Frank's spirit level. "Good Lord!" he exclaimed, dropping both coffee and biscuit into his lap. Luckily, the coffee was barely tepid and proved to be merely damp rather than dangerous.

The Dean's reaction was prompted because he had suddenly recognised Frank. Though he hadn't seen his face, it was obvious to him that the owner of that spirit level had to be Frank. There surely couldn't be two people wandering around London, checking everything and everybody with a spirit level?

A spirit level had figured prominently in the Dean's imagination during Frank's interview last Easter, and it was unquestionably the reason for Frank's appearance this morning. Frank's constant reference to the level during his interview, though obscure to the rest of the interviewing panel, had been quite obvious to the Dean. It was, of course, an aid to playing straight. And Frank's obvious commitment to its use had naturally marked him out in the Dean's mind as the most promising opening bat ever to have come the way of an improvised Art School XI.

Naturally, the Dean had brooked no opposition from the panel. Frank had been offered a place without the bother of having to open his folder and show his work. That he might never have wielded a cricket bat didn't occur to the Dean. As far as he was concerned, any student who insisted that the only way to play things was to play them straight, and who took the practical step of carrying a spirit level – to ensure that things truly were straight – simply had to be a natural opening bat.

It was the thought of losing such a heaven-sent gift, which prompted the Dean's exclamation, and similarly prompted him to rush to the edge of the balcony and start shouting and throwing biscuits at Zoe. It was a vain attempt. Proving rather conclusively that a distraught person is not the kind of companion one might willingly co-opt if biscuits have to be thrown with any accuracy. He might be admirable if a barrage were needed over a largish area, but accuracy? Unlikely. Which is why the Dean soon ran out of ammunition without interrupting Zoe's endeavours. Thus, he was becoming very distressed, when fortunately for him, the Art School XI and not least of all for Frank, Zoe let out a series of triumphant screams and then lay still, whimpering.

The Dean heaved a sigh of relief and passed out. The more knowledgeable of the spectators clapped politely; the freshers merely looked embarrassed.

Of course, it was now essential – for the sake of artistic integrity – that Ms Trope's under garments should be examined, catalogued and vacuum-sealed as quickly as possible. The diminutive Head of Art History, Miles Baker, who had taken to following Zoe around with video equipment, was on hand and took it upon himself to lead her away to the Art History department to complete the necessary formalities.

The crowd dissipated reluctantly, leaving Frank on his back in the middle of the quad. And as was usual, when he was in any kind of emotional state, he began to indulge in *Frank talk* with himself.

– Jesus, Frank! What a pair of thighs!

– That they were, *Frank*. That they were.

– Tell me now, Frank, why didn't you try to get hold of them?

– I was trying, *Frank*. Surely to God I was. If she hadn't been squirming like an eel, I would have got my level in there. But what about you, *Frank*?

– How's that then?

– Where were you when she was thrusting that rump of hers at you?

– Frank, I can only say that I was mesmerised. I think that's the right word.

– Oh, is that right? And what were you thinking of?

– Rear entry, Frank. Rear entry.

– That sounds coarse, *Frank*.

– Don't tell me it didn't cross your mind?

– No. Well, yes, but it was only a passing fancy.

– I don't know why you always try to act so innocent, Frank? I know you.

– Well, it just doesn't seem respectful.

– What's so disrespectful about it? Isn't that how our best friends do it?

– Well, that's true enough. I have to give you that, *Frank*.

– Too right, Frank.

– And it was a sight to behold. How much do you think it moved, *Frank*?

– I reckon it moved a full ninety degrees, Frank. No

question.

– Jesus!... Listen, *Frank*.

– Mm?

– We'll have to see about checking it properly next time it's passing by. A rump like that, *Frank*, especially with your close acquaintance with it, we should be able to spot it a mile—

"Excuse me," said a distant voice.

– Was that you, Frank?

– It was not.

"Are you alright?" continued the voice.

– I think somebody's talking to you, *Frank*.

– What would anybody be wanting with me? I'm just lying here minding my business.

– All the same, *Frank*. You'd better take a look.

– Why don't you go?

– Didn't I go the last time?

– Go on, Frank. Just take a quick look. You know I can't take company this early in the morning.

Frank opened one eye cautiously and saw a stunning-looking blonde peering down at him.

– Jesus, *Frank*, he sighed with a sense of wonder. That's a big girl, *Frank*. And tall with it.

– Some days, Frank, replied *Frank* matter-of-factly, only a big girl will do.

"Are you alright?" repeated the girl, in a voice that Frank thought husky.

A greater sense of propriety intruded into Frank's consciousness and, realising where he was, he heaved himself up and checked for broken bones.

"I'm a bit bruised and dusty but otherwise okay."

"Here, let me help you up," said the girl, offering Frank

a sympathetic arm. "What's that?" asked the girl, pointing to the spirit level in Frank's hand.

"Oh. Er, that's my level," said Frank, trying to sound matter of fact. He checked to see if it was still in one piece, and finding it so, breathed a surreptitious sigh of relief.

"Are you sure you're okay? You still look groggy to me. Look," said the girl, before Frank had a chance to reply, "why don't I take you to the refectory for some tea? I expect that would help."

Frank was never one to turn down the offer of tea. So, they set off for the refectory. While passing through the main entrance to the college, Frank's new-found friend, who had introduced herself as Prudence, happened momentarily to get ahead of him, and in doing so, gave him a first glimpse of her magnificent posterior: in motion. A momentary sense of déjà vu shimmered through Frank as he tripped into a new wave of *Frank talk*.

> – Jesus, *Frank!* Will you look at that? That must be the finest sight in Christendom.
> – Frank, I think you might be right, replied *Frank*, savouring the moment.

Fortunately for Frank, they were now inside the building, and he could therefore use the corridor wall to steady himself. It was fortunate the wall was there: Frank wasn't in a stable condition. Prudence, sensing his distress, came back to lend an understanding arm. She led him into the refectory and sat him down while she joined the queue.

As he took in the scene, Frank thought himself to be in heaven. All around him, the refectory was full of girls. They seemed to be everywhere, in all shapes and sizes. He drank in the scene slowly, savouring each discovered moment. There were girls with ponytails, girls with fresh faces, and girls with sparkling teeth. There were girls with slim, elegant hands, girls with slender, elegant necks and girls with their hair stretched tight in buns. Sporty girls in leotards and tennis rackets were grouped around the salad bar. Girls with musical instruments were serenading the flowers in the refectory garden. There was bustle and excitement as friends recounted what they had done over the summer and there was the anticipation of the new term. All around him fluttered a gentle blanket of femininity in which he wanted to enwrap himself forever.

Prudence came back with the tea and jerked Frank out of himself.

"Here you are," she said, placing a cup in front of him. "Do you feel any better now? Oh!" she exclaimed, noticing that Frank had gained a second spirit level. "You've got two of those things."

"Er, yes," said Frank, somewhat embarrassed. "I keep one as a spare."

"As a spare?"

"Yes, you know. In case I lose one."

"Yes, of course," said Prudence, still somewhat puzzled. "Tell me, what do you actually use them for?"

By now, Frank was feeling cornered.

"I, um, I use them in my work.... They help me see straight."

"Oh, I see!" said Prudence. It had dawned on her that she was talking to a fellow art student. "You're an art student."

"Yes, that's right."

"A fresher?"

"Well, yes and no. I'm going to be joining the third year."

Prudence gave a puzzled look.

"I've just transferred from another college."

"Oh! Anywhere interesting?"

"Well, no. That's why I transferred."

"So, what do you do?" said Prudence, changing tack.

Something inside Frank began to get nervous at this line of questioning.

    – Steady now, Frank, said *Frank*. She's only being friendly.

    – A bit too matey if you ask me, *Frank*.

    – I'm only saying.

    – Who asked you, *Frank?*

    – Suit yourself.

"I'm... a sculptor."

"Oh, really! I'm a painter. I'm in the third year here. Shake." She offered him her hand.

    – There you are, Frank. What did I tell you? A nice friendly girl, just trying to make you feel at home.

    – I'm ashamed of myself, *Frank*.

    – Think nothing of it, Frank. Just relax.

Frank shook her hand.

    – You know, Frank, said *Frank*, that's a very attractive looking young lady shaking your hand. In fact, she's got attractive looking bits sticking out all over.

    – There's no need to be coarse, *Frank*, said Frank censoriously.

    – Coarse! Who's coarse? You're just a prude, Frank.

That Prudence had shaken Frank's hand was not as innocent as it appeared. A handshake with Prudence always signalled the conception in her mind of a new piece: Frank was now a potential *portrait*.

During the second cup of tea, the conversation turned to Prudence's work.

"What sort of painting do you do?" said Frank.

"I paint underpants," said Prudence in a very matter-of-fact manner.

"Oh really?... As in Y-fronts?"

"Mmm."

"What's wrong with canvas?" he said, trying to take things in his stride.

"Men don't wear canvas underpants. I expect it's because it's rather a coarse fabric to be wearing round that part of the anatomy."

"True. But how does that relate to your paintings?"

"I paint underpants," explained Prudence, "while they're in situ."

– Jesus, Frank! What's she saying?

– Not sure, *Frank*, said a nervous Frank.

– Press her, Frank. Press her.

"Do you mean you paint underpants… while they're being worn by models?"

"No, I never paint models."

Frank wasn't sure what Prudence was implying and, given his recent encounter with Zoe, was hesitant about pressing the matter. *Frank*, however, was much more optimistic and pressed him to press on. He took a sip of tea to steady his nerves.

"Do you paint anything else?"

"No, just underpants. A small canvas I know, but there's nothing else I want to paint."

"Yes, I see what you mean. Have you been doing it long?" he said, trying to sound causal.

"Oh, ever since I was a sixth former. My first underwear painting was on my art teacher's undies. I used to have a terrible crush on him. He was Welsh, you know."

She gave his nationality as though it explained something. Frank couldn't work out quite what it explained, but he picked up the cue and nodded knowingly.

"He used to wear this dickey bow, and he had a lovely, lilting voice. Anyway, he took me into the stock cupboard one day – to show me some Japanese prints, or so he said. We didn't actually get round to looking at any prints, but I did discover this huge box of Windsor and Newton water colours, including some of the series 4. You know?"

Prudence paused to see if Frank understood the significance of what she had said. By now, Frank would have nodded to anything. He did so quickly, and Prudence continued. "They're pounds and pounds for a titchy little tube. Beautiful colours. Anyway, I had a sudden urge to paint with them and the most obvious thing to paint was his underpants."

Prudence took a sip of tea, knowing she had Frank hooked.

"So, what happened?" said Frank with a dryness in his voice, which betrayed his attempt at a measured response.

"Oh, not a lot. I was just getting into it when he shot his bolt."

"Oh," said Frank, feeling rather let down himself.

"Rather spoilt my painting. It doesn't always, you know. Sometimes it improves the work. Actually, it wasn't very good, anyway. He was wearing some of those horrible cheap briefs. Do you know the kind I mean?"

Frank nodded sympathetically. By now, he was on autopilot.

"You can get them from any market. They're about three to a pound: nasty little things. I've yet to find a pigment that will stick to them. Actually, the best things that I've come across are Marks and Sparks men's underwear. That's a lovely fabric: beautiful to paint on."

Prudence took another sip of tea.

"What happened to the art teacher?" said Frank, still trying to sound casual while concluding that, contrary to popular opinion, his lack of underwear could be a distinct handicap.

"Oh, I went off him after that," said Prudence dismissively. "He tried to get me to paint his underpants again, but after I'd seen him with his beer gut, I didn't fancy him at all. In fact, I can't see what I ever saw in him. I suppose it must have been his dickey bow and his artist's smock. Mind you, I kept the painting I did on his underpants."

"Do you keep all your paintings?"

"Oh, yes. I'm saving them up for my degree show."

"Oh? Do you have many?"

"Seven hundred and eighty-two," said Prudence, curator-like.

– Jesus, Frank! Seven hundred and eighty-two. That's more than all the hot dinners we've had between us.

"You must come up and see them sometime," said Prudence, getting up to leave.

– Frank!

– I know, *Frank*. I know. It's not every day a girl invites you up to see her collection of scalped underpants.

Chapter 2

Undergarments were also occupying the thoughts of Miles Baker over at the Art History department. Having recovered Zoe's bra and pants, Miles was now carefully sealing them in cellophane. This latest evidence of artistic endeavour was about to be added to a growing collection of Zoe's pieces. These, along with the videotapes of Zoe's performances, were by now a sizeable collection of objets d'art within the department. So much so that a second research assistant had to be engaged this term to help Miles with the growing task of writing up the collection.

The engagement of a second assistant to support Zoe's activities wasn't the only change this year. Miles had also gone to the trouble of fighting for resources to allow for the installation of a special bathroom to facilitate Zoe's post-performance needs. And of course, he had also insisted upon taking personal responsibility for ensuring that there was always an adequate supply of spare undergarments – for just such an occasion as today's performance necessitated. As he finished sealing Zoe's things, Miles reflected with some satisfaction on the day's events. Zoe's bathroom, as he liked to think of it, had been the source of some controversy during last year's budget proposals.

Today's events had totally vindicated his stance on the funding for the project. There was no way the artistic integrity of performing artists could now be challenged. Zoe's garments had been sealed within minutes of her performance. He doubted if there was an Art History department in the country with that kind of response time, and indeed, with the facilities the college now had for research into the work of such artists.

A clerical assistant had also been engaged this year solely to relieve Miles from some of the administrative demands of the department. This arrangement had been contrived to give him more time for the rather important task of following Zoe with video equipment. Again, in retrospect, that had been an excellent decision. Clearly, if the clerical assistant had not been in to check Miles's post this morning, Miles could not have been at the front gate to welcome Zoe after the summer break. Really, the whole thing had gone off terribly well. It was an auspicious beginning to the new academic year.

The Art History department had several roles to play in the college. Its primary function, however, was to provide the historical and academic context for the practical courses in the Art School. This was a difficult role to fulfil since the students were not particularly inclined towards academic study. Most of the students much preferred to spend their time making or doing something, rather than reading or writing about what other people had done.

The doing and making of things was not necessarily the doing and making that the common person might regard as useful. Nevertheless, the principle was there, and it underpinned the general attitude of many students. Certainly, most of the fine art students would have groped their way towards something like it. That is, they would have done, if only they had an inclination to articulate their thoughts on the subject.

Invariably then, this antipathy towards the Art History department led to all sorts of strategies for avoiding contact with it. Some students were discreet and avoided being confronted. They didn't attend lectures; they turned off into other corridors when they saw their *hat* (art history tutor) approaching; these students wrote the bare minimum when art history essays were required. Others were much more direct. They called the art history tutors a bunch of 'Effing parasites' and refused to have anything to do with *hats* who indulged in esoteric language and the inconsequential minutiae of 'Art History'. Not for them, the furtive sidling out the door when a *hat* approached. The students from up north were particularly inclined to this more direct attitude. Indeed, their posturing about art history had occasionally become almost a nationalist issue. Miles had spent the summer in wrestling with this prickly problem and had done a good deal of posturing himself (mental posturing, that is). And so, he was beginning this year with the firm intention of setting things to rights.

The Art History department occupied the ground and first floors of what was known officially as The New Art School Block; the old Art School building now housed the life class. Since life drawing was not mandatory, this space was a backwater.

The New Art School Block was built between the wars to a meandering design by the then Dean of the Art School. It was his way of saying that modern architectural thinking ought to be stood on its head. So where European architects thought in terms of cubes and cylinders, the so-called

Machine Ethic, he acknowledged organic influences in his design (creeping organisms in particular). Where his contemporaries made much of flat white exteriors, he was thinking in terms of chunky spiral staircases around the outside of his buildings. And where they were making much ado about functionality, he was making plain the idea that architecture should be fun. Which would probably account for his insistence that every building complex had to have a flat roof area: how else could one fly kites? The alternative was to risk an encounter with canine excrement at the local park; surely no one wanted that?

In celebration of this remarkable individual, who had almost single-handedly put St Sigeberht's on the artistic map, a bemused but grateful board of governors honoured the Dean by establishing a post in his name. Of course, in keeping with the Dean's style, the job description for the post required any new appointee to have a proven track record of unorthodox work. Unsurprisingly, this turned out to be a charter for eccentrics, and successive deans had been appointed solely upon an eccentricometer residing in the collective mindset of the governing body. What was surprising, however, was how this policy had enabled the college to establish an international reputation for its work, especially in the fine arts.

The current Dean was the fifth occupant of this particular post and was the most interesting to date. He arrived at the college with an aesthetic that reflected a preoccupation with the building industry. Developed, he claimed, during his formative student days when he enrolled on a building site over one summer holiday. His intention had been to develop enough muscle to lift his off drives over the head of deep mid-off during cricket matches – something he had found impossible to do, even with a rather short off side boundary. In the event, not only did he acquire the necessary muscle, but he also found that he had developed a deep-seated affinity with the solidity and dynamism of the construction industry.

The Construction Aesthetic, as the Dean liked to call it, informed a great deal of his physicality. It was made manifest, for example, in his insistence on wearing a yellow hard hat throughout the year. A donkey jacket with CHIEF stencilled on the back and red wellington boots were also invariant items of dress from October till the first nets in spring. He favoured red wellington boots, since these apparently made rather more *noise* than the traditional charcoal grey variety. The rationale behind this statement escaped most people, but it didn't matter. Everyone found the handles on the boots rather more intriguing than the fact the boots were red.

The hard hat, the donkey jacket, the red wellingtons, each of these hinted at the Dean's six-week spell on a building site in south-east London some thirty-odd years ago. However, nowhere was the Dean's affinity with the building industry more evident than in his choice of personal transport: an early model D JCB Excavator. He used this daily in travelling to and from the college. Since this journey took him along the Commercial Road, the main link between the City and the East, it invariably caused havoc in the morning rush hour. The Dean thought this was no bad thing since it gave the rush hour traveller a chance to reflect on the functional inappropriateness of their vehicles in the context of the city. It was his way of helping the unfortunates of this world to make a considered, perhaps even a spiritual, start to the day.

Some of the Dean's eccentricity inevitably rubbed off on the Art School staff and students. Miles, for example, had felt challenged to assert his individuality by taming something as larger than life as the Dean's JCB. Consequently, he had acquired a motorcycle that was visibly several sizes too large for him. In preference to the seven twenty-five from Brighton to Victoria, he made a point of riding up from the coast every day – a diminutive figure in black leather astride a roaring hazard. It was probably only a matter of time before Miles made a personal contribution to the road fatality statistics. This was no doubt the reason his colleagues in the department were so volubly envious of this rather daring steed of Miles's.

Miles had also opened up a second front in response to the Dean's challenge – as he saw it. It was entitled *New Movement* and was an avant-garde journal for the visual arts. This was, of course, a rather nominal function for this ad hoc publication. In practice, the journal was little more than an organ for Miles to demonstrate his editorial talents vis-à-vis Zoe's work. Each issue of the journal carried editorial articles by Miles on her latest piece/s, together, of course, with double page stills of her work. Hence, Zoe's output determined the publication of each issue.

Although *New Movement* was aimed at the more discerning Art History department, Miles would have been surprised to learn that his journal included amongst its readership some of the seedier elements of the East End. The reason for the catholic appeal of this journal lay in the stills of Zoe that appeared in each issue. Zoe with sheep, or Zoe with sewing machines, were combinations, which seemed to have a universal appeal.

The last issue, in particular, had been rather artistic. And since *New Movement* published details about itself, it had been a simple matter for the local villains to find out which room to target when they broke into the Art History department in order to borrow Miles's videos of Zoe.

The videos had been duly copied and returned the same night. The next day, Ron and his boys knew they had a gold mine on their hands. Copies of the videos were rush-produced and sent round to the regulars. They had proved to be an instant hit. By the end of that week, Zoe's artistic exploits were turning on punters all over the neighbourhood.

Chapter 3

Early next morning, Frank made a beeline for the refectory. There really wasn't anywhere else he wanted to be. Moreover, he wanted to make sure he found himself a decent seat. Frank viewed sitting in public places rather like visiting the theatre. So, it was important for him to *book* a decent seat, especially as the refectory promised to be the ideal spot to spend the next academic year.

In keeping with the ideas of a grander age, they had built the refectory on a large scale. It was both wide and long: it had to be to cater for the vast number of students that used the facilities. The refectory also had an exceptionally high ceiling. So much so, that in the interests of heating economy, the last administration had installed a false ceiling. Even so, because of the balcony area, which ran along two sides of the refectory, the ceiling remained high enough to make the chandeliers resemble distant clouds in a vast, grey sky.

Tall, gently tapering columns divided the refectory into two unequal parts, The larger part of the refectory housed the serving areas. These were located directly below the main run of the balcony.

At some stage, thin perforated screens had been used to

join alternate pairs of columns to make the other half of the refectory seem a more intimate environment. One could sit here quietly and to some extent feel like a spectator watching the main dining area. There was an altogether nicer view to contemplate if one cared to glance over at the enclosed refectory garden. This was a largish green retreat in the heart of the college and students often spilled onto it from the refectory, especially during fine weather. Sculpture students sometimes used the garden space to show their work.

The refectory itself was an exhibitionists' arena. Its central staircase, in particular, seemed to have been designed with theatricality in mind. The staircase descended from the balcony right into the middle of the refectory floor. Its positioning meant that for some it was a nerve-racking experience to come down from the balcony into the arena below. A measured, nonchalant approach was required to come down the steps with any kind of grace. Most freshers couldn't cope with it until well after the Christmas term. Some students never managed it at all and spent three years avoiding it. And yet, although it remained an exhibitionists' staircase, the overhang of this descent afforded a relatively secluded seating area where timid souls might find a quiet spot to hide.

Frank arrived just after the cleaners had left and spent half an hour trying out various tables for their strategic qualities. With the aid of his trusty spirit level, he eventually satisfied himself that a corner table near the rear entrance would provide the best vantage point. From here, he could survey the whole refectory; he could also look out of the glass panelling overlooking the refectory garden. And as he did so now, he was startled to discover a cricket pavilion with a Union Jack fixed at its apex. A moment later, he realised it wasn't in the garden: he had merely seen a reflection of it. The pavilion was in fact inside the refectory. Frank swung round and blinked in disbelief.

In one corner of the refectory stood a small wooden building raised on blocks. Half-a-dozen steps linked the structure to the refectory floor. Above it fluttered a Union Jack. On the front were the letters A.C.C. It looked for all the world like a cricket pavilion. It even had a veranda. A row of deck chairs lined the front. And now that he looked closer, he also saw a scoreboard to one side.

– *Frank*!

– I know, Frank, but don't worry about it. You're obviously seeing things.

– You think so?

– Stands to reason, Frank. It wasn't there yesterday. Was it?

– I must admit I don't remember seeing it.

– There you are then.

– Yes, but it's there now, *Frank*. Can't you see it?

– Yeah, but I reckon it's a figment of my overactive imagination.

– We can't both be imagining it, *Frank*, said Frank with a certain logic.

– Check it with the level, Frank, said *Frank* with the air of a man who knows how to deal with illogicality.

Frank pulled out first one level, then the other, and lined up the *illusion*.

– No good, *Frank*. It's still there.

– I bet it won't be there tomorrow.

– How do you mean? You reckon it's going to fly away in the night or something? Or perhaps you think its owner's going to come and take it back home tomorrow?

– There's no need to be sarcastic, Frank. All I'm saying is, it wasn't there yesterday. So maybe it won't be there tomorrow.

– I don't quite follow that. Anyway, you don't know it wasn't there yesterday.

– Don't you think I'd have seen it if it had been there? I mean, it's not as if it's inconspicuous.

– Well, I can think of one good reason you didn't spot it yesterday, *Frank*. I mean… For Christ's sake! exclaimed Frank, spotting a monkey on the roof of the pavilion. Will you look at that? There's a bloody chimp up there.

Frank held the spirit level up to the roof of the pavilion and smiled.

– Don't panic, Frank. It's not a real chimp.

– Not real? Give me that level.

Frank did a mental shift and took the level from his alter ego. He checked the figure on the roof of the pavilion. Sure enough, it was a mechanical chimp holding a large fan. It was using the fan to provide a gentle breeze for the Union Jack.

With that mystery of the chimp settled, Frank settled back to the business of the day. The unresolved rationale behind a cricket pavilion in the refectory slipped past his conscious mind as he turned his attention to other, more important matters. Just time, he reasoned, to polish the spirit level as the breakfast people began to arrive.

Since there was a hall of residence next to the college, the refectory was always busy at this time of the day. And as they poured in, Frank found himself transfixed by the femininity of the morning. It was like a gusty wind billowing into the room. Fresh eyes full of energy and lots of bouncy ponytails newly wrapped with every hair in its proper place. There seemed to be so much that needed to be said. Sounds, gestures and laughter – lots and lots of laughter – filled the refectory to overflowing. And Frank, though not an intimate part of this intimacy, was a witness to such a joyous place.

He sat entranced throughout the morning. Occasionally he got up to get a fresh cup of tea. Apart from polishing the level, there was nothing important pending. The refectory changed its clientele as different students came and went. Nevertheless, the atmosphere remained predominantly feminine, and Frank remained content.

He had a vague thought at the back of his mind that he had to see some tutor or other. But he couldn't remember when or where. Very possibly it was in the refectory. If so, it ought to be at this very table. It was obviously the best table in the refectory: it must be here. Well, in that case, he would wait. These tutors, as he knew only too well from his last college, were always late to tutorials.

Morning passed into midday. The refectory was now at its busiest. Most students ate there at lunchtime. There was something for everyone: an enormous main dining hall; a bar which served hot food and drink; and a balcony cafe which served great coffee.

As well as having traditional seating, the balcony also had a forest of stools, which allowed one to sit and overlook the main hall. As usual, at lunchtimes, it too was full to overflowing.

Amid the bustle and clatter of students eating and chatting, Frank faded in and out of a pleasant stupor. A rumbling noise in the distance woke him from his reverie. Vague at first, but then gradually getting louder and louder, till suddenly, it filled the whole refectory.

– Jesus, Frank! What's that noise?

– It sounds like an aeroplane to me, *Frank*.

– An aeroplane? In here? Don't be stupid. What would an aeroplane be doing in here?

– Flying?

– Oh, very droll, Frank.

Despite the unlikeliness of such an event, Frank realised there were other students at nearby tables with the same interpretation of this rather threatening noise.

To pinpoint the sound, several students started wandering in and out of the tables. They peered upwards expectantly, with hands held over their eyes to shield them from the ceiling lights. People on the balcony too were looking upwards. It was obviously coming from the ceiling; but what an odd thing.

The sound was coming from the east side of the refectory. But slowly, it travelled across the ceiling towards the front entrance. As it did so, five male students, dressed in cricket whites, sauntered down the steps of the cricket pavilion. One of them had a brand-new cricket ball which he was polishing absentmindedly on his trousers. Oblivious to the refectory throng, these *players* appeared to see the plane, which the rest of the students could only hear. They followed the trail of sound across the floor of the refectory. Eyes lifted heavenwards and occasionally pointing skyward to confirm the sighting to each other.

"I believe it's a Spitfire," shouted one of them to the others in obvious excitement.

"Possibly," bellowed the *bowler*, "but from this distance

it's hard to tell." And then after a pause added, "Actually, I'd be surprised if it's not a Hurricane. I believe they've got one stationed at Biggin Hill at the moment."

And so, they strolled through the refectory, seemingly unaware of the other students and the disruption they were causing.

By now, the refectory was in turmoil. Freshers were knocking into each other: the floor was getting covered in food and drink. The fine art students in the refectory had of course recognised the situation as a performance piece by The Five – as they liked to call themselves – and remained in their seats in order to *allow the piece room to breathe.*

The Five shared a passion for cricket, a passion which permeated all aspects of their work. This included adopting pseudonyms based on famous English cricketers. The Five were thus: Gilbert, Barnes, Hobbs, Hammond and Hutton.

Their latest piece, *The Interruption of Play by an Aeroplane*, like all their pieces, was making its debut in the refectory. This was natural because they had adopted the refectory as their working studio. The Dean had, of course, been most helpful in this respect. He had argued for them to be given complete artistic licence to develop their work in any way they felt appropriate.

This current piece was certainly being developed. The staff behind the counter, despite having served in the refectory for years, and having seen a good deal of odd undergraduate behaviour, were nevertheless curious about the piece. Several of them stood on chairs and leaned over the counter to get a better view of the *sky*. Not a good idea: Els' and Nel', who served beans on tos't and Welsh rabbit respectively, knocked each other off balance and demolished the filled rolls counter. The till cashier rushed over to help, but unfortunately, she slipped on a slice of tomato and went tumbling on top of the unfortunate pair.

Just as the plane and the players got to the middle of the refectory, the students were startled by a loud exasperated voice yelling, "OH–GET–ON–WITH–IT!"

This had a very unnerving effect on most people, and several students almost jumped out of their skins. One or two of the balcony students were startled to the extent they spilled drink and dropped food over the parapet. Down below, this was misinterpreted as an opportunistic attack by the balcony crowd – such things happened from time to time. As a result, several students felt obliged to retaliate by throwing food up at the balcony. This provoked a further response from the balcony, which consequently triggered off a chain reaction in the hall as students pushed back their chairs to avoid the rain of coffee and flying Danish pastry.

The refectory manager, Frost, who had been on the phone when the disturbance started, shot out of his office to investigate. However, since there were now a lot of students standing and milling around, he struggled to make any headway. But he did see enough to guess the cause of the problem. He had been haunted by similar outrages in the refectory over the past two years. Unfortunately for him, The Five enjoyed the support of the Dean. Thus, he was powerless to do anything regarding these episodes. He had complained bitterly to anyone who would listen. He had even been to the senate but had come away empty handed. Not only that, but he was he obliged to put up with a 'Bloody hut' in the middle of the refectory: one could not describe Frost as a 'cheerful bunny'.

He couldn't even consider damage limitation because they never told him in advance when they were going to stage an event. Several of his staff resigned after the last episode when The Five had rolled an imaginary pitch in the middle of the refectory: they had brought in a power roller during the lunchtime rush and had crushed most of the refectory furniture. He dreaded to think about the damage report from today's events.

Meanwhile, the exasperated voice came on again, shouting, "CAN–WE–PLEASE–GET–ON–WITH–THE–GAME?"

Students stood up to get a better look. Frank, likewise, pushed his chair back and stood up. People from the window side of the columns left their seats and came into the main hall and added to the audience.

Frost was by now in imminent danger of exploding with rage. Just as The Five got to the far end of the refectory, he broke through the cordon of students. He emerged into the central area to see the backs of the disappearing *players* as they sauntered out of the front exit. Behind them lay a scene of bemused chaos.

The freshers didn't know what to make of it all. A few of them had been present at Zoe's performance yesterday and were now very skittish. Would it be like this for the next three years?

Chapter 4

The refectory suddenly lost its charm for Frank. There was rather too much sound and movement for his liking. What with the noise and bustle, and Frost shouting obscenities and threatening to take the matter to the senate, he concluded it would be difficult to concentrate on the female form. He picked up his belongings and threaded his way to the rear exit. Given the chaos left by The Five, it seemed much the safest option.

Out in the corridor, he found himself at a loss. He had counted on spending the rest of the day in the refectory, but that was now a non-starter. However, he remembered he had to visit the registry about his grant. This seemed like an appropriate moment. Unfortunately, the registry had closed for lunch.

– Botheration's, *Frank*. What do we do now?

– Come back later, Frank: simple.

"Excuse me," said Frank, approaching the duty clerk. "What time will the registry be open again?"

"Oh, about two. But if it's about a grant, you won't be able to get an answer today: a virus hit us last week. It'll probably be next week before they've caught up with the backlog."

– Shit, *Frank*, said Frank to himself.

"Er, thanks," he said dispiritedly to the girl.

– What do we do now, *Frank?*

– Beats me. How much have you got on you?

– Bugger all, *Frank*. What do we do now?

– Didn't you ask me that a second ago, and didn't I tell you I don't know?

– Keep your shirt on, *Frank*. I was only asking.

A moment's silence reigned in Frank's mind as he pondered the consequences of a lack of funds.

– Overdraft, *Frank*, he finally admitted to himself.

– Yep, Frank. No two ways about it.

– Reckon we'll get one?

– Can only ask.

– True, *Frank*, but I don't rate our chances. Not after the last fiasco.

– No, but I don't see how else we're going to buy Marks and Sparks underwear.

He suddenly remembered Prudence and the fact that he had nothing in the way of Y-fronts.

– Oh!

– Yes, Frank. I thought that would make you straighten up.

It came hard to have to grovel to yet another bank manager but spurred on by the knowledge that he was ill-equipped to take up Prudence's invitation, Frank found himself waiting nervously outside the manager's office at his bank's local branch.

– Nothing changes. Eh, *Frank?* He mused to himself.

– Too true, Frank. Too true. Same old veneered chipboard pretending to be teak. Same old mock leather chairs. And the same old spotty cashiers wearing cheap and nasty suits. Doesn't it make you wanna puke?

– Steady, *Frank*.

Frank took out his level to comfort himself and found some solace in its familiar smooth edges. It was an old friend that never failed to help.

– You know, *Frank*, I wouldn't object to the grovelling, if at least the walls, or the wood were real.

– True, Frank. True.

– Even the walls here are only plasterboard. And check out those poxy oils. Are they the sort of paintings any self-respecting bank ought to have on its walls?

Despite his loathing for the paintings, Frank couldn't help but get up and straighten a painting with the aid of his level.

– They've obviously never heard of the Medici's, *Frank*.

– Who?

"Come in, would you, Mr Naylor," said a distant voice. Frank recognised the sound of a man who had the power of life and death over mere students.

"I've just been looking at your account, Mr Naylor," said an amiable-looking bank manager.

I've just been looking at your poxy paintings, mused Frank.

– How the bloody hell does he know about the account, Frank? We've only been in London two days.

"Your old branch emailed this report a few minutes ago," said the manager in reply to Frank's puzzled expression.

"Oh," said Frank, by way of a reply.

"Doesn't look too good, Mr Naylor."

"Er, no," replied Frank in a quiet voice.

"Well, Mr Naylor, I'm not a man to judge a new customer by his past record. I believe in starting with a clean slate. Especially as there seems to be a reference in this report to extenuating circumstances. And of course, the bank is well aware of the effect of the virus strike on St Sigeberht's registry. I'm therefore agreeable to your request for overdraft facilities, and you may draw the amount you requested."

"Oh," said Frank. "Is that it?"

"Did you want to discuss something else, Mr Naylor?"

"Um, no," was all he could say, though he then had the grace to mumble, "thank you."

"Good day then, Mr Naylor," said the manager. And then, smiling, said, "And if you have a few moments, I'd be most grateful if you would straighten the rest of the paintings with your spirit level: they do seem to move of their own accord!"

He was out in the street again before he quite realised what had happened.

   – Bloody hell, *Frank!* We're solvent again.

   – Nothing like it in the world, Frank.

   – And what a nice man, *Frank.*

   – There ought to be more like him. The world's a better place for that man being here.

   – Have to send him a card at Christmas, *Frank.*

   – He deserves it. I mean, I ask you. Have you ever met a bank manager like him?

   – I'll have to give you that, *Frank*, but then again, he's only the third I've met.

   – That's true enough, Frank. Though it feels like more. I wonder if he was an angel in disguise.

With a pocket full of cash, Frank headed off in search

of the nearest Marks and Spencer store. However, though his initial focus might have been M&S, that got pushed to the back of his mind as he explored the local high street.

The street was literally two minutes from the college. It was linked to it by a circular one-way system. The tube station bordered one end of this road; an overhead railway bridge some two hundred yards to the West, defined the other end. In the middle stood a recently renovated clock tower. This had been built by subscription to commemorate the coronation of Edward VII.

The clock tower occupied the middle of a square, which was set slightly back from the main road. A busy open-air market surrounded the tower. The sound of fruit and veg traders, shouting out apparently unbelievable prices, drew Frank into the space. He passed through these stalls to get a closer look at the clock tower.

The vigorous energy of the front stalls gave way to slower tempos as he penetrated the market. They reminded Frank of a gramophone record, rotating quickly at the edges, but moving slowly in the middle. And as if to confirm this image, he found the centre of the market to be full of very sedate looking traders. They barely blinked an eyelid as he passed. He tried to explain his gramophone imagery to *Frank*, but *Frank* had his own interpretation of the contrast between the traders on the edge of the market and these in the middle.

– The way I see it, Frank, he said expansively, is that it's a bit like the sea. You know?
– Frank shook his head.
– Yea. On the surface of the water, you've got this tremendous energy. While at the bottom, the water hardly moves. And near the surface you get this

tremendous battle going on for survival, with fish eating fish.

– Fish eating fish?

– Yea. Bit like dog eating dog. Anyway, at the bottom, you find these funny creatures that hardly move at all. They find a hole and they crawl into it and wait for the odd bit of food to float by. And that's how they get by. Their entire universe is about twenty square centimetres. Bit depressing, really.

Frank looked around him at the bits and bobs on offer. It was mostly second-hand bric-a-brac, and not very good bric-a-brac at that. There seemed to be a preponderance of old hair dryers juxtaposed with rusty single-bar fires; fading photographs in ornate frames offset against rusty tools that must once have been possessed by proud owners, and pots and pegs and pails and nearly new shoes. And amidst all the clutter, he noticed inhabitants with mollusc-like tendencies.

He came out of the market feeling somewhat depressed. However, he soon brightened up when he chanced across a side road which turned out to contain two real gems. The first of these was a library, which featured a spiral ramp for wheel chair users. Frank spent a happy ten minutes checking out its inclination with the aid of his trusty spirit level. He would quite happily have spent longer, but for the fact he was drawing attention to himself.

The second find of the road – a real bonus for Frank – was the discovery of a swimming pool. This building stood on its own. It was faced in shiny, green tiles (now faded with time) and was guarded by fatigued, ornate railings. Proud looking arches in yellow brickwork framed the double entrances: one for each of the sexes.

Frank was a keen swimmer and so paused momentarily to take in the facade. He now went in and badgered the receptionist for her last remaining photocopy of the opening times.

"No, no. I can't give you this. It's my last copy. I won't be able to make any more if I give you this."

"Well, can't you make some more copies?"

"I can't leave my desk."

"Well, where's your photocopier? I'll go and make some, shall I?"

"We don't actually have a photocopier."

"Oh?"

"We usually get them done at a shop round the corner."

"Well, I can do that for you."

"I'm not sure."

"Please," he said in his most pathetic manner.

"Well…, all right then. But be sure to come straight back."

"Right. Where's the shop?"

"It's just round the corner. You can't miss it. It's right next to Marks and Sparks."

"Marks and Sparks?" An urgency had suddenly surfaced in Frank's consciousness. He thanked the cashier for her trouble and shot out of the baths.

*

Emerging out of M&S, Frank reflected on the smart uniforms of the female assistants; quite unlike the tacky-looking overalls to be found on female assistants in other big-name stores. Musing thus on females and uniforms, he wandered down the high street in a blissful state. Since he was unfamiliar with the area, and uncertain about what to do next – especially with a carrier bag full of assorted underwear – he stopped for a moment to get his bearings. As usual, his level provided the means he used to locate himself.

It wasn't so much a question of locating himself in relation to his immediate surroundings, but rather, it was a ritual act of reassuring himself that he was still linked to the wider world of earth and sky. It was an impulse born of an innate recognition that he was a part of the earth and an infinite blue sky. However, since there wasn't a great deal of nature in East London, Frank elected to address the wide blue yonder. And to help him make a better connection, he climbed on top of a nearby bench. He held his spirit level up to the sky and attempted to locate himself in the wider scheme of things.

Of course, a ritual act is perhaps not the sort of thing to attempt in the middle of a busy London high street. One tends to lay oneself open to the prejudices of all sorts of cranks. In Frank's case, it was the culturally constrained eyes of the local constabulary, which happened to focus on his performance. A few minutes later, Frank looked down to see Detective Inspector Fogg of the local police station looking quizzically up at him.

"Might I ask what you might be doing, sir?" asked DI Fogg in his most polite and formal manner.

Frank, taken by surprise, answered in his most innocent and logical manner. "I was thinking what a fantastic place the sky is. And what a pity there's no grass to be seen anywhere in the neighbourhood. There's lots of grass where I come from.… I'll have to bring some more with me next time I go home."

This was obviously a perfectly simple eulogy by someone missing the countryside. Fogg however, missed the point completely and found a simpler solution. Namely, that Frank was stoned out of his mind and was no doubt referring to the weed itself.

"Grass?" said Fogg. He'd already had his suspicions about Frank, on account of him staring up at the sky and waving a spirit level for no discernible reason.

Five minutes later, Frank found himself in the interview room down at the local police station. Of course, Fogg found nothing in the way of weed on Frank, but he did find seventy-seven pairs of assorted Marks and Spencer underpants: size medium.

The discovery of so many underpants brought momentary relief to Fogg's mind. He reasoned that if he couldn't do Frank for possession of illegal substances, he would damn well do him for shoplifting. Especially as Frank seemed reluctant, very reluctant indeed, to explain why he was carrying all these underpants. The number seventy-seven too seemed significant: probably some sort of lucky number, which might protect a superstitious shoplifter from being caught.

Well, not this time, matey, thought Fogg.

Fogg was right about luck being involved somewhere in this affair, but he was completely off the mark regarding Frank's motives. Frank had originally intended buying seventy-six pairs. The number seventy-six was significant because he had anticipated blowing rather a lot of trombones in the near future round at Prudence's. He'd added the extra one just for luck. Of course, that wasn't an explanation he could offer to Fogg to account for the large number of underpants which were now spread across the table in the interview room.

Unfortunately for Frank, Fogg then found a cellophane

bag of grass clippings inside the lining of Frank's jacket.

"Bingo!" exclaimed a triumphant Fogg.

The grass clippings were actually Frank's way of carrying with him the scent of his home, and he often used it in the same sort of way that he used his level. He had missed them the last couple of days and couldn't work out where they'd gone. Fogg of course didn't see it that way and refused to listen to any sort of explanation. When Frank requested the bag, just so that he might take a quick whiff, Fogg was certain he'd got his man. The prospect of doing without the scent of home proved too much for Frank. He tried to take the bag from the table where Fogg had placed it. Not a good idea in the circumstances and he found himself being restrained by the assisting constable while Fogg read him his rights before he was marched down to the cells.

*

"Sarge, that prisoner we booked in day before yesterday," said a worried looking constable.

"What about him?"

"Well, he still won't eat anything. Says he wants an Indian."

"He wants what?"

"A take-away, sarge. He wants an Indian take-away."

"What does he think this is?" snorted the sergeant. "A bloody hotel?"

"I tell you something else, sarge," continued the constable, "he hasn't been since he came in."

"Been? What do you mean, been? Of course, he's not been anywhere. He's locked up, ain't he? Where the bloody 'ell's he meant to have been?"

"No, sarge. I mean he hasn't been to the bog. Not since

he came in here."

"What? Not even for a leak?"

"Oh, he's been for his leaks, all right. He's just not been to the bog. He just keeps saying that he wants an Indian. Says it's something to do with his religion to eat only Indian food. Sounds pretty desperate in all. Oh, and that's not all, sarge. He wants his spirit levels as well."

"His spirit levels! What on earth does he want them for?"

"I don't know, sarge," replied the constable. And then added jokingly, "Maybe he wants to check the level of the cell."

"Well, make bloody sure he doesn't get 'em."

"What about the take-away, sarge?"

The sergeant thought hard for a moment, but only for a moment. His inclination was to say no, but there'd been that incident last year when a Sikh prisoner had refused to eat the regular food. He wouldn't repeat that mistake. "Yes, alright," he said curtly. "See that he gets what he wants."

Forty minutes later, Frank was tucking into the tastiest curry he'd eaten in a long time. As he hadn't eaten for two days, he'd over loaded his order: prawn curry, aloo gohbi, dhal, bhindi, rice of course, a nan and several onion bajhis. He'd actually been able to order what he wanted since several members of the station used the local Indian take-aways and there were plenty of menus lying around the station.

Frank was a connoisseur of Indian food. Not surprising really, since he ate curry every day. That the London's East End had more Indian take-aways per square mile than anywhere else in the country had been the primary reason for Frank choosing to come to St Sigeberht's. He'd obviously made the right decision.

After the feast came the reckoning. Because he hadn't eaten for two days, it meant that there hadn't been much pressure in Frank's bowels, and he hadn't felt the urge to go. However, there was plenty of pressure now: urgent pressure.

He had to put to himself the question – what does a man in a police cell do with a lot of digested curry demanding an early exit and no convenience to hand? The only viable solution, if he doesn't want to upset his hosts, he reasoned, is to be discreet. Fortunately for Frank, there was a means to hand: the empty cartons of aluminium foil which till recently had contained the most delicious curry he'd eaten for some time. Somehow it seemed terribly appropriate. The lids and rubber bands, which had been used to secure his meal, now secured his motion. Just in time, too. No sooner had he finished than DI Fogg reappeared.

This, however, was a chastened DI. The lab had confirmed the vegetation in Frank's plastic bag was indeed common or garden grass. Frank's story about the underpants too had checked out at Marks and Spencer's. Consequently, Fogg had been given a dressing down by his superior. A resentful Fogg concluded he'd been well and truly stitched up.

"Right," said Fogg, throwing open the cell door. "On your feet and let's have you out, sharpish."

"What's happening?" said Frank, taken somewhat by surprise.

"You're free to go," said Fogg, gruffly.

Frank was in a contemplative mood after his prolonged motion, and this took a moment to sink in.

"Oh, right." Then, realising that Fogg meant he could

actually leave, he hurriedly scooped up the cartons and made for the door.

"Just a minute," said Fogg, his eyes narrowing. "What's in those cartons?"

"Er, nothing," said Frank, though he couldn't help looking anxiously at the cartons. A fatal look, as far as Fogg's suspicious nature was concerned. He demanded that Frank hand them over. Frank declined, pointing out that they weren't the sort of things that Fogg would be interested in. Really, they weren't. That clinched it. Fogg attempted to take the cartons by force.

"Hand 'em over," he demanded, taking one end of a greasy carton.

"I tell you there's nothing in there you want," pleaded Frank, desperately holding on to the other greasy end.

"Hold him," yelled Fogg at the assisting constable. As the hapless constable joined in the struggle, the rubber band holding the lid of one of the cartons broke. Inevitably, the contents of Frank's recent motion flew out of the carton and onto Fogg's startled face.

"Jesus! Oh my God," gurgled Fogg. "It's shit! Fucking hell, I'm covered in shit!!!"

– Shit, *Frank*, yelled Frank to himself. Let's get out of here.

– Too right, Frank. This is definitely not a place to be.

He bolted for the door and ran down the corridor, clutching his remaining cartons. A pounding heart and Fogg's screaming obscenities carried him up the stairs and out of the cell area. He was canny enough to slow down once he'd reached the outer part of the police station. Even so, he almost panicked into a gallop again when the duty sergeant called out to him as he tried to walk out the front door.

"Oh, Mr Naylor," said the sergeant as he was rushing past the booking-in desk. "Will you sign for your things?"

"What? Oh yes," said Frank, spotting his beloved levels.

*

As dusk fell, Frank strode out of his flat. Freshly showered and shaved, and with a clean pair of underpants on his talcumed bottom and waving his level to direct the sound of some interior melody, he strode down the street, confident of being able to pass muster in any hospital ward should the need arise. Through the busy back streets of this misbegotten little borough, cheerily on his way, to a rendezvous with fate, he went, carrying his carrier bag of goodies, for Prudence to admire. Admire what? The quality of his attire, of course. He whistled a jaunty ditty, making the notes spin like smoke rings through his lips. He considered doing a little jig to entertain the rush hour crawl, but upon reflection thought it prudent to reserve his energies, settling instead, for some unnecessary morale-boosting *Frank talk*.

– Yo, ho, ho, *Frank*, he said to himself, twirling his level where another man might have twirled his moustache.

– I couldn't agree with you more, Frank.

– Did this girl say she liked white cotton to paint on, or did she not, *Frank*?

– That's what the girl said, Frank.

– And have we got some cotton, *Frank*, or have we not?

– Just the odd one or two, Frank.

– Oh yes, we have some cottonannas, we have some cottonannas today.... You don't think we might be presumptuous, *Frank?* asked Frank in a moment of doubt.

– How do you mean, Frank?

– Well arriving like this with a carrier bag full of underpants.

– You know the trouble with you, Frank?

– Frank shook his head. Tell me about it, *Frank.*

– You're a drip, Frank. A drip. That's all there is to it. A bleeding drip. And I don't want to hear any more of your drip, drip doubts. You're dripping your life away, Frank. Just once in a while Frank, why don't you just turn it on full? Eh? Time to stop the dripping and flow freely.

– Well, I don't mind flowing freely, *Frank,* said Frank in a rather hurt tone of voice. What I'm saying is there's a limit. I mean a man can only do so much. Seventy-seven's perhaps beyond even your limit.

– Yeah, but don't forget, Frank, said *Frank* winking to himself, There's two of us! Anyway, he continued in a more rational vein. Who said we have to use all seventy-seven tonight? It'll just give Prudence a choice of fabric to work on.

– Hmm, said Frank thoughtfully.

– Don't worry about it, Frank. Anyway, too late now. Here's the house. Check the level.

Frank went into automatic mode and pulled a level out of his pocket. He sighted a large Edwardian house of umpteen rooms, raised and with a short path leading to the steps. Some loud rock music was skipping out of an upstairs window. While from somewhere indefinable, came the almost identifiable sounds of someone's fifth symphony. A summer of weedy neglect held the gate open for him as he skirted the bicycles chained to the railings and climbed up to the front door.

"Hello," said a vivacious looking creature as she jerked the doorknocker away from his hand. He recognised her from the refectory. "I saw you coming up the path," she explained. "I expect you're here to see Prudence." Her ponytail bobbed as she closed the door behind him.

"Er, yes."

"Straight up the stairs to the top. You can't miss it."

She disappeared into what he took to be the lounge. He recognised most of the faces in there and thought he detected something conspiratorial in their manner.

– Do you think they know something we don't, *Frank*?

– Like what?

– I don't know. They just look smug to me. You know what I mean?

– Yeah. Now that you mention it. The word smug does comes to mind.

– That's just what I was thinking, *Frank*, smug.

However, the level in his hand reassured him and eased his concerns. He spiralled his way up the well-trodden steps to the attic room. There were distinct signs of the presence of mice, but this was no time to be squeamish. He carried on regardless and found, at the top of the house, a white-painted door, with 'Prudence' writ large in bright red letters.

He huddled outside the door, but instead of knocking, found himself listening intently to the murmurs emerging from within. And as he listened, he became aware that he was no longer listening with his ears but with his stomach. Kneeling on the carrier bag of goodies, he peeped through the keyhole and espied the familiar figure of the Dean of the Art School: naked except for some long johns.

The Dean stood on a floor-mounted plinth with his hands secured behind his back. Frank was surprised to see he was also gagged. Obviously, Prudence had no intention of letting her subjects dictate the artistic course of events. Not that it seemed to be necessary, The Dean's eyes were closed; he appeared to be undergoing a transformative experience. Prudence, dressed in a paint splattered artist's smock and with a palette of blues and greens, moved the plinth rhythmically with her foot while she dragged and flicked a set of brushes across the lumpy parts of his anatomy. The Dean was doing his best to follow the force of the brush strokes, but Prudence was obviously intent on leading him a merry dance. Here was a genuine artist at work. Her brush strokes were now thoughtful and varied, whereas a moment ago they had been rhythmic and consistent. Frank found himself glazed and glued to the keyhole until interrupted by *Frank*.

– What's happening, Frank?

– Hard to say, *Frank*, said Frank rather hoarsely.

– Move over and let me have a butchers.

He shifted over mentally, and *Frank* sidled in to take a peek.

– Well now, Frank, he said to himself. That does look naughty.

– What's happening now, *Frank?* asked Frank, anxious that he was missing something.

– Well, Frank, let's just say this is no time to be paying a visit. I bet that's what those girls down stairs were so smug about.

– You think they knew, *Frank?*

– Bound to.

Frank remembered the fact that Prudence had mentioned that she'd painted almost eight hundred underpants.

– Oh!

– Exactly, Frank.

– A bit much, *Frank*.

– True, Frank, he said to himself reluctantly. Anyway, she looks to be tied up. Or rather he does.

– We could come back.

– Wouldn't be the same, Frank.

– True.

He sneaked down stairs and tried to go out the back door so as not to run the gauntlet of the lounge. But it was not to be his night. He trod on one of the umpteen residential cats just as he got to the bottom of the stairs.

"Oh, wasn't she in, Frank?" said an innocent voice from the lounge as he clattered down the last few steps.

"Er, no," was all he could say as he bolted past the giggling room and into the cooling breeze.

Chapter 5

The next day found Frank back in the refectory. It was midmorning when he arrived, and the refectory was therefore relatively quiet. He got his tea and wandered over to the clubhouse (while musing on the possibility of contriving another rendezvous with Prudence). Inconceivable now to imagine he'd overlooked a cricket pavilion inside the refectory.

Looking closely at its construction revealed it to be a work of art. Beautifully constructed from fine woods, it had been built with loving care. It was clearly meant to be a permanent structure.

Despite being in a very public space, the pavilion provided the occupants with relative privacy. That was because it was raised off the ground. The windows allowed the occupants to gaze out at the refectory floor; but no one in the refectory could easily see inside because the windows were so high.

Frank took all this in as he climbed the steps to the porch. He saw, just inside the doorway, someone without trousers ironing his cricket whites. Behind him, on deck chairs, sat the other cricketers he had seen a few days ago. Now, as then, they were dressed in whites.

– What's going on, *Frank?* How come there's a cricket pavilion in the middle of the refectory? And why are these students sitting around dressed in cricket whites?

– Well, yes, I see what you mean, Frank.

– The cricket season's finished, hasn't it?

– It is an art school, Frank. You've got to make some allowances.

"Um," said Frank, announcing himself.

"Hello," replied the trouser-less person, looking up from his ironing. "Come in. It's over there." He pointed with the iron towards the back of the pavilion. Then, turning to the others in the room, he said, in a very firm voice, "Could you straighten your bat please, batsman... Well... Yes, it's there or thereabouts." And then, after a pause, asked, "How did that sound?"

"Better," said a cricketer. "But there wasn't enough of a pause there, Hammond. Try it again, and this time give the batsman time to get himself into a muddle. If you jump in too quickly, it doesn't give the batsman time to get uncomfortable."

Hammond cleared his throat, paused theatrically, and then tried again.

"Could you straighten your bat please, batsman.............. Well... Yes, it's there or thereabouts."

"Yes, that's wonderful. Don't you agree, chaps?" said the cricketer.

– What's he on about, *Frank?* said Frank to himself rather nervously.

The other cricketers made approving noises concerning the delivery of this line, while Frank continued to ponder its significance.

– Dunno. What's over where? And what's going on?
Ask him, Frank.

"Um, what's over where?" he said in a measured sort of way.

"The stopcock," said Hammond. "What else?"

"The stopcock?"

"Yes, would you sort it out as quickly as possible, please? Only, we're rather short of water and we're all gasping for some tea."

Frank explained he wasn't a stopcock man. Nor had he ever been. He thought about going onto explain about the lack of stopcocks in his childhood, but *Frank* stopped him. By this time, Hammond had finished ironing his trousers. He satisfied himself that the crease was straight and then put them on.

Frank's admission of a lack of intimacy with stopcocks appeared to have ended the conversation with those present. Hammond appeared to have forgotten his presence altogether. He folded the ironing board and stowed it in a corner of the room. Frank had to announce his presence again.

"Um," was all he had time to say before one of the others called out.

"New man in, chaps."

That triggered some rather polite applause from the others. Still clapping, they rose from their seats and encircled him. After a short pause, one of them cupped his hands to his mouth and spoke quietly, as though he were shouting at Frank from some distance.

"Do you require a guard, batsman?"

It was all a bit much for Frank. He felt the room move ever so slightly. Instinctively, he raised the level up to his eyes and held it there. It helped. The room stopped moving. It also went down well with The Five. They congratulated him on his foresight in bringing along the level as an aid to taking guard at the crease. Someone suggested that the club ought to buy a pair of levels for the cricket bag for next season. They approved that unanimously; Frank found himself at the centre of discerning approval.

While explaining to The Five the merits of long and short levels, Frank became alarmed to see them abruptly freeze in unison. He needn't have worried: they weren't about to subject him to anything else. They had realised they were in the presence of the prodigal that the Dean had announced would arrive to open the batting next season. Apparently, he had informed The Five that Frank was the best thing since the invention of the thigh pad. And that he would transform the club's batting. Of course, this was news to Frank. He tried to put the record straight, but fortunately for him, *Frank* poked him in the proverbial ribs. After all, it wasn't his fault he had been miscast, and anyway, next season wouldn't start for another six months: plenty of time to think of something.

– Well, that explains a lot, *Frank*.

– About what?

– The interview, dummy. Last term. Don't you remember? All those questions about line and length and how would we handle an in-swinging ball.

– I thought he was talking about ballroom dancing.

– So did I, *Frank*. So did I.... Still, I ought to straighten things out. Otherwise, I'm going to end up in an awful mess. Can you imagine me playing cricket? I've never held a bat in my life.

– Stop wittering on, Frank. I'm thinking.

He couldn't do too much more thinking, however. The Five, delighted to have a player of such distinction in their midst, felt obliged to show their guest their latest piece: *The Consultation with the Square Leg Umpire*. Out on the refectory floor, The Five went through their paces.

"It's rather a subtle piece," said Gilbert afterwards. "I don't think many people will get it."

Frank certainly hadn't got it. But he'd been around art schools long enough to keep a po-face and nod appreciatively. *Frank*, on the other hand, often put his foot in it. Fortunately for *Frank*, Frank was usually on hand to keep him from doing anything too disastrous.

Chapter 6

He became friendly with all the refectory staff. And as he sat there, daily, thoughtfully polishing his level and checking the female form – with his spirit level glued to his forehead for the best part of the day – he came to be known as the *Level Headed Student*.

The days drifted by pleasantly for Frank. At first, he had been content to sit at one table, but he soon realised he couldn't simply ogle girls all day long without being labelled a crank or worse. So, to cover his activities, he explored the spatial references of the female form from all the tables in the refectory. He adopted a strict rotational sequence; and made this known to all by placing little numbered cardboard arrows on the tables. These were positioned at the ends of tables and acted as a guide to Frank's progress. They also indicated his possible imminent arrival at a particular table. Thus, a typical conversation at a table might be:

"Oh, he's at thirty-seven. He'll be here soon. Better make room for him, Chloe."

This rotational approach gave structure to Frank's activities and suggested that he was actually doing something interesting, and perhaps even technical. Some students concluded he was a surveyor of some sort.

It worked well for a while, but Frank realised that even with this structured approach, he couldn't disguise his ogling in this way for very much longer. He then had a brainwave: he would do it with mirrors. The Dean, who was a regular visitor to Frank's table in the refectory, had been rather helpful regarding getting permission for Frank to place arrows all over the refectory tables. He was equally willing to support this new idea of Frank's regarding mirrors. Indeed, when Frank started talking about the nature of reflective images, and angles of reflection and incidence, the Dean became very enthusiastic. He supposed it must have something to do with Frank's preoccupation with straightness.

With official blessing, therefore, Frank bought rather a lot of mirrors. Some of them were normal, full-size mirrors; some were fairly small: including tiny shaving mirrors. He also purchased several trick mirrors to add to the overall effect. He then spent several days in positioning the mirrors at strategic places around the refectory. Finally, he took another two days to align the mirrors with his levels and a theodolite.

He started doing complicated-looking calculations. First, in a traditional manner: on the backs of envelopes, then, as he revelled in his activities, on large rolls of paper. He used three calculators: all at the same time. They were clearly not enough. To compensate, he borrowed a computer from one of the science labs. An impressive looking oscilloscope followed soon afterwards. A technician helped him to set this up at his favourite table. By now, the column next to his favourite table had been given several shelves to support Frank's endeavours.

These *artistic activities* caused endless headaches for Frost. Not only was Frank constantly under everyone's feet – taking up more and more room with his mirrors, his instruments and his wretched calculations – but he was also setting new precedents regarding artistic licence in the refectory. The Five were now just one of two major problems in his life.

Eventually, after almost two weeks, Frank was satisfied with the positioning of his mirrors. He returned to his originally favoured table and proceeded from where he had left off studying the female form. For the first time since he had arrived at St Sigeberht's, he felt himself to be in control. Although, if truth be told, he was in a trance for most of the time he was in the refectory.

– So much femininity, *Frank*.

– *Frank* corrected him: So many feminine posteriors, Frank.

– Don't you ever think of anything else, *Frank?*

– Do you?

– No comment, *Frank*, was all that Frank would admit to.

It didn't matter, though. He was enjoying being a student. To add to his act, Frank made notes in a little exercise book. It looked very interesting. Except that now people started leaning over his shoulder to see what he was writing. His growls about privacy helped little. People's curiosity got the better of their sense of propriety. In any case, he couldn't expect privacy in such a public space. However, since he was only writing gibberish, he couldn't afford to be scrutinised too closely. He solved this minor problem by dropping the writing and using hieroglyphics instead.

– See what you make of that, you nosey bastards, Frank said to himself.

– Steady now, Frank. They're only curious about what you're doing.

– Not curious, *Frank*. Just down right nosey.

– Wouldn't you be nosey, Frank?

– Maybe, but I wouldn't go poking my nose over someone's shoulder.

That settled, Frank got down to some serious scribbling. Uninhibited by the fear of being read, he began to lose himself in the role of artist at work. His output flowed freely as he left his conscious mind to meditate on things feminine. To accommodate his expanding output, he graduated from the little exercise book to larger sketchpads.

Because he was now using sketchbooks for his activities, Frank's *work* took on an extra dimension and added to his credibility. However, this was not all. There were unexpected developments arising from his scribbling. After another week, he discovered, to his horror, that his meaningless scribbles had morphed into expressive life drawings. Since Frank had been taught to regard life drawing with suspicion, he reacted violently to the discovery.

– Jesus, *Frank!* exclaimed Frank to himself in a mixture of panic and amazement. I'm doing life drawings.

– Cut it out quick! Frank shouted *Frank* in an equally panic-stricken voice.

Shaken out of himself, he tried to gather up what he had been producing. However, before he had a chance to do anything, several people arrived at his table, including Hendricks, the life class tutor. Not unnaturally, Hendricks was attracted by the almost mythical nature of Frank's drawings and complimented him on his expressive line. Frank tried to grab all the drawings and push them under the table, but it was too late: he had been discovered!

In fact, Frank looked so credible that people talked about him beyond the bounds of the refectory. The artistic community assumed he was doing a major piece in the refectory. Both staff and students often came to see him in action. The balcony became especially popular for checking out *Frank's piece*. It was almost like free entertainment. Except that it was more than that. It was *High Art*. Especially as seen from the balcony. In between sips of hot coffee, or nibbles of croissants, the conversation invariably turned to Frank's activities. Thus, a common remark might be:

"I wonder what he's looking at right now?"

Or,

"How can he concentrate with all that noise and bustle around him?"

The answer, of course, was that Frank didn't so much concentrate as go into a trance. Hence, he heard very little. As far as seeing was concerned, he had a one-track mind, and it was very focused. There were, of course, questions also about his spirit levels. For example:

"What do you think's the significance of having two spirit levels?"

Or,

"How can he look along two spirit levels at the same time?"

These and other questions formed part of the small talk of the artistic community of the college. Frank and his refectory piece cropped up in conversation everywhere. One or two students bought their own spirit levels and tried to see for themselves what Frank was seeing. Others followed their example. Suddenly, a rash of students started wandering around the college with spirit levels. Some of them found spirit levels small enough to be worn like pens clipped to outside jacket pockets. This was considered very chic. Some students went to the other extreme and started carrying metre length spirit levels. This was considered rather manly. The sculpture students especially favoured this ploy since they worked with manly materials like steel and concrete. The Jewellery department then scored something of a coup: a group of students produced working miniature levels and began wearing them as ear rings. These devices came to be seen as especially useful in maintaining a level head when all around were losing theirs.

The rest of the college didn't know what to make of it at all. One thing was certain, however: Frank's activities were assuming artistic importance. The social nature of the refectory environment helped and indeed promoted Frank as a developing major artist. Quite apart from the high profile that such a situation afforded, there was also the opportunity to grow by association with other major artistic figures. In Frank's case, there were two important associative contacts: the Dean and The Five.

The Dean was a frequent visitor at Frank's table, usually stopping to keep Frank abreast of developments regarding the New Zealand tests. Not that Frank had any particular interest in how the 'lads' were doing down under, but he liked the Dean and always tried to give him his undivided attention. And since Frank was one of the few people around the college who showed an interest in the game, the Dean spent a fair part of the day at Frank's table.

Other regular visitors included The Five. Indeed, since they had a clubhouse in the refectory, they were actually neighbours. When all five were present, as well as the Dean, together with associated girlfriends and pets, it was hard not to see that this group represented the avant-garde of the Art School.

Although many people now claimed they *understood* Frank's piece, not everyone felt comfortable about being au fait with his *oeuvre*. Some of the first-year students, in particular, found it difficult to put it into context. Some of the bolder ones began asking their tutors to explain Frank's work.

Not unsurprisingly, someone asked Frank's tutor to comment on Frank's *Refectory Piece* – such was by now its common name.

The head of sculpture, Colin Dunne, had been assigned as Frank's tutor. However, since Frank hadn't been to any of the tutorials or responded to notes in his pigeonhole, Dunne had to comment on a piece of work he knew nothing about and a student he hadn't seen since his interview. This wouldn't have mattered too much if it were only students asking the questions, but he was tackled by all and sundry, including the Warden. Frost had raised the matter with the Warden, and it had consequently come up at a senate meeting. Difficult as it was for a head of department to go looking for a student, Dunne had to check out Frank in the refectory.

"Er, hello. It's Francis, isn't it?" said Dunne, sitting down right in Frank's line of sight. Frank had been estimating the declination of a rather elegant posterior and didn't take kindly to Dunne's arrival.

"It's Frank, if you don't mind," said Frank brusquely.

There had been rather a lot of distractions lately, and he was finding it difficult to concentrate on the job at hand. Dunne's was the umpteenth interruption that morning.

"Oh, I'm so sorry. Yes, of course. Frank, it is then. Er, Frank," said Dunne, introducing himself, "I wonder if we might have a chat sometime."

"A chat? What about?"

"Your work, Frank."

"My work?" repeated Frank, sounding like a parrot.

"Yes, you know. Your sculpture."

"Oh, right," said a thoughtful Frank.

"Shall we meet in your studio? Say, at ten, tomorrow morning?"

"My studio?"

"Yes, if that's convenient?"

"But I haven't got a studio," said Frank in a hopeful sort of voice.

"No studio? Everyone has a studio here. Third years especially have quite a lot of space. Don't you know about your studio allocation? You should have received a note in your pigeonhole at the beginning of term about your space."

Frank pleaded ignorance. Though he omitted to mention he hadn't checked his pigeonhole since he had arrived. Likewise, he thought it prudent not to mention he didn't know he had a pigeonhole. Dunne promised to look into the matter. In the meantime, Frank reluctantly agreed to a rendezvous at the studio the following day.

Chapter 7

That afternoon, Frank located the Art School pigeonholes. And sure enough, he found the letter regarding his studio space. Armed with his allocation slip, he made his way to the studios. These were housed in an old textile factory, and hence students referred to the building the *Factory*.

The Art School had bought the building some years back to augment its studio space. It was now used only by the fine art students. It was rather cliquey. Any visitor, who wasn't a painter or sculptor, got a very frosty welcome.

The building was situated just off the Manchester Road on the Isle of Dogs. It stood out from the other grim looking buildings and the wharves, because of the flags and bunting that hung from every window. It stood, box-like, square on to the road and occupied a considerable frontage. As a result, it provided a useful reference point for travellers going round the isle.

Like most buildings, unfortunate enough to stand near major roads, the Factory had become coated with layers of grime and dirt. Even so, visitors could see traces of virgin brickwork in isolated spots where students had attempted to clean the surroundings to the entrance and windows. The windows were especially noticeable on the ground and first floors where the college had installed white security shutters over them.

Because the original design of the building had been conceived with horsepower in mind, vehicular access to the building for large vans was rather tight. It all contributed to the charm of the place. Except, of course, when students wanted to move substantial sculptures in and out of the building. And then the fact that the entrance was only designed to accommodate horse-drawn wagons became a problem. Notwithstanding this handicap, the college persevered with the building because it was possible to move large pieces by lowering them onto barges at the rear of the building.

As a communal building, the Factory had little going for it, especially as it was some way from the main college. However, from the students' point of view, its saving grace was that it backed onto the Thames. Over the years, the students had built a little jetty and spent a good deal of time swimming and boating during fine weather.

On the inside, the Factory was painted white from top to bottom. The lack of colour on the walls gave the best possible foundation against which to see students' work. The worthiest examples, particularly of past students' pieces, lined the foyer. It was, in effect, a small gallery and acted as a spur to student aspirations.

Posters advertising current and forthcoming exhibitions took up a fair bit of the wall space. There were also pigeonholes, notice boards and timetables. A couple of vending machines for drinks and snacks completed the scene.

The Factory comprised four floors. Admin had offices on the ground floor. This area also housed the Art School's foundry and workshops. The other floors were allocated one per year group, with the first years on the first floor and the thirds on top. The layout of the three floors were identical.

On each of the upper floors, they had split the large amount of floor space into individual studios. At the end of each floor, a gantry allowed students to shin down to the jetty. It was a facility much used whenever students expected tutors to make an appearance and weren't too keen on entertaining them. This exit provided a convenient escape route to Greenwich across the river.

Upon entering the building, Frank encountered a friendly technician who pointed him in the right direction, and he located his studio on the top floor. He paced out the space.

– It's a big place, *Frank*. And its empty.

– Too right, Frank.

– What are we going to do here, *Frank?*

– Beats me. What do you reckon?

– There's nothing I want to do here at the moment. I'm tied up in the refectory.

– Well, that bloke, what's his name, Dunne, is it? Wants to see what we've done so far this term. Not a lot, is it, Frank?

– Well, I've only been here six weeks, *Frank*. A man's got to have time to think. And remember, the police took up a bit of that time.

– The important thing, Frank, is to appear as though you're doing lots of things. Right?

– Right, said Frank, wandering what *Frank* was getting at and therefore not totally committing himself.

– Well, all you have to do is to fill the place with some

work and no one'll know the difference.

– Yeh, but where do you propose we get hold of some work?

– That's easy, Frank. You don't get work, as such. You get some packaging. That way no one'll think about the work they'll just focus on the packaging.

– I don't get it, *Frank*.

– Look, Frank, said *Frank* patiently. You know that automatic cellophane wrapper I've been using at the flat?

– Mmm.

– Well, all those take-away cartons I've been wrapping with it, they look good. Right?

– You mean sort of like parcels? said Frank sarcastically.

– Exactly, said *Frank*, missing the edge in Frank's voice. Parcels look good. They're sort of mysterious because you don't know what's inside them. And great art's always mysterious. You've told me that yourself, Frank. Mona Lisa's smile's mysterious, isn't it? Well, I'll just bring that wrapper in here, and I'll start wrapping things up in cellophane. We can call it Mystery Art, or maybe Mysterious Art. Or, better still, *Art Mystérieux*. That'll confuse the buggers.

– What sort of things would you wrap up?

– Does it matter? Anything just so long as it's bulky. Right? It'll soon fill the place up.

– Cellophane's transparent, *Frank*, said Frank spotting the flaw in *Frank's* logic. There's nothing mysterious about a transparent parcel. Anyway, I'll still have to explain to Dunne what it's all meant to mean.

– No, you won't, and I'll make sure that the parcels

aren't transparent. I'll wrap them up in brown paper first.

– What do you mean about not having to explain to Dunne?

– I mean you won't need to explain because it'll be *Art Mystérieux*. You can't go round explaining away mysteries. They wouldn't be mysteries any more, would they? Eh? I could do mystery paintings, Frank. No one would know what was on the canvas, or whether I'd used oils or acrylics. In fact, I wouldn't even use canvas for painting. It's too expensive. And how about sculpture made from of soft stuff? So, you'd be able to sit on it. In fact, you probably wouldn't be able to tell the difference between what I'm thinking of and an armchair. I could...

Frank sensed himself reeling under *Frank's* onslaught. He needed time to think. He certainly wasn't happy being there in a great empty studio. And the prospect of filling it with work seemed daunting. *Frank's* idea sounded neat enough, but he knew from bitter experience that *Frank's* ideas usually got him into trouble. He drew out his spirit level and gently stroked his forehead with it. Slowly, he recovered his composure.

Frank, meanwhile, was giving the matter some serious thought. He decided that as the first course of action, he really ought to shift the take-away cartons that were accumulating at the flat and move them into the studio. He reasoned that, at a carton a day, he would soon be swamped at the flat. And of course, a carton could burst open accidentally. A terrifying prospect. The studio seemed like a good place to store his cartons. And it would put something physical into this enormous space.

At least it would look as though he was doing something. But he wondered: dare he leave it to Frank to explain to Dunne their artistic content. Artistic content? He burst out laughing at that thought.

– What's so funny, *Frank*? asked Frank, looking puzzled.

– Oh, just a thought, Frank. Listen. That idea of mine? About the parcels?

– Yes, alright, *Frank*, said Frank in a resigned tone.

– And listen, Frank.

– What?

– I want to move the take-away cartons into the studio. It'll give us a start in filling the place and it'll also give us a bit more space at the flat.

– Good idea, *Frank*, said Frank, suddenly finding himself to be enthusiastic. You going to get them now?

– Can do.

– And what about Dunne? asked Frank, trying to tie up loose ends.

– Leave him to me, said *Frank* confidently. It'll be a pleasure. And don't worry about a thing. I'll soon have this place looking like the Tate.

The next morning, Frank was back at the Factory. He had worked hard the previous day and had made the studio seem inhabited. However, as he now reflected on Dunne's imminent arrival, he felt rather nervous about how he would tackle Dunne. He had felt confident enough yesterday, but then he always did when he was trying to make a point with *Frank*.

– *Frank*, he said, calling his other self.

– I'm not here, Frank.

– What d'you mean, not here? I can hear you, *Frank*.

– I mean, I'm not available, said *Frank* testily.

– What d'you mean, not available? Are you on the bog or something, *Frank*? said Frank equally testily. Come on, I just want a quick word.

– No can do, maestro. You're on your own here.

– Bloody peasant, Frank muttered to himself. Just wait till you want something, he said a bit more volubly.

Frank may have been having his problems regarding this tutorial, but so was Dunne. He had seemed very business-like in arranging the meeting, but in reality, Dunne was rather more nervous at the prospect of this tutorial than Frank. A cursory investigation into Frank's artistic background had been enough to show they had nothing in common.

Why was it, Dunne reflected, that the Art School didn't take on students who truly showed an interest in art? *Real Art.* The honest-to-goodness study of the human form using proper materials like clay and bronze. These young men and women nowadays seemed not to have the slightest idea of anything. Least of all, of form and content. It was all very well doing these clever arty-farty jokes, but you couldn't do that for a living. And most of these people couldn't even draw. What was one to do?

"I blame the Dean, of course," he would explain to his wife every time he faced this kind of problem. "The man's an absolute idiot. How he ever got the job, I cannot imagine. I mean, have you ever heard of anything so ridiculous as an art school Dean, who does nothing except go wittering on about cricket all day? He even attends senate meetings dressed in whites! And when he's not dressed in whites, he's dressed as a labourer: complete with a hard hat. I mean there is a limit."

Like Frank, Dunne wasn't in a happy frame of mind this morning. He didn't see why he should go on with what was sure to be a farce. Yet, he had to give some sort of account of Frank's work. As Head of Sculpture, he really couldn't avoid the issue. Driving moodily along the Commercial Road, Dunne mused rebelliously on the possibility of declaring a foul, of calling someone's bluff. In this, unusually for him, lateral frame of mind, he had something of a brain wave. He realised he had a problem because he could not relate Frank's work to that of any other student he'd taught. He couldn't do so, he argued, because Frank's work followed none of the widely accepted canons of *Real Art*. Therefore, he further argued, it wasn't art. As Head of Sculpture, he ought to know! *Ipso facto*, it couldn't be his responsibility!

"Brilliant, Colin," he said to himself. "That'll fix the fucking Dean. In fact, it'll fix quite a few people. Yes," he mumbled to himself as he pondered the consequences of UDI, "that'll fix the fuckers."

Up on the third floor of the Factory, Frank was by now getting desperate. He knew Dunne would arrive at any moment, and he still hadn't worked out how he'd handle a formal tutorial. He started pacing up and down the studio, but that didn't help matters. It was no good. He had to get out of the building. He bolted out of his studio and shot over to the window overlooking the street.

– Shit! he said, espying Dunne getting out of his car. *Frank*! What are we going to do? He'll be here any minute.

Frank was still being aloof.

– Not my problem, Frank.

– Not your problem!? Listen, you bloody pleb. We're in this together and if you don't get your thinking cap on pretty damn quick, I'm going to tell Dunne exactly what you're doing with those fucking cartons.

Frank turned pale. He reached for the spirit level, but Frank cut him short.

– There's no time for that, *Frank*. He'll be here any minute. His car's just pulled up outside. Come on. What are we going to do?

– Fire escape, *Frank* yelled triumphantly. There's got to be a fire escape.

– Fire escape! Frank yelled in turn and started running around like a demented chicken. Fire escape. Where's the fire escape? My God, *Frank*, there's no fire escape. We're trapped!

At this time of the day, there were never very many students around the building, especially third-year students. Just as well for Frank, since he demolished quite a lot of work as he zigzagged around the entire floor looking for a way out. There was, however, one other person on the floor and inevitably Frank bumped into her. As he did so, Zoe yelled out something mystical and, in one swift movement, threw Frank onto the floor. Before he realised what had happened, she leapt upon him and wrapped her sturdy thighs around his neck. This was too good an opportunity to miss; she launched herself into the new *Pfaff piece* she had been sketching out in her mind.

Luckily for Frank, he had his spirit level in his hand. As she dragged him around the floor, he got the level between Zoe's thighs and prevented certain suffocation. Zoe for her part didn't take kindly to Frank shoving something hard in between her thighs and so stepped up a gear to grind it to dust.

An ebullient Dunne arrived on the scene to find a frenzied duo rolling around the studio floor. Stopped in his tracks, he tried to take in the scene. He wasn't sure whether to be excited or appalled at the spectacle. His truer instincts started to get the better of him, but he found a more civilised response and backtracked out of the room. It seemed the sensible thing to do. As Dunne retreated down the stairs, Zoe climaxed amidst the ruins of someone's still life. Whimpering, she now lay still. Frank prised his head from her thighs and got to his feet. He staggered over to a nearby chair and collapsed into it.

– Jesus, *Frank*. That's the second time she's nearly choked me to death.

– I know, Frank. Nice!?

– Nice? I'm nearly choked to death, and you call it nice?

– Well, someone enjoyed it, Frank. Even if you didn't.

– What do you mean, someone?

– Take a butchers, said *Frank*, nodding towards Zoe lying on the floor, smiling.

– Oh, he said, before he lapsed into a semi-comatose state.

He awoke with a jolt with the realisation in his mind that Dunne had been there a moment or two ago.

"Dunne!" he exclaimed.

"Don't worry. He won't be back for a bit," said Zoe, sealing her undies in some cling film. "Dunne's seen me performing before; he always gets embarrassed."

"I'm supposed to be having a tutorial with him."

"Lucky you."

"No, you don't understand." And Frank explained his problem.

"Come with me," motioned Zoe, hoisting a bag over her shoulder. She led him to the gantry and pulled out a rope ladder. "Quite safe," she said, as he looked apprehensively at her. "Goes down to the jetty. Everyone uses it to avoid tutors. There's one on every floor. And if you're really desperate, there're usually a lot of boats down below. Most students have one. Come on. I'll give you a lift."

"A lift?"

"Across the river. To Greenwich. Everyone's usually over at the Buoy at this time of day. Come on. At least it'll get you out of Dunne's way."

Frank didn't need to be asked twice.

Chapter 8

The Billy Buoy, or more commonly the Buoy, was more than just a pub. Many of the art students spent a good deal of their waking hours in this establishment. They did their best work here. This was where they developed ideas, as opposed to the Factory, where they were merely implemented. Apart from the refectory, many of the students refused to do creative work anywhere else.

The Buoy was also the natural place for many of the extra-curricular activities that an art student might want to indulge. If someone needed money, for example, they came to the Buoy: a student could always find temporary labouring work. If you wanted a game of bar billiards, this was where you'd find a table. The Buoy boasted a genuine bar billiards table with authentic ceramic toadstools. If you wanted to play skittles, the Buoy boasted unique facilities. You would probably have to go up north to find an alternative venue for a decent game of skittles. And if you wanted to hear music, proper music as opposed to the plastic variety, the Buoy played the *right stuff*. The landlord insisted on playing only the music of the great rock and blues bands of the late sixties and seventies. This was probably also the reason that several rock groups used the Buoy as a recording base. Invariably, they were art students who planned to spend three years developing their musical skills. For them, art, certainly fine art, was very much a second fiddle.

A large circular bar divided the Buoy into two halves. Art students dominated the front part of the pub; the locals haunted the back half. A keen rivalry had developed between the two sides on everything from darts and bar billiards to football and cricket. Hence, the pub ran two teams for everything. Of course, the Art School XI also met here. On match days, the Dean arrived in his JCB with a long trailer for the team. Perhaps not the most efficient means of transport, but according to the Dean's reckoning, as an intimidatory ploy, the JCB was probably worth as many runs as extras.

When Frank and Zoe arrived at the pub, he was surprised to see a gathering of fine art students waiting to go in.

"What are they doing here?" he asked.

"It's opening time. Everyone comes here at opening time."

She seemed to think this covered everything. Frank wasn't in a terribly inquisitive mood and didn't therefore pursue it any further. His mind still lingered in the middle of the river – watching her rowing. She had been magnificent. Her strong hands had pulled the boat effortlessly across the river. The water, the gulls, her smooth taut skin glowing with vitality. It was all there in his mind.

He remained engrossed in his thoughts while Zoe tried to say something about her work over a pint of Guinness. After the umpteenth glass, he finally concluded that he could appreciate what she had been trying to say regarding her work. She had spent almost two hours in trying to explain herself, but only now did he really understood.

"I'm sorry for being so slow," he said, almost tearfully. "What must you think of me? Don't you think so, *Frank*?"

"Who's Frank?" said Zoe, looking around.

"I'm Frank," he said with a guilty look in his eyes.

"Yes, but you sounded as though you were talking to someone else?"

This had an immediate sobering effect on Frank.

> – Steady now, Frank, said *Frank* as he mumbled his way to some sort of explanation.

They drank and played bar billiards and darts and skittles and then they went back to playing bar billiards. Frank had a vague recollection he ought to have been somewhere else, but he couldn't remember where. The refectory seemed to have been wiped from his memory – though he could still remember the close encounter with Dunne earlier that morning. He shivered as he thought about it now.

"What am I going to do about Dunne?" he said, half-aloud.

"Dunne?" said Zoe. "Oh! You mean *Laurel*. Don't worry about him. He's harmless."

"How do you mean?"

"He's one of a double act. The other's Wheeler. Head of Painting. Otherwise known as *Hardy*. Both potty."

"Laurel and Hardy?" said Frank with a wry smile.

"Exactly. They're both absolutely ancient; ought to have been put away years ago."

"I'm supposed to be showing Dunne my work."

"*Laurel*," said Zoe, correcting him. "Just ignore him."

Frank wondered why he hadn't thought of this himself. It seemed like a brilliant solution to his problem. He ordered another pint to drink Zoe's health. They drank and played bar billiards till closing time and then wandered back to the college via the foot tunnel; they left the boat behind for the evening.

*

During the evening session, Frank and Zoe were sitting drinking with The Five. Towards the end of the evening, in the best traditions of the Buoy, Zoe floated an idea that seemed inspired. It quickly took hold of the imagination of everyone at the table.

"An Art School panto! Brilliant," hiccupped Frank. "I wanna play the Dame."

"I absolutely must play the Slipper," said Barnes.

"Don't be daft, Barnes," said an authoritative Gilbert. "You're not the right size. Better leave it to me. I'm the man for the Slipper."

"What d'you mean, not the right size? I'm just the right size."

"Here, let me show you," said Gilbert. He took out a tape measure from his pocket and waved it in Barnes's general direction. "There! You see! The Slipper's got to be a size 10; you're only a size 8."

"Oh," said a deflated Barnes. "Well, I never. Well, in that case, I insist on playing the Scarecrow."

"The Scarecrow? I didn't know he was in Pinocchio," confessed Hobbs, suddenly coming to life.

"No! No! Stop! You don't understand," explained Zoe. "I didn't mean that kind of panto. I mean something like—"

"Pinocchio! That's what we've got to do," said Hutton, standing up and pointing to his nose.

"No, you Pillock. Why don't you just listen for a minute? I was thinking of—"

"Of Dalmatians?" interjected Hammond. "Hundred and One Dalmatians. That'd make a great panto. We could go down to Battersea Dogs Home and borrow some dogs. They may not have a hundred and one Dalmatians to spare, but we could soon paint a few spots. Most of us paint spots every day! It'd be a piece of cake."

"You are definitely a pillock, Hammond," pronounced Zoe. "A complete pillock. Here, this'll help you think straight," she said, as she slowly poured a pint of bitter over his head. And then, having got the admiring and undivided attention of the gathering, she outlined the plot of a breath-taking panto based on Snow White.

"Snow White and the Seven Academicians? Brill," said Frank. "I wanna play the Dame."

"I wanna play the Scarecrow," said Barnes, thumping the table.

"Bags I play the Slipper," said Hammond.

"Christ! Not again," said a weary Zoe. "You haven't heard a word I've said. Right. See if you can take this in through that haze of alcohol. Listen," she said, with an air of tipsy exasperation. "I'm going across to the Factory, right now. I'm going to write out the plot tonight. Anyone who wants to be in it, be there tomorrow night. After closing. Sharp."

"Wait for us, we're all going over too," yelled a chorus of drunken voices.

Everyone got up at once and lurched towards the door. No one wanted to be left behind in the dash for the Factory. It was the same every night: a drunken mob would emerge from the Buoy around midnight and stagger down to the river; they would pile into a flotilla of rowing boats and then row dementedly for thirty metres before the oarsmen ran out of puff and started puking over the side.

Given the state of the students, it was surprising no one had drowned. This was almost certainly because so many boats went across at the same time that there was always someone on hand to pull drunks out of the water. And of course, being an art school mob, they inevitably sheltered the odd crank or two who didn't drink. These sober individuals came into their own around midnight. By the time they had crossed the river, the drunks had sobered up to some extent.

Most of the students would then work for several hours before trudging home. This was the best time of day for working. It was the only time of day the Factory came alive. A hard core worked through the night. A useful arrangement for all concerned: it suited the students who could get their drinking and socialising in before getting down to some work. It suited the Art School, since by keeping the building open, they at least got some work out of the students.

The journey across on this evening was especially lively. Everyone seemed fired up about the panto. Casting for the parts continued to dominate the conversation. Zoe wouldn't say anything more about her thoughts, but the revellers seemed intent on shouting it out for the minor roles. About half way across the river, someone shouted a claim for Grumpy.

"No! I've already bagsied Grumpy," shouted someone else.

"No, you didn't. I was sitting right next to Zoe, and I got in first for Grumpy."

"Bags, I play the Slipper," shouted another voice.

"I wanna play Sleepy," shouted someone else. "I'd be

good at that."

"Has anyone bagsied the Witch?" shouted someone else. "I know just the person for that."

"You're a bloody liar," shouted the second claimant on Grumpy. "You were nowhere near Zoe when she started talking about the panto."

"Was so!"

"Was not!"

"Are you calling me a liar, you moron?" said would-be Grumpy Number One, standing up threateningly in the middle of the boat.

"SIT DOWN," yelled a chorus of passengers.

"What if I am?" retorted would-be Grumpy Number Two, squaring up in his boat.

"I'll show you," said Grumpy Number One, as he started rowing towards a would-be Grumpy. "You're definitely going to be grumpy by the time I've finished with you."

"Grumpy! Grumpy!" yelled the chorus of lurching passengers as the rolling boats manoeuvred for position.

Clearly, the Grumpy issue would have to be settled. The passengers in both claimants' boats joined in the spirit of things and started hurling abuse at one another. There wasn't much else to throw. The other boats shouted encouragement and tried to make a circle around the protagonists. Not an easy thing to do, considering the circumstances. Fortunately for the revellers, the pitching of the boats and the general lack of coordination ensured that boats didn't collide. Though, inevitably, several of the students fell into the river.

With Zoe rowing again, Frank lay face down in the boat's rear: a limp figure with one hand dangling in the water and the other holding the level out straight. He fancied he was engineering the boat towards the other bank. Clearly a case of reverse engineering, he thought, and giggled inwardly.

When they got to the other side, Zoe lurched off muttering something about, "Bloody art students."

Frank turned over onto his back and held the level up to the spinning moon. He decided it was spinning too fast, and he ought to stay to level it. He hummed a little tune as he set about trying to steady the moon with the aid of his trusty level.

At this stage *Frank* butted in to his endeavour:

– Just look at the state of you, Frank.

– What?

– You're paralytic, Frank.

– Who are you calling a parrot?

– That's the last time I go drinking with you.

– What d'you mean, *Frank*, said Frank in an indignant voice. You drank just as much as me.

– Yeah, but I can hold my drink. You're like a wet fart. A few jars and you can barely stand up.

– Can't I? We'll see about that.

Frank staggered to his feet and swayed his way over onto the jetty. He lurched to a nearby road, dragging *Frank* in his wake, and started looking for a white line.

– Hold on, Frank, said *Frank*, desperately trying to keep up with Frank's lumbering limbs. What's the rush?

– What's the matter, *Frank?* Can't you keep up?

– *Frank* could only gasp in reply.

– Right, *Frank*. Now just watch this, said Frank as he stumbled upon a dotted line in the middle of one of the side roads behind the Factory.

Stooping with one hand on his knee to catch his breath, he looked along the line. For some inexplicable reason, the line appeared to be moving – albeit slowly. Frank blinked, but it didn't seem to help. He lay down on the floor and tried sighting the line. This looked more promising: the line looked dead still.

– Got it, he muttered.

– What's the matter, Frank? You tired? said *Frank* sarcastically.

– Don't give me any of your lip, *Frank*. I'm gonna do it now and then we'll see how you perform.

However, no sooner did he get up than the line started moving again. He took out his level. Unfortunately, it didn't help. In fact, it simply confirmed the line was moving. It swung like a pendulum, arcing across his line of vision. Frank pulled out the spare level. Holding one level against each eye, he controlled the movement, so the line didn't deflect beyond the two levels.

– Got it! he exclaimed and started advancing along the road.

By now, the other boats were pulling in towards the jetty. Several of the students spotted Frank and came running over to see what he was doing. Whatever it was, it looked jolly interesting. Everyone decided they wanted to have a go. Within a few minutes, fifty odd students began swaying down the main road. From there it didn't take long before a lurching conga came to life – with a reluctant Frank at its head.

He hung on grimly to his two levels and tried to steer a straight course. Not an easy thing to do, especially through a haze of Guinness and a retinue of vociferous back-seat drivers. The conga careered all over the road, narrowly avoiding several fatal collisions with speeding late-night traffic. Desperate to escape from the main road, Frank swung round and headed towards the pavement. Suddenly, he was free and spinning towards some bollards. The rest of the conga veered off towards a nearby restaurant. A derailing train of drunks burst into a somnambulant Taj Mahal and collapsed into several giggling heaps. The commotion shook the sleepy waiters out of their joss-stick-induced stupor. They rushed to find tables for this unexpected flood of late-night diners.

Frank found himself on his back again. Seemingly where he had started. The Moon reappeared. Still spinning madly, threatening to fall at any moment. *Frank* was crowing about something or other.

He didn't really care for this rather vulgar side of *Frank's* character and was about to tell him so when someone interrupted his thoughts.

"Are you all right," said the voice.

"Who are you?" said Frank, peering into a shadowy face.

"It's me."

"Ah, hello," said Frank, thinking it best not to press the question of identity lest an explanation was required about the Moon.

"Here, let me help you."

He found a comforting arm around his waist and was happy to be helped onto his feet. Somewhere in the distance, he could hear a jumble of music. He tried to pick out the tunes but found it difficult to concentrate. It seemed much more sensible to just let it float over him. A little later, he fancied that a nurse was examining him. He couldn't understand what had happened, but he'd obviously been in an accident. He didn't know where *Frank* had gone. The nurse assured him he was all right. His trusty levels were clenched tightly in his right hand. Thank goodness. He lay back as the anaesthetic seeped into him.

*

He awoke to find himself in a white room in a large brass bed. There were small paintings all over the walls. He glanced to his left and saw his clothes neatly folded over a chair.

– Where am I, *Frank?*
– Don't recognise it, Frank.
– I thought we ended up in the Factory last night.
– I thought we ended up in hospital.
– This is someone's bedroom.
– Quick as usual, Frank.
– Do give it a rest, *Frank*, said Frank wearily.
– You must have got lucky last night, Frank.
– Yeah, lucky I didn't drown.

The door opened and Prudence walked in, carrying mugs of tea.

"Hello," she said, "I'm glad you're awake. I've got to go out in a minute."

"Oh," he said as realisation flooded into his mind.

– Are you thinking what I'm thinking, *Frank?*
– Check your underpants, Frank.

He lifted the bedclothes to find himself totally naked.

"My underpants, Prudence?" he asked, though he knew the answer.

"They're drying over by the window."

"Prudence! You didn't?"

"Mmm." She smiled coyly. "Numbers eight hundred

and eleven, eight hundred and twelve and eight hundred and thirteen," said Prudence, pointing to the three brightly coloured underpants hanging on a makeshift line by the window. "They came out very well. I'm going to make a triptych out of them."

"Three times! You did me three times? Prudence, that's totally out of order."

"Why? Isn't that why you left all those underpants here when you came round the other day?"

"Yeah, but it would have been nice to have been awake," he said ruefully. He realised now why he felt sore.

Chapter 9

News of the panto had spread throughout the college within a couple of days of Zoe announcing that she intended to put something together for the Christmas party. The announcement coincided with Miles's deliberations on the publication of the second issue of *New Movement's* autumn edition. Thus, he devoted a good deal of the issue to discussing the implications of this major work for Zoe's development.

Of course, he didn't actually know very much about the panto. Like everyone else, he knew the title and had gleaned some scraps of information from what had emerged from the pub. Other than that, he knew little. But that didn't stop Miles from speculating on the form the plot might take, and on the relationship between the plot and Zoe's work in general.

He was helped, to some extent, by the insistence of some cast members in indulging in ad hoc rehearsals at every opportunity. The two would-be Grumpys, in particular, added to the atmosphere by having a slanging match at every opportunity. Not that this was giving anything away, but it stirred people's imaginations and emotions. Zoe made matters worse by forbidding anyone to talk about the panto outside the rehearsal rooms.

Perhaps because he had no way of knowing the details of the plot, Miles rather indulged himself in the imagery he used to paint some plausible scenarios for the panto. Miles's imagery had, of course, to be drawn from Zoe's past work. Thus, he felt justified in thinking he could perhaps see, in ways that others couldn't, what Zoe might be contemplating. His editorial dwelt for some considerable length on the symbolism of sheep and reproduction in some of Zoe's earlier work. He also fancied he gave a good critical account of the imagery of speed and violence in her work, as exemplified, for example, by the sewing machine performances. The second series, the so-called *Pfaff pieces* in particular, were dealt with in some depth. These were regarded as particularly fine examples, so he was on sure ground there. A major part of his article explored a more contentious issue: the castration of the rubber man and the implied relationship with the limp libidinal tendencies reported to be central to the plot of the panto. He argued convincingly that this was an attempt by Zoe to draw together several important strands in her thinking and to arrive at a new synthesis of art through the act of procreation. The net result was a rather exciting and evocative piece of journalism that probably wouldn't have looked out of place in the Sunday tabloids.

A couple of days later, a copy of the journal landed on DI Fogg's desk. Ever since that unfortunate incidence with Frank's take-aways, Fogg had instructed his minions to 'Keep an eye' on the Art School. The surveillance, it seemed, had paid off.

Fogg read Miles's piece with considerable interest. He noted with Machiavellian satisfaction that the article mentioned Frank as a probable member of the cast of *Ms White and the Seven Academicians*. There was a heavy score to settle with Frank, and Fogg fancied that he found himself in the agreeable position of being able to anticipate the settling of this score.

He little doubted his crystal-ball gaze was made possible by a conjunction of auspicious heavenly circumstances. Being of a generous nature, he made a mental note to put a ten-pence coin in the next begging bowl he encountered.

The reason for Fogg's good humour stemmed from the fact that an old friend from the Drugs Squad had contacted him. His colleague had been particularly interested in enlisting Fogg's support on raids involving local nightspots. Fogg, of course, had been keen to help. Being an experienced officer, he knew that a favour given was a favour banked. He hadn't expected to cash in his favour quite as soon as this, but there was no point in saving if you couldn't cash your cheques when you wanted. This was the line Fogg used to argue the point with himself and hence used to rationalise an additional joint operation with the Drug Squad. Thus, was born operation 'Fairy Godmother'.

*

Most colleges have some sort of celebration at the end of term. Typically, there's a group of some sort or other; perhaps even two. A late extension can usually be counted upon. Sometimes there are minor disk jockeys to help jolly things along, together with rather tacky light shows. These are used to hide the all-too-depressing decor. Art School end of term celebrations were different. The Art School held nothing as common as discos or dances; the Art School gave parties. Musical groups were invariably not included in the bill of entertainment. However, bad ventriloquists, incompetent string trios or ageing fire-eaters went down rather well. Home entertainment too was well received. The Art School students were a tight-knit community and considered themselves to be a family. And in the best of family traditions, they liked to produce their own entertainment. This year, the main event would be the *panto*.

The original idea for the panto had, of course, come from Zoe and indeed she had written a large part of it. However, with an active and vocal cast, the plot inevitably became more of a collaborative effort. Rehearsals for the panto had been going on for the past three weeks.

Rehearsals should have been held in the Factory, but since everyone was so enthusiastic about the panto, impromptu rehearsals had been occurring all over the place. Even students not involved in the panto got in to the spirit of things by practising shouting the traditional responses in the refectory:

"Oh yes he is."

"Oh no he isn't."

The college had seen nothing like it. Art students in bizarre costumes started swanning around the refectory. The two would-be Grumpys launched *Support Me for Grumpy* campaigns. Both of them started wandering around the college in *authentic* dwarf clothing. This too was problematic, because the two protagonists had very clear and necessarily divergent sartorial views on what the modern, well-dressed dwarf should be wearing. It all promised to be good fun.

Zoe's plot was, in fact, only the main reference point for the panto. Most people who were in it entertained clear ideas about the panto and had every intention of acting out their interpretation. Consequently, rehearsals had been difficult and fractious. Several major rows followed about the dwarfs, or rather, the lack of them. Neither of the potential Grumpys had been happy about that: totally in character. However, Zoe was firm on the issue: there would be no dwarfs in the panto.

The would-be Grumpys were, by now, very grumpy indeed. Neither of them would be in the panto unless they made up and considered other parts. But since both of them insisted on acting out the part of Grumpy, neither of them had any intention of making up. On the contrary, both of them intended on taking a starring role in the panto. It was all very trying.

*

After settling the dwarf question, casting for the major parts proved to be a relatively straightforward affair. Zoe would obviously play the part of Ms White. Frank, despite his reservations, had been persuaded to play the part of Prince Hardwood of the New York School. Zoe insisted he was the only person capable of playing the part. Frank hadn't been able to work out quite how she came to that conclusion, but *Frank* wasn't going to argue. Miles had been desperate to play the other major part: that of the Critic. But the Dean pulled rank on him. Miles had to accept his disappointment and settle for the part of the Critic's cat. He was not happy, but what could he do? The Five were to play the academicians, together with a couple of third-year students.

The dramatis personae were then:
Ms White – Zoe
Prince Hardwood – Frank

The Critic – The Dean
The Critic's cat – Miles
Mac – Back gate porter
The Fool – Jon (third year sculptor)
The Model – Melissa (third year painter)
The Mirror – Jasmine (third year painter)
Academicians:
Abel – Gilbert
Alaric – Hammond
Alistair – Hutton
Ambrose – Hobbs
Aubery – Barnes
Aidan – Ivor (third year sculptor)
Albert – Bunny (third year painter)
Extras as sheep

After all the rows and the rehearsals, the end of term finally arrived. It had been an eventful term for most people, not least of all for Frank. And it wasn't over yet. In the case of the Art School, it definitely wasn't over yet. The last week dragged by interminably as excitement built up over the end of term party and the panto.

For *Frank,* the last day of term couldn't come soon enough. He declared himself ready, willing, and able to make a complete spectacle of himself. Frank, by contrast, became progressively suicidal. He hadn't slept properly for the last couple of weeks, thinking about what he would have to go through. *Frank,* rather helpfully, kept telling him not to think about it. But it didn't seem to help. He got through the last few days by strapping his levels to his forehead. It didn't make for sociable behaviour, and eating and drinking had been a problem, but it did at least help to get him through the days – at least those parts of the day when *Frank* wasn't going on about something or other.

The day of the panto finally arrived. *Frank* got Frank into a stupor at the Buoy over lunchtime. That hadn't been hard to manage. Frank had been only too willing to co-operate.

*

St Sigeberht's had two halls for staging events: the main hall and the drama hall. The college used the main hall for official functions and for staging concerts. It was a gigantic, airy affair with lots of classical trimmings. The drama hall was a smaller, more spartan venue. However, with its purpose-built stage and more intimate feel, it was much more suited for staging something like the panto. Even though it would be a tight squeeze to get everyone in.

The drama hall was used for a variety of events. Its primary purpose was to support the college's drama courses, of course. But the college also used it for a multitude of other things. Every lunchtime, for example, it became a spill-over area for the union bar, situated directly opposite. The Chinese Society used it to host table tennis tournaments. A dozen table tennis tables could fit easily along the hall. And then there were the Adult Education ballroom dancing classes every Tuesday and Thursday evenings. And of course, the Friday night discos ran throughout the year.

All in all, the multi-purpose use of the hall militated against it becoming a specialist area for the Drama department. However, what the department lacked in the way of an auditorium, it made up for in the excellent facilities and support that was provided for its students vis-à-vis the stage.

The support included the services of two full-time

carpenters. To prepare for the panto, a third hand joined these chippies to help in the construction of some special features. In particular, and first, they extended the stage by two metres. Second, they constructed a large open-faced balcony on the right-hand side of the stage. And finally, they built a gangway high on the back of the stage, so that players could make their way from one side of the stage to the other.

*

In retrospect, Frank would have no recollection of this evening prior to his walking into the drama hall. For *Frank*, the evening began as he entered the hall carrying a pint of lager. He paused just inside the doorway and was surprised and exhilarated by the discovery of the magical atmosphere within. Silhouettes and shapes of bodies dancing filled the hall. Around the sides stood groups of friends – obviously telling each other jokes of some considerable hilarity. A classic beat drove and sustained the dancers and spectators alike. He savoured the atmosphere for a moment longer. And then, like an exuberant swimmer divesting himself of excess baggage, swallowed his lager in one long draught before diving into the throng.

An intoxicating pool of flickering lights and sounds filled the hall. So strong was the impression of being underwater, that *Frank* turned for a moment to look back through the doors to the scene outside the hall. A tired, yellow light outside confirmed his perception, and yes, the people standing outside really looked as though they were standing on the edge of a pool looking in at the scene below. The reason they were standing outside, he realised, was because they weren't art students. They belonged to the main college and were probably doing something like sociology or teacher training. The further realisation that he could distinguish non-art students added to his sense of belonging to this swimming evening.

The freshers in the hall too sensed something similar. They had made it through an unnerving first term. And perhaps, for the first time, they understood what it meant to be an art student. They would no longer feel uncomfortable in the face of visual provocation. They knew now it was simply a matter of taking things in one's perceptual stride. Many of them were certainly taking large strides at the moment, making rather idiosyncratic movements to the beat in a way that only a tuneless art student can manage. One student – a keen footballer – had invented a dance called *Crossing the Ball to the far Post*. He was busy demonstrating the steps; he had been practising all week in the Factory. It had obviously been worth all the preparation: he had a ring of admiring spectators around him shouting encouragement. The dance had every chance of being the move of the evening. **Frank** picked and skipped his way through the crowd without recourse to his level. He made his way to the front of the hall and climbed back-stage.

*

The curtain opened and revealed a set containing a large four-poster bed surrounded by easels. This almost professional-looking beginning silenced the audience. Until, that is, the Fool walked on to deliver the prologue. A semi-drunk audience greeted him with all the voluble good humour that a semi-drunk audience has at its disposal. The Fool blinked momentarily as he took in the decorations and the jolly heaving mass in front of him. After the cheers and whistles had died down, he raised his hand solemnly and began to deliver the prologue.

"Once upon a time, long ago—"

"Get on with it," shouted a drunken voice from the crowd.

"Quiet!" hissed the audience as they craned to hear him.

"Once—"

"We know that bit," shouted the drunk.

"Once upon a time," repeated Fool slowly. He was determined to make a sound start to the panto. "Long ago, in a far-off country, lived seven academicians."

"Seven piss artists you mean," shouted someone.

The sound of sniggering broke the tension at this aside from the audience. The Fool, trying not to smirk, carried on with his prologue.

"Each of these academicians dreamt of spawning a vigorous *New Art*."

Hoots of laughter greeted this alleged aspiration. The panto was obviously getting off to a good start. There were, however, two aspiring academicians on the staff at the Art School: Dunne and Wheeler. They were present in the audience and became distinctly uncomfortable at this unexpected beginning. This should have been the beginning of no more than a high-spirited Christmas party with a traditional panto.

"Each day," continued the Fool, trying to make himself heard above the bubbling audience. "Each day the academicians took their paintings to the Critic and asked if this work represented the *New Art*. The Critic, who never lied…"

By now the Fool had the audience listening intently to his every word. Dunne and Wheeler strained to pick up the nuance of the Fool's delivery.

"The Critic, who never lied," repeated the Fool, "always replied:"

Though your paintings are fair and all

They are funny and, well, small and

In truth, I must recall

They are not the New Art at all: at all

This brought further hoots of laughter from the audience, as well as loud and generous applause. Dunne and his co-aspirational colleague suddenly felt rather exposed and half-decided to leave, but then stayed to see what other slanderous aspersions might be thrown around. Clearly, it was in their interests to be present in case a disciplinary case needed to be made.

"This is getting a bit much," said an indignant Wheeler.

"We ought to record this," said Dunne to his Companion. "Might be important to have an accurate transcript after the event."

"Good idea. I've got a pocket recorder in my office. I'll just be a tick."

Wheeler shot off towards the rear as the Fool walked off to a further round of cheers.

The lights dimmed momentarily and then brightened, exposing the opening set again. This time, however, the set showed seven academicians painting a reclining nude. The hubbub died down as the audience anticipated the start of the dialogue. However, this was a pseudo beginning. In the best traditions of performance art, the first act was completely without dialogue. The audience didn't twig straight away. Wheeler certainly didn't, as he scurried back from his office and barged his way through the audience.

Because the audience was standing, and because a

standing audience, especially a tipsy one, finds it difficult to restrain at least a gentle murmur of sound, there developed a feeling at the back of the hall, that they were missing out on the dialogue because of the noise from the front. Inevitably there began the imploring "shhhh's" and hissed "Quiet's." The people at the front couldn't see the stage very well because it was raised, but they could tell there wasn't much happening – apart from the odd academician holding his brush at arm's length to get a decent vertical over the model's anatomy. After a couple of minutes of this, the audience became very restless. It was clearly not the occasion to try out this sort of performance art. But just as the audience was getting cheesed off, help arrived stage-left in the form of a grumpy person.

Off-stage, the cast groaned at this unexpected turn of events. But the Dean had a better grasp of the situation and advised against any action. It seemed like a heaven-sent intervention and ought to be played out.

Out on the front, the said Grumpy marched to centre-stage with the aid of some rather flappy arms and legs: dwarf style. He stood, legs akimbo, confident in himself, and then leant forward conspiratorially.

"I'm Grumpy," he confided to the audience.

The audience cheered. There was going to be a role for them in this panto.

"Oh no, he's not," shouted an exasperated voice entering stage-right. "There's only one Grumpy round here, and it's me. I'm your man."

"Oh no, you're not," shouted the first Grumpy, shaking his fist at the advancing figure from stage-right. This was a tactical blunder; the audience picked up on it straight away. Not for nothing had they been practising for this moment.

"Oh yes he is!" they chorused.

"Oh no, he's not! I'm Grumpy," he shouted back, clearly hurt by the rejection.

Back came the deafening chorus, "Oh yes he is!"

"Please," he implored. "You don't understand."

"Off! Off!" they thundered.

Grumpy Number Two clasped his hands in the air and did a little jig. A premature gesture because it wasn't over yet. Grumpy Number One had a trick up his sleeve. He motioned for the crowd to be quiet.

"I can prove that I'm Grumpy," he announced confidently.

This was an unexpected claim, and the audience was suitably impressed. Grumpy Number Two smelt a rat and didn't hesitate to say so.

"Methinks I smell a rat here," he said, holding his nose theatrically.

"Phew," responded the crowd.

"It's true," said the first Grumpy. "I can prove it. You wanna know how?"

"Yes!" they chorused.

He beckoned them to come closer, as if about to confide a great secret.

"The real Grumpy's got a birthmark."

"A birthmark," whispered the amazed throng. "Where?"

"On his bottom!" screamed Grumpy Number One.

Grumpy Number Two went pale under his makeup. He guessed what was coming next.

"Let's see what this impostor's got on his bottom!" demanded Grumpy Number One, pointing dramatically at his rival.

"Off with your pants! Off! Off!" they shouted.

Since Grumpy Number Two had no intention of dropping his trousers in public, Grumpy Number One invited some support from the audience to help unmask this *impostor*. Suddenly Grumpy Number Two didn't fancy making a spectacle of himself and bolted stage-right. Grumpy Number One was left triumphant in the middle of the stage. And to the delighted cheers of the audience, he did a little striptease to reveal a large G sign on his posterior.

This seemed an appropriate time for the *genuine* Grumpy to be removed from the stage, and indeed he came off willingly as the heavies zoomed in from either wing. No matter: he was triumphant. He had made the role his and there was no more to be said on the matter.

This left the academicians exposed again. However, having been thoroughly grilled by Zoe over the past four weeks' rehearsals, they hadn't reacted at all during the Grumpy episode. The audience again hushed briefly. They hadn't realised that the Grumpy double act wasn't part of the panto and were now waiting expectantly for the next scene. It was obviously going to be as good as the last act and they were therefore willing to be patient. At least for a moment or two. Again, the Dean read the situation and motioned for the players to get on with it.

Chapter 10

"Well," **said Abel,** standing back and admiring his painting, "I think that's about there." Then, by way of confirmation and invitation, added, "This really looks the part. Come and take a gander at how it should be done, chaps."

Nobody moved. However, one of the other academicians voiced much the same sort of opinion about his work. A third was then prompted into asserting the quality of his work.

"Art?" said Aubery, advancing to centre-stage. "Don't talk to me about art. Come and feast your perceptions on this, you lucky lot."

Of course, the other academicians didn't take this lying down and started bleating on about their paintings. In fact, the bleating became realistic as the sound of sheep was switched in to take over the academician's ranting. To add to the sheepish metaphor, the academicians started gesticulating and wandering around the stage as if addressing some potential neophyte.

Suddenly, the model got off the bed – wrapping a drape around her modesty.

"I've had enough of this bleating," she declared loudly as she tossed the last curl of the drape over her left shoulder.

The academicians were startled at this unexpected interruption, which was made more dramatic by the sudden loss of the sound effects. "You lot are pathetic," she pronounced. "Bloody pathetic. Aren't they pathetic?" She looked at the audience for affirmation.

"Oh yes they are," they shouted back, and then broke into giggles at this revelation.

"And it's the same picture every day," she said, storming around the stage, scattering academicians in her wake. "You paint the same rubbish over and over. Except the spots are in a different place on the canvas. And speaking of spots and splodges. When are we going to see some content that isn't miscellaneous spots and splodges of paint? Spots, splodges and damn spots. That's all you ever to paint. You see any spots or splodges on me?" she demanded, baring a shoulder to the audience.

"No!"

"You see any spots or splodges over here?" She bared her other shoulder. "Or on here?" she added, baring a thigh.

"No!!"

"And what do we have here?" she said, marching to the first canvas and turning it to the audience.

"Spots and splodges!" shouted the audience.

"And what have we got here?" she said, turning the second and subsequent canvases to the audience.

"Spots and splodges!!" they shouted to each exposé.

"I mean, haven't you twigged yet?" she said, turning to the academicians at last.

The academicians, huddled together, barely managed a collective, "What?"

"You're all sheep. All bloody sheep. Not one of you've

got any bollocks."

The sound effects of sheep bleating were switched on again. The audience sensed an opportunity to contribute. Within moments, the hall was echoing to the dulcet sounds of bleating sheep and giggling students.

This also seemed to act as a cue for haranguing the academicians on stage, especially as there now appeared to be a score of extras on stage all dressed in sheep's clothing. They had materialised on stage and were busy rummaging around the academician's legs. Several of the sheep were trying to mount the academicians. It all looked terribly camp.

Back in the audience, Wheeler became very irate. He felt especially vulnerable because he was a noted exponent of the Spot and Splodge movement. Indeed, he was currently showing some large canvases in a one-man exhibition in the college gallery. Two years and two hundred litres of the best quality acrylic daubs of varying hues and sizes were a testimony to his commitment to the S&S vernacular.

At least one academician on stage thought he'd had enough of this haranguing.

"And what do you know about art?" demanded Ambrose, as he broke out of the involuntary huddle of academicians and advanced towards the model.

"Yes," muttered Wheeler, looking to Dunne for confirmation. "What do you know about it?"

"We may not know much about art," said the model conspiratorially to the audience, "but we know about splodge merchants. Don't we, boys and girls?"

The audience's loyalty was never in doubt and the academicians cowered together as the audience made vocal their views. The academicians and the audience then launched into the standard,

"Oh no you don't."

"Oh yes we do," routine.

Eventually, one academician raised his hands and beckoned for silence. "There's only one way to settle this," said Abel. "We must have a consultation with the Critic."

The other academicians gasped. Several of them threw up their hands in mock horror and started backing away from him. However, after a pause, the others nodded in agreement.

"Yes, Abel's right," voiced the nodders.

"We ought to go," said Albert. "We haven't been for ages."

The others remained unconvinced.

"I can't see him giving the nod to any of us," said a reluctant Ambrose. "He never has to date. Why would he this time round? And last time we went round he said some horrid things about my paintings."

"Oh, that was just his way of being playful," said Abel. "I'm sure he meant nothing by it. He's quite a nice chap, actually."

"You're just saying that, Abel, because he wasn't as rude about your work as he was about the rest of us," said Aubery.

This struck a resonant chord in the others, and they all started muttering dark thoughts about the Critic.

"Bloody cheek," hissed Ambrose.

"Who does he think he is?" said Alaric, pacing back and forth across the stage.

"I wanted to strangle him after the last consultation," said Alistair. "He said his cat could paint better than me. I'm definitely not going round."

Before anyone could say anything more, the model, who till now had been wandering round the stage silently laughing at the paintings, began making clucking noises, and with hands akimbo started flapping her elbows as well. The front line of the audience followed suit almost immediately. Before long, other squawking students were trying to find room to flap their elbows. Given that the hall was packed, that was quite impossible. Those that couldn't flap like chickens squawked even louder. On the stage, the reluctant academicians tried vainly to retaliate by shaking fists at the audience, but it was a lost cause. The squawking eventually subsided into giggles as the academicians capitulated.

"All right, all right," yelled Alistair. "But I'm warning you," he said, wagging his finger and retreating backwards from the audience, "If he compares me with his cat again, I'll… I'll… I'll get very cross."

"Oooh," responded the audience.

The technical help backstage took this as a cue to play music. Near the front of the stage, a large canvas painted with song lyrics was lowered from the ceiling. As it did so, the cast moved to the front to stand on either side of the giant *lyric sheet*. Behind them, the curtain closed unnoticed as the cast broke into song.

The song appeared to be based loosely on the Wizard of Oz – some way removed from the apparent base of Snow White, but no one minded. In the best traditions of pantomime, the stage players encouraged the audience to join in.

When the song finished, the audience rewarded the cast with loud cheers and generous applause. The academicians, led by the model, skipped off the stage in triumph. Before the audience had caught its breath, the curtain rose directly after the last academician left the stage.

In contrast to the previous scene, which was bright and bobbish, and cluttered with easels, brushes and other accoutrements of the jobbing academician, the opening moments of the new scene augured a restrained continuity amidst refined and subtle-looking surroundings.

The design brief for the Fashion and Textiles department had been to create a mysterious set for a modern-day Wizard Critic. What they produced was a cross between a Bond Street gallery and a Japanese watercolour, but with references to Frank Lloyd Wright thrown in as well.

Prints of famous twentieth-century paintings covered the right-hand side of the stage. A long window defined the left. The framework of the window was modelled on a sideways view of Wright's Robie House of 1901. The carpenters had covered the whole thing in a translucent material. They had lit the window from behind to cause soft, diffuse patches of light-overlays to be cast onto the stage. The strong horizontals of the house contrasted against several white plinths placed around the stage. Giacometti-like figures were mounted on these stands. They stretched upwards, pulling the eye towards a cream-coloured canopy spread high over the stage. This was angled upwards from the rear of the stage. It, too, hinted at higher ideals. Images of Mondrian's Composition in White, Red and Yellow adorned the canopy. The spotlights at the front of the stage picking out the rectangular motifs. The set and its lighting had a thoroughly calming effect on the crowd. Within a few moments, they fell quiet.

As the last whispers died away, the academicians entered stage-right, in single file, centipede style. Shushing each other and clutching their paintings, they tiptoed on to the stage, giving the impression of small boys entering a headteacher's study.

"Doesn't look as though he's in," whispered Aidan, peering over the right shoulder of his forward neighbour. "Why don't we come back later?" he added, in a beseeching treble in his upper register.

"Much later," echoed Albert, who was behind him.

"Much, much later would be best of all," added Alistair.

Abel, at the head of the file, appeared to lose his bottle. He tried backtracking off the stage. The academicians behind him sensed his discomfort and resisted the backward pressure. In fact, they responded with some pressure of their own. As a result, Abel was propelled, unwillingly, towards the middle of the stage.

As he got to centre-stage, a loud explosion hurled the academicians in all directions. The puffs of smoke cleared to reveal a tall enigmatic figure in dark glasses. He was wearing a severe-looking grey suit with a black velvet floor length cape. It was, of course, the Dean – but quite unrecognisable as such. The audience fell completely silent and held its collective breath. The academicians dropped their paintings with a clatter and huddled up tight for comfort.

"Well?" boomed the Critic, as he rounded on the cowering group. "What visual drivel have you brought this time? I hope it's an improvement on the nonsense you delivered last time. My cat could have done better. Couldn't you, Doris?"

"Meow," replied a bewhiskered Miles, emerging from the Critic's cape to a rousing cheer. The whiskers perked up as Miles basked in the audience's unexpected affection.

This was an unusual experience for him and one that could no doubt be developed. With his tail a-curling, therefore, he moved to centre-stage on all fours. Miles prepared to pronounce on the subject of painting, and on these paintings in particular, but the Dean had no intention of standing there listening to Miles burbling on about art. He decided that the one line from Miles was quite enough. One had to get things into perspective. After all, he was only the cat.

"Come on. Come on. I haven't got all day," said the Critic, as he grabbed the cat's tail and swept him unceremoniously back under his cape. And just to make sure he stayed there, thumped him with a cricket bat, which had magically appeared in his hands.

"Yes, sir."

"Straight away, sir."

The academicians broke out of their huddle and started scampering round the stage like so many demented clowns. They lined up their pictures along the back of the stage and waited, hands-a-wringing, for the Critic to pass judgement. A hush fell over the audience as the Critic moved towards the paintings. He was hampered to some extent by a comatose Miles, but this didn't prevent him from making a cursory inspection of the paintings.

He moved briskly from one work to the next, jerking his cape to accommodate Miles's formless mass. Inspection over, he drew himself up to his full height, cleared his throat, and broke into verse:

> Though your paintings are fair and all
> They are funny and, well, small and
> In truth, I must recall
> They are not the New Art at all: at all

"Same as usual," said Alaric.

"We're never going to get this painting business right," said Aubery.

"Wait," called the Critic imperiously as they turned to leave. "There is more."

"More?" said Ambrose.

"Perhaps he's going to give us some tips on getting it right," said a hopeful Alistair.

The Critic advanced to centre-stage and removed his dark glasses.

"I've never seen him without his dark glasses," said Albert – as an aside to the audience. Aubery threw up his hands in theatrical amazement as the Critic slipped one hand in his pocket and pointing with his glasses added:

There is one who is fairer
Whose vision is clearer
Ms White is her name
Not painting by numbers is her game
Whosoever penetrates
her well-guarded gate
Will doubtless find himself at the Tate

After delivering these enigmatic sounding lines, the Critic disappeared in a puff of smoke to the accompaniment of loud guffaws from the audience. Dunne and Wheeler, who both nursed ambitions of getting a piece into the Tate, became somewhat embarrassed. The Critic's last line had been rather near the mark. The deflated duo didn't feel quite so inclined to make an issue of the panto.

Back on the stage, the academicians tried to work out what the Critic had meant.

"Well," said Abel. "I've been coming to see him for yonks and yonks and that's the first time he's mentioned anyone called Ms White."

"Who do you think this Ms White could be?" said Albert.

"She can't be anyone," replied Ambrose. "I mean, stands to reason, doesn't it? We'd have heard of her if she were anyone. Right?"

"Too right," added Alaric.

Suddenly, the sound of thunder filled the hall. The academicians scattered to the sides of the stage, as a second peal was followed by a flash of lightning. Smoke billowed down from the ceiling and rolled over to the edge of the stage. As the sound of thunder subsided, the Critic's words were heard again, booming out across the stage:

There is one who is fairer

Whose vision is clearer

And in answer to the obvious question, a large screen descended from the ceiling above the rear of the stage. It flickered into life to reveal a video image of a girl wearing paint-splattered clothes working energetically at a large easel. The audience recognised Zoe straight away; the academicians had to be informed. Cue the distant booming voice of the Critic:

Ms White is her name

Not painting by numbers is her game

Whosoever penetrates her well-guarded gate

Will doubtless find himself at the Tate

The Critic's voice died away slowly with the last couplet. Just before it finally faded, another bout of thunder and lightning hit the stage. The academicians looked suitably helpless. They were finally driven off the stage by the commotion. All very impressive stuff. And to underline the fact that the audience with the Critic was over, the curtain swept in to close off the stage – just as the last academician went tumbling into the wings.

*

The academicians, who had been so sheepish in the Critic's presence and who had stood transfixed at the image of a revealed genius, were now reanimated in a new scene back at the Academy. No doubt the bottles of tasteful wine circulating around the stage were the reason for this jolly atmosphere.

The slower among them started wondering about the possible form and content of Ms White's work. For others, however, form and content were mere abstractions. Vague distractions which missed the point altogether.

"What do you think he meant when he said that bit about her, 'Well-guarded gate'?" said Aubrey.

"Only one thing he could have meant, old boy," replied Abel. "No two ways about it."

"What? You surely don't think he meant that, do you, Abel?" said Alaric, sounding suitably shocked.

"What else could he mean, old boy?"

Despite the rather thoughtful hint from the Critic, the academicians still had no clue about Ms White. They stood about the stage, scratching their thinning heads and prompting each other for a clue. All to no avail.

"There's nothing for it," said Abel, eventually. "We'll have to send for Mac. He'll know who she is."

"Who?" said a chorus of academicians.

"Mac: the porter," said Abel. Then, as if to lend authority to his remark added, "He's in charge of the back gate."

This brought forth a mixture of boos and giggles from the audience. Mac was a part-time porter but had taken the role to heart. He tried to convey the impression that he was in sole charge of the rear entrance to the college. Clearly, the panto had found him a role in which to play himself.

"Why would he know?" chorused the puzzled group.

"Mac knows everyone," said Abel. "If he doesn't know who this Ms White is, then she doesn't exist."

"Yes, but why would our back gate porter know her?" said Aubery.

Mac was, in fact, a German postgraduate art history student named Walter Gropius. However, although he had a famous namesake, he much preferred to be called Mac. No doubt it had something to do with his research on Charles Rennie Mackintosh. At any rate, he was also something of an expert on Modern Art. After explaining all this to his fellow academicians, Abel rushed over to the stage phone and called the back gate lodge. Thanks to the magic of the theatre, no sooner had he put the phone down than Mac wandered onto the stage.

A mixture of boos and cheers accompanied his entrance. The cheerers were undoubtedly glad to see Mac because his attempts at a Scots accent were always worth listening to; the booers were no doubt recalling the incident during the staff versus student cricket match last summer when Mac had been given out for a clear LBW decision but had refused to walk. It was the only time since he had arrived at St Sigeberht's that he had let the Scots accent go and had lapsed into Teutonic fury. They had resolved the incident by allowing him to continue to bat. By mutual agreement, the two captains discounted his subsequent contributions, such as they were. It had all been very embarrassing.

"Yoeuse sent furr me, surr," he said in an almost incomprehensible Scots accent, while scowling at the audience trying to pick out booers against the glare of the footlights.

"What?" said the academicians, almost in unison.

"I'hm herr at yurr raquest, surr."

"What?" said Aubrey in his most exasperated sounding type of voice. As one of the older academicians, he was supposed to be especially slow in comprehending foreign-sounding accents. Someone from the audience thoughtfully tried to act as an interpreter and shouted out a translation. Unfortunately, the interpreter was a Scot whose accent was almost as impenetrable as Mac's. Several members of the audience seized the opportunity to play a part. The more active members took their cue from the lone Scot and started shouting out a tolerably good translation of Mac's responses to the academicians.

"He said you sent for me," shouted a chorus of helpful voices.

"Oh, right. Now then, Mac," said Abel, half-looking at Mac while directing his question to the would-be translators in the audience. "What can you tell me about a Ms White? She's supposed to be a painter. Have you heard of her?"

"Ahh yes, surr. That'll be the lassie in the furst-yeer stoodios. A verry good painterr she be, surr. A verrry good painterr indeedah."

The academicians turned to the audience in obvious desperation.

"She works in the first-year studios," shouted several translators. "And she's a very good painter."

"What do you mean she works in the first-year studios," said Ambrose, turning from the audience to confront Mac.

"Ahh mean no murr an no less. The lassie's a student

heerr at the Academy. Though wha' she's doing heerr's beyon ma ken. She's furr betterr than enny o' the tutorrs heerr."

This time, the translators' contribution prompted a dramatic response from the stage.

"Good God, man," said Alaric, before the translators could respond. He advanced theatrically to centre-stage, and pausing for effect, said, "Do you mean to tell me that this, this Ms White, or whatever her name is, is actually a student here, at St Sigeberht's?"

"No, you idiot," hissed the academicians. "Not at St Sigeberht's; at the Academy. Ms White is a student at the Academy."

"Oh," said a deflated Alaric, but he recovered quickly. He retraced his steps back to the huddle while waving his arms as if to cancel the last bit of dialogue. A bemused audience took the situation in its stride and responded with a tolerant cheer. The academician waited for the noise to die down, then advanced again to centre-stage as if nothing had happened, and simply repeated the last bit of dialogue. This time, with lots of emphasis on the correct institution:

"Do you mean to tell me that this, this Ms White, or whatever her name is, is a student here, at the ACADEMY?"

The audience rewarded Alaric with another cheer. Meanwhile, the other academicians looked at one another rather meaningfully.

"A student at the Academy, eh? First-year student, is she? Are you all thinking what I'm thinking, chaps?" said Abel, looking around at the group.

They all nodded like a row of donkeys.

"Last one there's a cissy," said Abel.

They bolted stage-left to avoid that fate. The clattering of their footsteps followed them off stage and faded slowly; then grew stronger again. A moment later, the group reappeared high up on the stage, running left to right with wildly gesticulating arms. As they crossed the stage, they were picked out by a spotlight, which followed them disappearing stage-right. The spotlight paused by the wings, waiting for them to return. They dutifully reappeared a moment later and lurched across the stage in the opposite direction; a moment later, they came back the other way again. As they ran backwards and forwards, they got louder and more frantic, trying to keep each other from being first in line.

All of this provided a convenient moment to dim the lights on the stage and allow the stage crew to change the scene. Eventually, the academicians clattered off stage but then failed to reappear in the expected place. Instead, they emerged, rather breathless, on the balcony overlooking the stage. Down below, they could see a studio. It obviously belonged to a real painter.

Someone had gone to a lot of trouble to create this set. There was so much to see; yet it would have been easy to miss the richness of the detail. A casual observer might have started with the autumnal colours of the dried grasses scattered across the stage. He might have lingered over the sketches pinned to the walls: studies of form and function. He might have been entranced by the tonal ranges of the pebbles that filled a collection of wicker baskets. They lay, like eggs, in a patchwork of grey shadows, and were echoed in compositions hung around the studio. But there was colour too: in the working drawings of plants, landscapes and figures; in the folds of hessian draped about the studio;

in the bits of scientific apparatus, in the warmth of toys arranged on various tables. And then there were the scores and scores of tubes of colours – arranged neatly in rows next to the main painting area: reds, blues and greens, but also ochres, crimsons and violets. Each echoed in parallel trays of soft luxurious pastels: a fortune in colour paraded unashamedly for the delight of any artist who might chance to pass by.

The studio was lit from above with a bright neutral light. It produced a tremendous feeling of space. A space that was clearly defined and, hence, tangible; it seemed as physical as the objects on the stage. The academicians froze briefly to take in the scene. It was an arresting moment before the action continued, but it was also meant to be a statement in its own right, and indeed, it seemed to be appreciated by the audience. They fell silent and were content to gaze for a while.

The casting of two spotlights on to the stage signalled the cue for further action. Within the undulating lights, a voluptuous female figure, dressed in the briefest of bikinis and wearing knee-high boots, strode onto the stage and was seen to be accosting an easel with strong purposeful strokes. The audience let out a cheer as they recognised Zoe.

"Cor!" exclaimed the academicians in inebriated unison.

"I concur," hiccupped Alistair.

Even Ambrose, who was supposed to be the model of propriety, managed a roguish, "My word!"

"Well, chaps, duty calls," said Abel, as he hooked one leg over the balcony to climb down to the stage below.

"Whoa, Abel. Just hang on there, old boy," said Aidan, grabbing him by the shoulder. The others joined in and hoiked him back onto the balcony.

"Let go, you miserable bunch of wimps."

"No good struggling, old boy," said Albert.

"Hopeless springs to mind, Abel," added Alistair.

They finally subdued him by sitting on him.

"Just wait till I get my hands on you."

"Calm down, Abel," said Ambrose.

"I'll make mincemeat of you," asserted Abel with a last puff of defiance.

"Abel, you'll just do yourself an injury," said Aidan.

"That's the general idea, dummy," said Abel. "What a way to go!"

"What makes you think that you're first?" said a babble of voices.

"Because I'm the only one with any balls around here," shouted Abel. "And besides, I'm the best painter. I ought to go first."

This brought forth a predictable chorus of howls from the other academicians. Naturally enough, they felt compelled to give him some bumps to express their displeasure. It was a chastened Abel who apologised and begged for mercy.

"Well, how do we decide who goes first?" said a breathless Ambrose.

"Only one thing for it, lads," said Aubery. "We'll have to take it in turns."

The others looked at him, and then at each other.

"Pillock!" said Abel.

"Just what I was thinking," said Alistair.

"Just thought I'd mention it," said Aubery, sounding rather hurt.

In the event, they tossed penny pieces at the wall

– nearest the wall to go first.

The lights dimmed as the academicians crouched over their bouncing penny pieces. A moment later, the main stage was lit again, and Ambrose entered stage-right. His penny had clearly won the game; he was now looking for his destiny. But like the proverbial groom, he was nervous about the prospect. Especially as there didn't appear to be anyone else on the stage. He looked to right and left, but bikini-clad girls were in short supply. Up on the balcony, the other academicians were watching intently. Ambrose turned to look at them. He shrugged his shoulders as if to say, "Now what?" Their reply didn't matter because the next moment, he, along with practically everyone else in the hall, almost jumped out of their skins as the lampstand which had been standing quietly to one side of the room, rotated dramatically to reveal a female figure in a magnificent wedding dress.

Ambrose jumped back as the figure swept past him, carrying a palette of bright clean colours. She strode to a canvas mounted on an easel in the centre of the stage. With deft strokes, she swept paint from the wood with a palette knife and onto the canvas.

"Um, hello," said a sheepish Ambrose.

The figure swept past him to collect more paint from a table at the rear of the stage.

"Um, Ms White?" said Ambrose, trying to introduce himself.

"Yes?"

"Oh!" exclaimed a surprised Ambrose. "Um, Ms White."

"Get to the point," said the figure. She grabbed a large tube and squeezed paint on to her easel.

"Um," said Ambrose yet again.… "Would you mind

terribly if I made a pass at you?"

The figure stopped squeezing the tube of paint and slowly lifted her wedding veil.

Chapter 11

"You wanna make a pass at me, Romeo?" said Ms White, advancing on Ambrose. "Well now, let's see what you're made of, shall we?"

Ambrose took a backward step as the audience picked up the cue from Ms White.

"Yes," shouted a strident voice. "Let's see what he's made of."

"Yeah, let's see what you've got, Romeo," echoed a chorus of semi-drunk helpers.

"Oh dear," said a whimpering Ambrose. He began backing off in a theatrical retreat. "What have I let myself in for?"

As he retreated, a bemused looking Ms White snapped her fingers in a dramatic gesture, whereupon a largish canvas descended from high above the lights. To the accompaniment of a "Wheee" and a "Pop" – courtesy of the Sound Effects department – it came to a stop in the middle of the stage.

"Let's see what you can produce with that, Leonardo," said Ms White, handing him her palette and brushes. A nervy Ambrose fumbled with his brushes, while Ms White arranged herself on the model's couch. A very provocative pose, it was.

However, Ambrose clearly didn't know what he was expected to do. He started by mopping his brow, but that didn't seem to help. After a pause, he glanced at the palette and brushes in his hand; then he looked at the canvas; finally, he looked at Ms White. Most of the audience, too, were befuddled. Cue Ms White.

"You got to say it with paint, blue eyes," she said, gesturing towards the easel.

Ambrose got the picture. "Oh! I've got to paint you, Oh, Goody!" he said with obvious glee. "I'm good at that."

He lost his nervousness, and, with a hop and a skip, shot over to the canvas. With the palette on his left arm and a twirling brush in the other, he lifted a dollop of paint and began prodding the canvas with short jerky strokes. However, he hadn't got far before it became apparent that this was no ordinary canvas. Every brush stroke that he applied to the canvas seemed to carry the stroke through to the writhing figure of Ms White on her couch. And it also became apparent very quickly that Ambrose was making a poor job of touching up Ms White – so to speak. Every prod and poke of Ambrose's brush produced sharp exclamations from the couch.

"Ouch! Oooh! Careful, you dummy."

Considering that Ms White's couch was behind the canvas, and that therefore she couldn't see what Ambrose was doing, his prodding, and her responses were well coordinated indeed. The audience in the front rows tried hard to see how the trick was being done but were left puzzled.

Since the concept of a living canvas was such an important part of the plot, the players gave the audience several minutes to appreciate the idea that the canvas and Ms White's body were essentially the same thing.

"Oh, for heaven's sake," said an exasperated Ms White after the umpteenth exclamation. "It's no good. You'll have to go."

"Go?" said Ambrose, looking around. "Go where? I've only just started."

He didn't have long to ponder his destination. Ms White snapped her fingers, and the ground opened up beneath the hapless painter. The palette and brushes flew out of his hands as he threw up his arms to maintain his balance. Brushes and palette clattered to the floor as his screams echoed away into the depths of the stage. The canvas, presumably his last on this mortal earth, followed without ceremony. The symbolism of this descent was not lost on the audience. Ambrose's departure went down well. So well, in fact, the audience burst into spontaneous applause. And for good measure, several members of the audience stuck in the proverbial boot.

"Ha! Ha! He deserved that," shouted a manic sort of lead.

"Good riddance to bad rubbish. That's wot I say," said a second.

"Call that painting? Pooh. My granny could do better with one hand tied behind her back."

"One hand?" said another. "Mine could do better hanging upside down with both hands tied behind her back!"

"'Nough said," said the lead.

Before the audience could offer more, the lights shifted the action to the balcony. The scene revealed a bunch of disconcerted-looking academicians.

"My God! Did you see that?" said a trembling Albert.

"Poor Ambrose. He didn't have a chance," said Aidan.

"What a terrible way to go," added Alistair.

"Gulp. Gulp and more gulps," said Alaric, pacing back and forth.

"I don't know about you chaps," said Alistair with arms outstretched, "but I'm off. I've gone off the idea of penetration."

"Poor, poor Ambrose," said Albert, tugging thoughtfully at his straggling beard. "Looks like the only thing he'll be penetrating is six sodding feet of soil."

"Poor Ambrose, my foot," said Abel, striking a discordant note. "He just wasn't very good. And we can't go by what happened to him. I mean, just think about what's at stake: a piece at the Tate!"

"I'm not sure it's such a great idea, Abel," said Aubrey, trying to sum up the pros and cons. "I mean it's all very well for the Critic to rabbit on about the Tate, but this is a non-starter. No one's going to get past this particular gate. That's for sure. Look what happened to Ambrose."

"Yes, but Ambrose is an idiot."

"Was an idiot," said Aidan, correcting him.

"Whatever," said Abel, dismissing a minor irrelevancy. "We won't make the same mistake that Ambrose made. Eh? I mean, we'll steer well clear of that trap door."

"Whatdaya mean steer clear of the trap door?" said Aidan. "Can't be done, old boy. The canvas came down directly above the trap door; don't see how you can avoid it."

"It's easy. Don't you see?" said Abel, trying to work up some enthusiasm. "Two of you come with me. We'll tie a rope round my middle, and you can then hold on to me while I work the canvas. If the trap door opens, you can pull me out."

"Forgive me for asking," said a sarcastic Albert, half addressing the audience, "but what's in it for the two mugs who're holding the rope? Eh?" He had spotted the obvious flaw and was milking the audience for all he was worth. And they weren't slow in responding.

"Yeah!" shouted the lead with a dozen others close on his vocal heels. "What's in it for them?"

"Easy," said Abel. "We all get to paint the canvas."

"Thanks, Abel," said Alaric, "but I've never been keen on group canvases."

"Me ne-neither," stammered Albert quickly – perhaps too quickly. The others looked round at him quizzically while the audience sniggered, as though sensing something naughty.

"Come on, chaps," said Abel, pleading with the group. "This is our chance to create new and exciting art."

"Sooner you than me, old boy," said Aidan, lighting up a pipe.

"Couldn't agree with you more, old chum," said Alistair showing a keen sense of self-preservation. "That trap door is huge."

Meanwhile backstage, Frank was being prepared. However, he had other things on his plate. In particular, he was now regretting the speed with which he'd knocked back several pints of lager before going on stage. He wouldn't normally have drunk that quickly, or indeed to have drunk lager, believing it to be a woman's drink. He had done so because there wasn't any Guinness available, and he'd made the mistake of making known his views on the feminine nature of the most popular brew in the college. His comments hadn't been allowed to go unchallenged, and he had to demonstrate his mastery of the amber nectar. And now, the drink and his nervousness about going on stage were having a thoroughly diuretic effect on his metabolism. He had already made two journeys to the loo but was now trapped back stage without hope of relief till the end of the performance. He loped around, seeking for a solution to a growing need.

Amidst the props and in semi-darkness, it was easy to imagine that he was in a wood of some sort. It occurred to him that if he had been in a wood, a suitable tree wouldn't have been hard to find. This thought led him to look for a friendly equivalent. By chance, he espied some tracery in the rear wall. He couldn't work out why it was there but peering through, he could see the lamp posts across the road.

– What do you think, *Frank?*

– Looks promising, Frank. And I am busting to go.

By now Frank was in dire straits. His bladder felt like a balloon about to pop. He simply had to relieve himself. He didn't even look behind to see if he was alone.

Outside and directly below Frank, stood DI Fogg. The DI raised himself on an empty beer crate (to check the activities backstage) just as Frank's urgent member came poking through the wall. One in the eye took on a whole new meaning for the hapless DI. In astonishment, he opened his mouth to utter an obscenity, but he was cut short by a jet of the amber nectar coming out in reverse.

"Arghhhaaah," gargled Fogg, falling backward. A bubbling curve of hot liquid followed him in close pursuit. Trying desperately not to swallow, he landed with a thud and an unfortunate gulp. "Jesus Christ! Oh, fucking hell. Argaaah," he spluttered, rolling over to avoid further dowsing.

In between bouts of coughing and spitting he tried to make himself sick by poking a finger down his throat.

"My God! I can't believe what I've swallowed. Fucking hell."

He stomped off in search of something to wash the burning taste in his mouth. "Some fucker's going to pay for this," he announced for the benefit of anyone interested. The other members of the police contingent made sympathetic noises at the receding figure before collapsing into hysterical fits as soon as he got round the corner.

In the meantime, Frank, oblivious to the scene outside, was getting dragged off towards the stage. Apparently, he was in danger of missing his cue. Fumbling with his flies and his props, he let himself be shepherded towards the proceedings.

– Are you ready for this, Frank, said *Frank*.

– Are you kidding, *Frank*? I'm never going be ready to parade in front of hundreds of people with this sticking out of my flies. And what I'm supposed to say when I get out there?

– Don't worry about the lines, Frank. Look, I've got them written down on this roll of paper.

– Well, that's you taken care of then. What about me? How am I going to remember my lines?

– Trust me, Frank. I'll see you right.

– *Frank*, I wouldn't trust you with an effing what's its name.

– Now, now, Frank.

– Don't you, 'Now, now' me you bloody peasant. I don't want to go on.

– Look, Frank, said *Frank* in a soothing tone. You just

take care of the accent. Leave the lines to me.

– It isn't just the lines, *Frank*. Jesus! It's this fucking thing I'm sporting. I've got to have another drink, he said in desperation. "Maybe I'll get used to it if I have enough to drink.

Frank wasn't the only one reticent about going on stage. The academicians were still arguing the toss about the wisdom of attempting to follow in Ambrose's footsteps. Abel by now was pretty cheesed off with his fellow academicians.

"Well, that's it then," he said in a hurt voice. "I'm going on my tod. Anyway," he added defiantly, "I don't know why I'm arguing the toss with you wimps. If anyone's going to pull this off it's going to be yours truly. And never mind one piece at the Tate; it'll be a bloody retrospective by the time I'm finished."

Before Abel could expand further, the spot lights on the balcony were dimmed to focus attention on the main stage. The set revealed a restless Ms White with knitted brow. Pausing for a sigh here and a sigh there, she criss-crossed the stage several times and eventually approached a full-length mirror at one end of the stage. With hands akimbo and in obvious frustration, she addressed the mirror:

Mirror, Mirror on my studio wall,
With your face so sparkling clean and all
Who is the fairest male painter of all?
And tell me, when can I expect him to call?

The Mirror, despite its huge size, replied in an unexpectedly shrill Brummy accent. "How do you expect me to know that?"

"Well, what a fat lot of use you are."

"That's not fair," retorted the Mirror. "I've bent over

141

backwards tryin' to help you. It's not my fault if you keep getting tuppenny ha'penny painters chasin' after you."

"Tuppeny ha'penny's about right," said Ms White in a bitter tone. "Look at the last pillock who showed up. Just clueless."

"Was he, dear?" said the Mirror. "Never mind. I expect he couldn't help himself."

"What do you mean?"

"Probably his classical training," explained the Mirror. "It gets to their libidinal tendencies you know."

"Really?"

"Oh, yes. Well known is that."

This remark brought forth a wave of sniggers from the audience. Particularly from those members of the audience close to Dunne and Wheeler. The duo glanced at each other again and made yet another mental note for retribution.

"You know what you need?" continued the Mirror in a cheery vein.

"What?"

"You need a modern painter. Someone from the Modern World."

"Where's that?"

"The U.S. of A. of course. I hear there're some very good modern painters over there."

"Well, I've never heard of any," said Ms White.

"Oh, yes. I'll tell you what," said the Mirror as if making an offer that no one could refuse, "I'll fetch someone for you."

"You can fetch someone for me? From America? What, just like that?"

"Oh, yes," said the Mirror with assured confidence.

"Just watch this."

The next instance there was a muffled explosion. When the smoke cleared. Frank appeared at the other end of the stage in a bathrobe. Despite the doubts behind the scenes, he had made it onto the stage with perfect timing. At the sight of Frank, the audience, who had been tipsy and bubbling for the past half an hour, erupted like a gathering of hysterical chimps. Though primed and agreeable they were, they were nevertheless surprised and delighted at the sight of Frank wandering on stage sporting an erection which looked as though it belonged on a working dray horse. A huge, bobbing thing, it projected from his loins at a telling angle and must have been fully a metre long. With his trusty spirit level attached to the side of the protrusion, Frank wandered around the stage in order to give the audience the opportunity to study his member from all angles.

Frank basked in the audience's admiration; Frank, by contrast, was hanging on grimly to the level with his eyes half shut. It was the only thing he could think of to minimise the acute embarrassment he felt – even with the best part of half a bottle of vodka inside him.

His walkabout brought him face to face – so to speak – with Ms White. She had slid behind a screen when Frank came on. She now reappeared and confronted Frank and his member.

"And who are you, big boy?" she asked coyly.

"Howdy, miss," said Frank in an appalling American accent.

– For Christ's sake, Frank, hissed *Frank*. Can't you do any better than that? You're playing the role of an American. A hard driving Yank of the New York School.

143

– Well, how can I concentrate with everyone staring at me? And this thing?

"Er, Yeah. My name's Prince Hardwood," said Frank in a more authentic tone of voice as Zoe prodded him for the next line.

"Oh, really," cooed Ms White. "And what exactly do you do, Princy?"

"I'm a painter," said the Prince with a flick in his voice.

"Oh, really?" said Ms White with a slight question in hers and with a sideways glance at the mirror.

"Cain't you tell?" he asked pointing meaningfully at his protrusion.

"Can't quite see the connection."

"This here's Excalibur. My main paintbrush. I never travel without it. Tool o' the trade, as they say."

"Er, quite," said Ms White with sympathetic understanding as the males in the audience tried to stifle their guffaws.

"I was just giving it a rub down," said Prince Hardwood. "You know? Have to keep them well oiled," he explained to a nodding Ms White.

By now, *Frank* was fully in his stride and was playing the audience like a seasoned trooper; in marked contrast, Frank was busy digging a hole to crawl into. But no matter how much he burrowed, he made no headway.

"The thing about paint brushes," continued the Prince, "is that you never know when you might have to beard a canvas or two. 'Stay alert, Princy. Stay alert.' That's what my daddy always used to say."

"Yes, I see what you mean by *alert*," said Ms White, and to the delight of the audience, stroked the paintbrush rhythmically with the tips of her fingers. "It certainly looks

144

like it could beard my canvas."

"Satisfaction gua-ran-teed," said the Prince, with the kind of authentic assurance that only a seasoned salesman can provide.

"Well then," concluded Ms White. "You must show me how well you can use it."

She took hold of his tool and, to cheers from the audience, led him like a bull with a ring through its nose to centre-stage. She paused momentarily to give the member a last lingering look, and then she brought down the magical canvas with a discreet snap of her fingers.

"Let's see what you can do with that. I'll just be on this couch," she said invitingly, sliding on to the chaise longue behind the canvas.

"Do you want anything particular doing," said Prince Hardwood, peering over the large canvas. As he did so, the tool inevitably knocked against the canvas. Ms White shivered visibly and let out a squeal of approval. The contact between brush and canvas seemed to help her decide exactly what she wanted.

"I'd like an all over sort of canvas," replied Ms White, as though instructing a trusted hairdresser.

"An all over canvas?" echoed Prince Hardwood in a puzzled sort of voice. He turned to the audience and shrugged his shoulders to communicate unfamiliarity with this quaint English custom of *an all over canvas.*

"Yes, you know," said Ms White, with a touch of impatience as she nestled into the chaise-longue. "Paint all of it."

"All of it," he said, echoing the confirmation to himself.

"Every little bit, please. Leave nothing out," she added with just a touch of urgency.

"Well now," said the Prince, warming to his task. "Don't say you didn't ask for it. This is gonna be some paintin'. It so happens that I'm fully stocked up today. You are in for a treat."

The audience could well understand the idea of Prince Hardwood being fully stocked up and shouted their encouragement.

Just as Prince Hardwood was about to start on the magical canvas, Abel appeared stage-left. He'd obviously decided to risk the trap door without support. He was wearing his best artist's smock and carried a huge bunch of paintbrushes in his hand. Clearly, he'd hunted out his entire collection of brushes: no way was he going to be unprepared as far as brushes were concerned.

No way, José, he'd thought to himself. However, as he now skipped onto the stage in obvious anticipation, he was surprised to find that Ms White was entertaining someone else. He wasn't too pleased.

Shouting aloud, "Blood and thunder," he pulled out his longest brush and raised it to his forehead: cavalier style. Prince Hardwood and Ms White looked at each other in mock amazement.

"Sir, I demand immediate satisfaction," said Abel, raising himself to his full height.

The audience cheered the double entendre.

Like a good trooper, Abel waited for the noise to subside and then with a sudden cry, he lunged at Prince Hardwood. The Prince countered neatly with his tool and then pushed Abel away with a great show of style. According to the script, a 'Breathtaking fight' then ensued with the protagonists careering all over the place. To frenzied shouts of encouragement, they cut and thrust their way around the stage, over tables and chairs, swinging from ropes and chandeliers.

The Prince's tool was a versatile piece of hardware. It was equipped with a motor, thus allowing it to move in all directions. It could squirt discrete blobs of paint or a continuous spray. And of course, the head was detachable. A demonic Abel nearly skewered the Prince several times as he demonstrated the various attachments that came with his tool. However, he wriggled out of the tightest of spots to foil his attacker. Eventually, it became clear the Prince was merely toying with his protagonist. With Abel exhausted and on his knees, the Prince blasted him off stage with a final percussive barrage of heavy-duty blobs of paint.

Judging by the deafening roar from the audience, the result was a popular outcome. Prince Hardwood too, seemed pleased with himself and did a victory jig up and down the stage. Halfway across the stage for the second time, he paused and raised a finger to indicate he had remembered that he had unfinished business. The audience fell silent as he approached the canvas again.

Wearing a mischievous expression, he began the task in hand. He gave a masterly demonstration of how to apply paint to canvas. Gently, vigorously, passionately. He worked the canvas while Ms White writhed and wriggled in harmony on the chaise-lounge. After the loud and exciting scene with Abel, this performance of Ms White's generated its own excitement with not a few of the males in the audience getting hot in the nether regions. As Ms White approached her climax, the Prince took a few steps back and then ran forward with a dramatic yell to skewer the canvas with his tool.

As the Prince's protrusion penetrated the canvas, Ms

White let out a piercing scream and began to inflate like a balloon. Within a few seconds, she had grown to resemble a large cow lying on its back. There was something odd going on within Ms White's stomach.

As the audience stood gaping at the ballooning figure on the couch, suddenly, to everyone's amazement, Ms White stood up and waddled on to an inclined area of the stage. Here, she opened her legs and started screaming hysterically. The academicians came running back on stage to see what was happening. They stood around clutching each other and covered their ears with each scream. The audience too caught something of the experience of what was happening onstage and became rather quiet. *Frank,* still holding on to his member, looked on with a bemused expression which he had been assured was de rigueur for such an occasion.

The sound effects provided a sustained drum roll as Ms White delivered something from within. Little by little, it emerged. Eventually, with a final earth-shattering scream from Ms White, it landed with a thud on the stage. The delivery uncurled itself to reveal a six-by-four canvas with legs and head protruding either side of the long edges. Just to make sure everyone understood what this was, the new arrival had a banner in its hand proclaiming *NEW ART* in large red letters. The painting was a succession of hard-edged lines terminated at the ends by circles enclosing soft colours; there was not a spot or splodge anywhere on the canvas.

The surprise of the event was broken by the reappearance of Abel. He reappeared on the scene and demanded to know what was going on. Upon seeing the new baby – now howling for its mother – he made a beeline for the figure.

"Gimme!" he exclaimed.

"You keep your hands off that, you shrimp," said the Prince, getting in his way.

"Come on, chaps. Quick. Gimme a hand," shouted Abel, taking hold of the left arm of the baby. "Quick. We can be out of here in a jiffy."

"You let go of that, you cretin," shouted the Prince.

"You let go yourself," shouted Abel as the Prince took hold of the other arm. A tug of war ensued with the Prince at one end and the academicians at the other.

With the protagonists shouting abuse at each other and the audience shouting "Heeaavve," it was surely only a matter of time before something gave way.

Meanwhile, outside the hall, DI Fogg had arrived back at the scene of operations. He had finally got rid of the awful taste in his mouth with a mixture of whisky and chocolate. And now, someone was going to bloody well pay.

"So, what's the effin' score?" he said, while looking around for anyone smirking at his expense.

"Nothin' much, sir," replied his sergeant, poker-faced.

"What nothin'? You can't have been looking. There's bound to be someone doing a bit of dope, at least. I mean, it is a student party."

"Nothin,' sir. We've got four men on the inside and none of them's seen anything in the way of dope, pills, crack or anything else."

"I don't believe it," said the DI. "Here. Give me that radio."

"Come in, Bright," he snapped. The radio crackled as Bright came on the air.

"Bright here, sir."

"Wilson here tells me you and the others have seen nothing since you've been in there?"

"Yea, that's right, sir. It looks clean in here. The only thing we've seen is a couple of people rollin' their own and you can't arrest people for that, can you?" he said, chuckling.

"Rollin' their own," snapped Fogg. "Rollin' their own and you say you've seen nothin'. Well, that's got to be it. That has got to be it! Don't you agree, John?" said Fogg, turning to his companion from the Drug Squad.

"It sounds thin to me, George. But you're calling the shots."

Fogg thought hard. For a brief moment, he was on the point of standing the men down. Then he remembered the burning taste in his mouth.

"There's got to be something there. What's happening in there now, Bright?" he said trying to find a straw to clutch.

"What, sir?... Oh!" said Bright, thinking that a progress report on the panto was being asked for. "Well, sir, there's a bit of a tussle goin' on."

"What do you mean?"

"Yeah, they seem to be fightin' over a baby, sir."

"A baby!?" said Fogg. "At this time of night? Why would anyone be carrying a baby around at this time of night? Especially to a party." The phrase *social services* clanged a bell in Fogg's head. There would definitely be brownie points to be picked up from *social services* if there was a baby in there which ought to be at home tucked up asleep; there would definitely be flak to be picked up if he didn't follow this through. Suddenly, Fogg was very alert.

"What's happened to the baby now?"

"They're still tuggin' at it, sir. Oh!"

150

"What? What!?" shouted Fogg.

"They've pulled off one of its arms, sir. Oh my God! There's blood everywhere."

"Shit," said Fogg. "Fucking shit. Why does this have to happen to me? Right. Go! Go! Go!" he bellowed at the waiting troops. And someone get an effin' ambulance up here: fast."

*

The next day the panto made the evening television news as an illustrated feature, courtesy of Miles's video. The video had somehow gone missing from the Art History department almost as soon as the story broke. Television reporters described it as the 'Provocative Panto' that had perhaps gone a little too far.

The tabloid press gave a detailed and lurid account of the proceedings on the following day. There were outraged headlines and fantastic stories about pornographic pantos and Art School orgies. Grave concern was expressed about the desecration of Christmas and the pillaging of children's stories. There were also lots of pictures. Miles's video had made someone a lot of money.

The sight of a naked model on stage surrounded by 'lecherous' old men and a flock of sheep featured in all the tabloids. There was plenty of scope here to stir the imaginations of discerning readers. But the dominant image to burn itself indelibly on the public psyche, was the picture of Frank with his spirit level strapped to his member. The Art School found itself besieged by reporters and three-man camera crews.

A reporter doing a standard follow-up struck lucky in finding a disgruntled refectory manager. Frost, after years of frustrated bureaucratic machismo, saw a chance to get revenge; he was rather obliging about the goings on in the refectory. The cricket pavilion and of course Frank's mirrors aroused a lot of curiosity. That was all very well, if a little bizarre. It kept the story wriggling for a while. A second reporter then scooped the real follow-up story. He chanced to make the link between Zoe's more dramatic pieces and the X-rated videos that Ron's boys were circulating around the East End. Cue a second day of revelations in the media.

The Warden was absolutely livid. After years of painstaking effort to build up the academic reputation of the college, he felt betrayed by the *outrage*. The Dean, by contrast, found the whole affair rather amusing. That angered the Warden even more, and he called the Dean a blatant anarchist. That was perhaps an overreaction. True, the Dean had been amused, but that was because he was an artist. He couldn't help but be amused at the chaos lurking so close to the day-to-day reality of ordinary life. However, the Dean also saw a golden opportunity to put the future of the Art School XI beyond doubt.

He abandoned his regular donkey jacket and hard hat and instead took to wearing cricket whites and playing with a cricket ball during the subsequent interviews with the press. He avoided questions regarding curricular content and insisted on talking instead about quality, especially the quality of play during the last season. And here, to his credit, he was more than generous about the quality of the opposition during the last season. He also adopted the lofty chairman of selectors ploy – intimating that there was always room in the Art School XI for a quality batsman, but that the standard was rather high. Try as they might, the reporters couldn't get round this obtuse strategy. Especially as the Dean took the precaution of having the Art School statistician (as he liked to call him) by his side during these little get-togethers with the press. Consequently, any tricky question regarding the pornographic content of the Art School syllabus could always be countered by an engineered reference to the averages. These showed real gains in the performance of the Art School XI over at least the past five years. Contrary to the reality of last season, the bowling was made to look particularly impressive. The visual aids that illustrated these statistics were computer generated in-house. Thus, emphasising the Art School's commitment to avant-garde ideas.

Compared to the Dean, the Warden was a poor communicator. He suffered at the hands of the press and made matters worse by trying to defend the indefensible. He came off rather badly in trying to explain away the cricket pavilion and Frank's mirrors in the refectory. And when reporters quizzed him about the panto, he made a hash of things by suggesting, rather tetchily, that he would be quite happy to take his children to see *Ms White and the Seven Academicians*. He still hadn't any idea of the panto's contents.

It was all very wearying. Not least because of the general tone of indignation related to profligacy at the taxpayer's expense. The Warden found it impossible to defend the situation in the face of aggressive reporters, and of course, the person who should have been answering challenging questions was playing the eccentric card and invariably burbling on about cricket.

A variation on the theme of indignation was that the Art School was little more than a school for training kinky citizens and why couldn't more of us enrol. Nudge, nudge. It was this thought-provoking line of questioning that provided the final impetus for the Warden to agree to a proposal by a television journalist called Peter Fairly.

Fairly had made a reputation as an in-depth reporter. His approach was to adopt the role of a person and let his camera crew record him and his thoughts in the subject's environment. The recording process would normally go on for weeks. Naturally, his work was terribly sympathetic towards his subjects. In his time, he had done in-depth work on everything from lolly-popping to lion taming. Being an art student, he explained to the Warden, wouldn't present any problems.

"Just think of it, sir," explained Fairly, sensing the Warden's discomfort, "This will be the college's chance to set the record straight. People will see for themselves that the recent incidents have been blown up out of all proportion. They'll understand that the reality of being an art student is very different to the image the media has portrayed in recent days."

"Will they?" wondered the Warden half aloud to himself. *On the other hand*, he mused, this might be a good way of getting rid of the Art School. After the nightmare of the last few days, he felt inclined to give the Art School as much rope as they needed. He allowed himself a ghost of a smile as he entertained the thought of the college without the Art School. They could at last concentrate on really developing the college's academic standards; no more *Mickey Mouse degrees*.

Spring

Chapter 12

Frank had found himself short of funds over the Christmas holidays, and so contrived to land some labouring work via the Buoy. It meant leaving London for a week, but he was glad of the opportunity of getting away from the flat. Fogg, too, was advised to disappear for a few months while the fuss died down. In his case, his chief inspector insisted on escorting him on to a plane to get him out of the country.

"Don't read anything into the fact you've only got a one-way ticket, Fogg," said the chief inspector. "We'll send you a return ticket in good time."

"In good time for what, guv?"

"In good time for your disciplinary hearing."

"You are joking. Aren't you, guv? Guv...."

Fogg's words fell on deaf ears as the chief inspector about turned and motioned to his sergeant.

"Good riddance," muttered the chief under his breath as they walked away from a worried-looking Fogg.

"Sir?" said his sergeant.

"I said let's hope Fogg can make himself useful over in New York."

"Sir?" said the sergeant again.

"With any luck we won't need a return ticket for him."

"You mean you think he might decide to stay over there, sir?"

"Quite possibly, sergeant," said the chief inspector, thinking that his sergeant was even slower than usual that morning.

*

The spring term opened to a cold spell of weather. Frank, who had spent a freezing Christmas helping with some unseasonable architectural repairs, was exhilarated to get back inside the refectory. The Christmas job turned out to be a real cowboy affair. He and a couple of sculpture students had been offered a job to carry out roofing work for a wealthy sheikh down in Godalming. Apparently, some workmen the sheikh had employed for minor repairs to his roof got rather drunk one evening and, finding the local to be lacking in the most fundamental of facilities – such as a decent skittles table – went back to the job to play skittles with the sheikh's balustrade. The sheikh was minus sixty odd balusters before his bodyguards got to the roof. The story had raised lots of laughs in the Buoy. Disarmed by the humour of the story and with the promise of lots of cash – if they could repair the damage within a week – Frank and a couple of others piled into a van and drove down to Godalming in high spirits.

He realised, in retrospect, that it had been a mistake to rush into accepting the job. It was Christmas week and virtually nothing to support the building trade had been open. They had to improvise to make half-a-dozen moulds for the balusters. That had been difficult enough, but then they discovered they didn't have access to a concrete mixer: they were forced to mix concrete by hand.

And because of the cold weather, the concrete took ages to set – even with the help of liberal doses of concrete hardening accelerator. The chap who'd hired them omitted to mention the central heating had been shot to pieces when the bodyguards chased the workmen off the roof. And then there'd been the problem of the coping stones: the workmen had thrown these off the roof because, apparently, they hindered the falling action of the skittles. They had all smashed after falling forty feet off the roof. Since there was no prospect of getting replacement stones in a hurry, they again improvised to make fake stones out of fibreglass. Frank had expressed doubts about the fakes, but afterwards, looking up from the ground, he had to admit that – after being painted and screwed down onto the balusters – he couldn't tell the difference between the real coping stones and the fakes.

Reflecting over the holiday, Frank felt as if he'd spent it hung upside down inside a cold storage chamber. Still, at least he was solvent again. The warmth of the central heating hit him as he walked into the college. It made him realise how cold he was and had been over the break. He felt himself thawing as he made his way to the refectory, to the first cup of tea of the new term.

"Ello, darlin'," said Florence, smiling at her best customer. "Nice to see you back…. You want the usual, love?"

"Hello, Flo," said Frank, nodding and thinking that Flo should have been a nurse. He huddled around the steaming tea. Watching the hot liquid, he reflected with renewed embarrassment (and not a little anguish) at a very unsatisfactory end of term conclusion.

It was all somewhat hazy: especially the bit about the

panto. But he did vaguely recollect going back home with Zoe. Both of them had been tipsy; he rather more than she. They had somehow found each other during the confusion and had giggled in each other's arms as the boys in blue burst through to the stage. Neither of them had felt inclined to say anything, but it had been understood there was unfinished business between them and so they skipped out of the college, carrying a celebratory bottle of vodka.

They missed the hysterics by slipping out through a convenient fire exit. She rode piggyback on him as they lurched down the high street and into the estate where Frank rented a flat. Although Zoe was driving him hard, he stayed on his feet all the way home. However, the effort made him rather light-headed as well as very thirsty. As a result, he knocked back most of the vodka and several bottles of beer from the fridge. Not unsurprisingly, he spent the next few hours sitting on the loo, feeling rather sorry for himself.

He had woken to find himself on the bathroom floor with Zoe long gone. What made it worse was that she would spend the whole of next term on an exchange visit to America. It would be at least another three months before he'd see her again. And as for unfinished business? Well, that was probably a non-starter now.

He would probably have remained in this morose state, except that his eye caught hold of something unusual in the refectory:

    – What's that, Frank?

    – Eh? replied Frank, shaking himself out of his stupor.

    – What's that camera crew doing in here? I'd have thought all that would have died down by now.

– Beats me, *Frank*. Maybe they're doing another follow-up. Or maybe there's some other scandal brewing.

Frank's first guess was, in fact, pretty near the mark. The public hullabaloo regarding the panto had died down. However, there were questions to be answered and an extraordinary meeting of the senate had been convened before the start of the new term to discuss the matter. The most visible, practical outcome was the camera crew Frank had just seen wander into the refectory.

The Warden had been particularly pleased that the Dean had been enthusiastic about the idea of letting Fairly become an art student for the rest of the academic year. Notwithstanding the eccentricity card the Dean had played during the senate's deliberations, it was primarily because of the Dean's support for the Warden's idea that the Dean emerged rather well from the post-mortem on the panto fiasco. Miles emerged as the unwitting dupe who had allowed the name of the college to be brought into disrepute. He was told in no uncertain terms to secure the Art History department against further break-ins. In the meantime, he had to deposit his videos of Zoe for safekeeping in the college vault. Losing his videos was a savage blow, and Miles had said so in no uncertain terms. He became rather distraught at the prospect of losing the videos, especially since Zoe would be away for the whole of the spring term. A furious Miles emerged from the meeting muttering dark things about everyone and the Dean in particular.

Miles would have been even more upset if he had been privy to the Dean's thinking about an in-depth reporter wandering around the college with a camera crew in attendance. Contrary to the impression he gave, regarding his support for a necessary public relations exercise, and hence a concomitant restoration of confidence in the college's academic reputation, the Dean had seen straight away, that a half-decent camera crew would be very useful in helping to record and remedy the problems of technique during the winter nets at the local sports centre. These indoor nets, useful as they were in preparing for a new season, had never really developed the team's potential. That was because of the difficulty of giving players meaningful feedback on defective technique. But here was a chance to remedy the problem for bowlers and batsmen alike. The Dean had no doubt the coming season would see the Art School XI strike terror into the hearts of every team north of the Thames. As for the Challenge Cup, that was surely a foregone conclusion.

In the soothing warmth of the refectory, Frank soon forgot about his cold Christmas and tried to drop back into his ogling routine; but it wasn't the same. The refectory was practically deserted because so many students were on school placements. This term, they would only come into college for lectures one day a week – and then only in a stagger. There was no prospect of reliving the atmosphere and excitement of the past term. It looked like being a long, bleak spring term.

The other thing that forcibly intruded itself into Frank's thinking was the realisation that he would soon have to mount an exhibition for his degree show.

The degree shows gave art students a chance to show off their best work. These shows were the final formal examination of the student's artistic endeavours. The art work that students exhibited reflected the best they had produced over the past two years and two terms. However, since most students either did nothing very dramatic for the first two years or were rather embarrassed at what they had actually done, work for the shows tended to be completed in the autumn and spring terms of the final year – with the greater emphasis on the spring term.

Frank, like all the other third years, now faced the prospect of preparing his degree show. He had found a letter in his pigeonhole that morning, outlining the form of the examination, together with his space allocation. It had been a sobering read. As if that wasn't bad enough, he also had to produce a five-thousand-word essay on, 'Any Artistic Theme of your Choice'.

What he found especially galling was that *Frank* was looking forward to putting on a degree show. Not only that, but he had sketched out a complete set of pieces. It sounded appalling. And talk about sailing close to the wind.

– It's all very well to talk about Mystery Art, *Frank*, remonstrated Frank, but it won't do.
– What d'you mean?
– I mean, you can't just go round wrapping things up and claim that it's Mystery Art.
– Why not?
– Well, what are you going to wrap up, anyway?
– I can't tell you that, said *Frank* in a protective tone of voice. It wouldn't be a mystery any more. Would it?
– Oh, for Christ's sake, *Frank*. It's me you're talking to. Not some nosey parker from the Inland Revenue.
– Hmm, said *Frank*. Well, it's no big secret. I'm just going to wrap up anything that comes my way. It actually doesn't matter what it is.

– Why not?

– Because it doesn't.

– Well, what's that got to do with art? asked Frank in exasperation.

– Art? Don't talk to me about art, Frank, retorted *Frank*. The art bit is supplied by the imagination of whoever's looking at whatever I've wrapped up.

– And that's it? You're going to present some parcels you've wrapped up.

– Don't be daft, Frank. That's just the beginning.

– Oh, said Frank, sensing something worse.

– I going to have a mystery quiz show, said *Frank*, trying to sound casual.

– What's that when it's at home?

– Quite simple, really. I'm going to have a quiz show as the centre piece of my degree show: complete with mystery prizes.

– Like what? said Frank falling, into the same trap.

– This time, however, *Frank* was cagier and refused to tell him.

– *Frank*, said Frank, trying to reason with his alter ego, You can't do it.

– Oh, and why not?

– Because it's got no content, Frank.

– Content! Don't talk to me about content, yelled *Frank*. What d'you know about content, Frank? Eh? What do any of them know about content? Where's the content in what's-his-name's bathroom tiles?

This was a reference to a set of off-white tiles arranged in the shape of a safety pin, which had recently won a major sculpture competition. Apparently, an eighty-metre version of the said object was to be mounted somewhere along the Thames embankment.

> – Anyway, said *Frank* defiantly. What are you doing for the degree show? Mmm? What little arty number are you dreaming up? At least I've got some ideas, old boy. What about you?

Frank couldn't reply because he didn't know; he became confused and irritated. Something like panic set in until he realised he had a level in his hand. He used it to stroke his forehead gently. There was also the reassuring fact that there were nearly four months before the degree shows had to be mounted. Something was bound to turn up. In the meantime, he had to ensure that *Frank* didn't get too far ahead. He knew from bitter experience that if he let *Frank* have a head start, he wouldn't be able to catch him.

> – I'm also going to have some go-go dancers, said *Frank*, intruding into Frank's thoughts again.
>
> – What? said Frank with a jolt.
>
> – Go-go dancers.

This took a moment to sink in. Even then, Frank wasn't sure what *Frank* had said.

> – Go-go dancers, said *Frank* again, rather slowly. What's the matter with you today, Frank?
>
> – How do they fit into your grand scheme of things? said Frank, trying to regain his composure.
>
> – They'll be there for the glamour, Frank. They're going to dance around my *Mystery Pieces* for the TV promotions. You know, like they do on the bingo promotions on the telly.

Frank shook his head in disbelief. He couldn't believe what he was hearing. *Frank* seemed to be in bonkers land.

> – *Frank*, he said, trying to sound rational, You can't advertise a piece of sculpture like it was a bingo

card, or, or a packet of soap powder.

– Why not?

– It's just not done, *Frank*. It wouldn't be art, he added, trying to insert something ethical into his argument.

– Bullshit, retorted *Frank*. You wanna sell your work, don't you? Well, how's it gonna sell if you don't promote it? No one else will you know, Frank. I'm gonna make sure my pieces are sold before the end of the term.

Frank walked away from it. There was no point in arguing with *Frank* in this mood. Clearly, though, he needed to sort out his own show to avoid being shown up by *Frank*. He gathered up his things and set off for the Factory in a pensive mood. Florence watched him leave with concern.

That was the first time that she could recall Frank leaving the refectory so early.

*

Over in the Factory, Fairly was also having artistic problems. He had arrived at the college that morning full of excitement at the prospect of becoming an art student. He recorded a suitable first scene at the main college entrance, describing for a future audience his excitement at the prospect of training to be an artist for several months:

"No doubt some of you will recognise the name of St Sigeberht's School of Art. It was – it still is – a controversial institution. If I mention the word 'Panto', you may have an inkling as to what I'm talking about. I won't say any more than that," he said rather generously. "That would be to pre-judge the issue. Or should I say issues? And what are the issues?" he said, gesturing with both shoulders and raised eyebrows. "That is perhaps a controversial issue. Let us say, for now, that these are they: Is what goes on in here," he said expansively, waving his arm behind him to take in the broad sweep of the college's entrance, "of any relevance to you and me? To the man, or woman, on the Clapham omnibus? Is what goes on in here," he enumerated by ticking off his second finger, "related in any way to the work of the great masters? To Leonardo, to Botticelli, to Van Gogh, to name just three? Does what goes on in here," cue the third finger, "have anything to do with the making of art and, perhaps more importantly, with the making of fine artists? These, as I see them, are the big issues. And for me, perhaps the most important of these, is the idea of a man or woman, as an artist. And by that, I mean an *Artist* with a capital A."

He paused with a practised eye to let his declaration sink in. Then, as if encapsulating the essence of what he was saying, he raised his right hand, his fingers seeming to hold the point at issue, "Becoming an artist is something that perhaps many of us dream of. I must confess that I have, on occasion, indulged in such fantasies. But for most of us, that is all they are: fantasies. However, over the next few months, I hope to make my fantasy become real. I hope, too, to reveal something of the process that is involved in the making of a fine artist in the twenty-first century. And I hope to address some of the issues that need to be addressed, here, in London's East End. Here, at St Sigeberht's School of Fine Art." He turned theatrically and once again swept his hand expansively over the panoramic view of the college's formal entrance.

As Fairly mused, yet again, on his opening remarks, he congratulated himself on the eloquence of his opening scene. The camera crew, too, had seemed more than usually attentive. It augured well for the future. Of all the roles that Fairly taken on, this was the one he empathised with the most. However, now that he was in the Factory, in his own studio, together with several hundred pounds worth of paint and virgin canvas, he found himself a loss as to what to do next. He flicked a brush moodily across his hand as he paced up and down his large, very empty studio. His camera crew dutifully settled down to record this obvious search for inspiration.

Three-quarters of an hour later, both he and the camera crew were thoroughly bored. They decided it would be useful to record a second interview, with Fairly explaining to the camera how he was looking for inspiration but had failed so far to find any. With a suitably humble expression and looking quite the part in his brand-new artist's smock, Fairly gestured to the empty canvas and shrugged his shoulders.

"I have been struggling," he explained, trying to convey something of the artist's frustration, "and that is not too strong a word, for almost an hour now, to begin the act of creation. I am sorry to say that I have failed. Failed miserably." He paused to stroke his chin. "The canvas, as you can see," he gestured with his head, "is still in a *virginal* state. Apparently, that's a technical term," he added hastily, remembering the panto and the fact that he had to tread warily on sexual connotations in his presentation.

He tried to say something else, but clearly found the process too painful. He gestured to the canvas again, scratched his chin and then his head and then shrugged his shoulders again before he started pacing the studio once more. The camera crew congratulated Fairly on his candour before clearing off to the refectory for some tea. Fairly decided he'd endured enough angst and that perhaps he ought to get some professional help.

As he came out of his studio, he caught sight of Frank wandering up and down in the studio next door. With his level in hand, Frank appeared to Fairly to be going through the same mental process that he himself had been going through only a few moments ago. This student was obviously searching for inspiration. Knowing that he was billeted with third-year students – students approaching the end of three years training – Fairly realised with something approaching relief that what he had been experiencing next door must have been quite normal. Surely?

"Excuse me," said Fairly, interrupting Frank in his perambulations. "I wonder if I might ask you a favour?"

Frank, who was in a fragile state of mind after the refectory tête-à-tête with *Frank* and who, had only just avoided being run over by a camera crew as he came up the Factory stairs to his studio, dropped his level with a clatter at the unexpected appearance of this rather odd-looking person from what he had assumed to be an empty studio next door to his own.

"Oh, I'm so sorry," said Fairly, introducing himself. "Look. About that favour? I just want a bit of advice about my painting. Well, not my painting exactly. I haven't done anything yet. That's just the point. I mean, how does one actually start?"

> – What's this idiot burbling on about, Frank? said *Frank*, waking up to the fact that Frank was talking to someone. And who is he, anyway?
>
> – Not sure, *Frank*, said Frank, replying simultaneously

to both questions. He just popped up from next door.

"How do you start your work? These things, for example," said Fairly, pointing to *Frank's* takeaways cartons and brown-paper parcels. "How did you come to put them together? I mean, what's the thinking behind them? Or come to that, what's in them?" he muttered, catching a whiff of something emanating from the cartons.

Frank made a mental note to wrap an extra layer of cellophane over the take-aways. Clearly, the present wrapping arrangement wasn't adequate. In the meantime, he manoeuvred Fairly away from the growing stack of takeaway cartons and let himself be persuaded to examine his work.

"You see my problem," said Fairly, with a wave of his hand.

Frank found himself in two minds at this point. He didn't want to encourage this reporter, since inevitably he would start wanting to snoop into *Frank's* work. On the other hand, *Frank,* with his declared intention of a high-profile strategy, realised that a media person as an immediate neighbour could be a valuable friend. An inner tussle took place before a comprise was reached and Frank suggested some modest advice, designed to remove the reporter from the Factory: at least for a while.

"Why don't you try the life class?" he said innocently. "Just to get you started on developing your perceptual skills."

"The life class. You mean working from a model? I didn't know that sort of thing went on in art schools anymore."

"Oh, yes. I'll take you down there if you like."

169

Chapter 13

A circular annexe next to the main Art School block housed the life class. One reached it via a narrow twisting passage. En route, one could look into half-filled lecture rooms and – if so inclined – into the college dustbins. Many students spent a surprising amount of time rummaging through these bins. Not least of all the sculpture students. They were always on the lookout for bits of *Found Art*. The local tramps were also regular rummagers. In fact, sometimes it was hard to distinguish the former from the latter, especially as the sculptors had recently taken to scrounging at the same Oxfam shop as the tramps. There was little love lost between these two groups of rough lifers.

One could, invariably, also find Mac, the back-gate porter, lurking somewhere near the bins and the bike-sheds. This was his domain – so to speak. He bore the grand title of Keeper of the life-studio. In effect, this meant he opened the studio in the morning and made sure it was vacant when he locked up at night. He occupied a shed somewhere amongst the nooks and crannies that made up the rear end of the college, but it was extremely well camouflaged. Anyone who wanted to get hold of Mac usually had to whistle a tune. He was said to be particularly responsive to highland jigs, though, apparently, some students reported that he also responded well to Wagnerian themes. Of course, students familiar with Wagnerian themes tended not to broadcast the fact.

This was the setting for the college's life-studio. It was described by students as a nether-world place. But anyone who took the trouble to tackle the slightly menacing approach to the life-studio was rewarded by a pleasant surprise. While the exterior appeared cramped by being juxtaposed so close to the rear of the college, the interior boasted a delightfully airy and beautifully proportioned space. It was ideally suited for life drawing.

The life-studio was like an anachronistic hostel, which students visited at some stage during their three years at the college. It was never a popular place to spend one's day. Although, the studio did occasionally become very popular indeed. This was sometimes in response to the prevailing artistic climate but was more likely to be in response to the sensuality of a particular female model. On this morning, the life-studio was definitely on the list of popular destinations. Hendricks, the life tutor, had recently engaged a stunning French language student and word was getting around.

After Frank's recommendation, Fairly and his team arrived at the studio next day full of purpose. At least, Fairly was full of purpose; the camera crew, having insisted on stopping off at Bella's cafe, were full of eggs, bacon, two slices and tea with two sugars. Fairly had to wait for them to stock up with fuel and was now just a touch impatient to get cracking. Yesterday's fiasco was something, he decided, he would not dwell upon. He'd also made a faux pas as regards his togs. He'd arrived at the Art School dressed in what he fondly assumed was the appropriate *uniform*: check jacket and check shirt with a soft woollen tie with corduroys and a half-decent beard, which he'd spent all Christmas growing. However, one had to give him credit for realising he'd made a gaffe. As a savvy media man, he was quick to change his image for the following morning. The beard was replaced with a stubbly growth and the corduroy and check were replaced with a lumberjack shirt and paint-spattered jeans. The paint clearly defining the palette he'd been using in his work of late. Except, of course, since Fairly hadn't produced any work as yet, the paint had to be painted on. He'd spent a couple of happy hours the night before in engineering a result on his jeans.

He'd started cold yesterday, but he was going to put that right. Some disciplined life drawing was obviously what he needed to get his mind tuned to looking at things like an artist. He was ready to *pay his dues*, as he had expressed to the camera at the entrance to the life-studio. Then perhaps he could think about something more substantial, a little more creative.

He spent some considerable time in setting himself up in the studio. Hendricks, who was not averse to free publicity, had been most helpful in getting Fairly set up. Especially regarding cordoning off a little area around Fairly so his film crew could get in close to his work.

"It's very important that the crew be able to rotate around me freely," explained Fairly to a bemused Hendricks.

"I quite understand."

"It's a question of being able to, to...," Fairly tried to find the right words, "to capture the sweat from my pores if necessary. If that's what it takes to convey the moment. You understand?" Hendricks nodded absent-mindedly as he adjusted the seating around Fairly's position.

After the setting up, the pencil sharpening, the adjusting of the paper, and of course, the final visit to the loo, so as not to disturb the flow of concentration when he began to draw, Fairly eventually had to confront a large blank sheet of cartridge paper. Its crisp whiteness and lack of flaws had an arresting effect on his ability to make a start. For just an instant, he felt himself sweating. A feeling of panic swept over him as he remembered what he'd said to Hendricks. After a few moments, he glanced around furtively to see how other students were going about the business.

He was surprised to see how active the students seemed to be. His neighbour on his immediate left, in particular, was scrubbing the paper with aggressive sweeps of his arms. The chap on his right was doing some sort of jerking dance with his head. He would stare at the model for an instant before jerking his head back to his paper. It looked as if he was trying to project the captured image of the model onto the paper. And when he had done so, he would sweep the paper with his charcoal in a swift movement before the image disappeared.

Fairly found the whole thing rather disconcerting. Eventually, however, the charcoal in his hand crumbled and made a mess of his paper. With the surface thus spoilt, Fairly found himself able at last to attempt some rather timid marks on the paper.

"No! No! No!" shrieked Hendricks, as he spotted Fairly committing a cardinal sin on the paper. With one eye on the camera, he wrested the charcoal from Fairly's hand. "That will never do. You must be committed to your line. Look. Like this," pronounced Hendricks, shouldering Fairly out of the way. With a firm jaw and controlled energy, Hendricks swept across Fairly's paper and showed him what it meant to make committed lines. "There! That's how it's done. You don't have to get it right first time," said Hendricks, trying to reassure a stupefied Fairly. "Just make sure you tackle the drawing in a firm manner. Show it who's boss. Hmm?"

Fairly looked at the camera and grinned rather sheepishly. Then, he pulled in his chin and stomach, drew himself up to his full height and, looking masterfully at the paper, plunged in with a view to committing some committed-looking lines. Hendricks smiled approvingly before moving off.

A few minutes later, Fairly stood back to examine his drawing. It was without doubt full of committed lines, but they didn't seem to work together very well. He looked in vain for the model's form in the drawing. After making absolutely sure that she wasn't there, he looked at the camera and shrugged his shoulders. He glanced out of the corner of his eye to check on Hendricks's position before sliding his drawing surreptitiously into his folder.

"I think I'll let that one go," he whispered to the camera. "It's not quite I'd intended."

The next half a dozen drawings went the same way. Each accompanied by a sheepish aside from Fairly to the camera.

As the morning progressed, Hendricks found himself squeezed out by a spreading rash of easels and drawing boards. With word getting out about the new model and a mysterious television camera crew, the life-studio suddenly seemed to be very popular. Indeed, by mid-morning, numerous students were crammed in there. Hendricks found it impossible to move around freely and offer instruction in his normal way. His initial instinct was to become somewhat cross and retreat behind the encircling line of students, but this left him with a very peripheral role. It was very unsatisfactory. Especially because the camera appeared to be concentrating on and around centre-stage.

Wally, the cameraman, had a standing brief to concentrate on Fairly. But not, of course, to the extent of missing out on the context. The context, on this occasion, was obviously rather more important than the meaningless scribbles on Fairly's paper. He felt sure Fairly would not thank him for lingering on his exploratory technique. Consequently, he gave rather more attention to the model. This, of course, made him unpopular with everyone. Everyone except the model. She was clearly enjoying the attention of the camera and forgot that she was supposed to be playing a still role. Her body became restless and moved almost imperceptibly to keep abreast of the camera's advances.

The model's movement caused a mixed reaction amongst the students. Some students, those that could see the model in a way that revealed her as a series of planes and angles, realised straight away that she had moved. They found it a straightforward matter to accommodate for the movement.

Lesser mortals, however, found the entire business rather frustrating and resorted to wholesale corrections with the aid of erasers and white chalk. Others simply started again on a fresh sheet of paper.

Hendricks, grizzling at the edge of the circle, sensed the restlessness in the room and decided that the periphery was definitely not where the life tutor ought to be. He squeezed past the layers of would-be draughtsmen, claiming to have spotted something wrong with the cage.

The cage was the name of the elaborate wire and plumb line structure that Hendricks had constructed to house the model. It was an aid to accurate drawing, but from the students' point of view, it was often more trouble than it was worth. The model was forever getting tangled up in it, and invariably, it meant a hold up while Hendricks sorted out the problem. Either that, or some of the abler students, who could produce a drawing in two minutes flat and therefore rather despised it, would make a point of stumbling into the cage, disturbing any number of the lines.

Notwithstanding the students' antics, Hendricks persevered with his teaching aid. Unlike some of his colleagues, he actually was master of his material. He could judge if any of the plumb lines on his cage were out by as little as two millimetres and *retune* them without difficulty.

This keen spatial sense meant that Hendricks invariably spent a good part of his time in *tuning* the cage. And when he wasn't doing that, he would poke and prod the model with his cane. Of course, this centre stage role meant he invariably interrupted someone's line of sight, no matter which bit of the cage he was trying to adjust. On this occasion, there were rather a lot of students who wished that Hendricks would get out of their way. The model too got rather tetchy, especially as Hendricks was hovering in between her good side and the camera. And Wally, the cameraman, was getting upset because he constantly had to adjust his position in order to ogle the model, while the students behind his meanderings were totally fed up with their lot. One way or another, there was a good deal of shuffling going on.

Inevitably, an exasperated student at the back threw some charcoal at nobody in particular. Someone else decided that under the circumstances, throwing charcoal seemed like a pretty good game. He started throwing his charcoal with an aggrieved sense of direction at Hendricks. It caught the mood of the moment and in next to no time, Hendricks was being showered by charcoal from all directions.

A surprised Hendricks started and twirled to fend off this apparently unprovoked and unseasonable attack by the wasps that nested in the studio. Inevitably, he lost his balance and, with an anguished cry, crashed through the plum lines and onto the model. She took exception to being leapt upon by a hairy madman and started screaming for him to get off. In trying to calm her down, Hendricks found himself groping her magnificent breasts. Her worst fears about Hendricks's intentions surfaced, and she screamed for someone to help get this lecherous man off her. Protesting his innocence, Hendricks tried even harder to pin her to the spot to calm her down. He looked around desperately for support in trying to calm her. It wasn't a wise strategy. She struggled free and landed him a kick in the groin before she and Hendricks crashed out on opposite sides of the cage. They knocked down several easels and boards. An inevitable domino effect followed as crashing boards and easels knocked students, and they in turn fell on adjacent bits of drawing kit. Within a matter of seconds, the twin shock waves created by Hendricks and the model had clattered around the room, leaving very little standing.

The model was the first to get to her feet. She stopped only to pick up her gown before she clambered over the wreckage and bolted out of the door. The students – charcoal throwers in particular – decided that this was the best strategy and followed in her wake. A minute later the studio was deserted except for a confused-looking Hendricks still protesting his innocence to an equally confused and battered-looking camera crew. Fairly was the only one who salvaged something from the situation: he realised with a sigh of relief that he wouldn't have to show his scribblings to anyone. He turned his face up to the heavens and thanked anyone who happened to be listening.

Chapter 14

After Christmas, along with other mundane hopes for the New Year, the Art School XI could look ahead to the new season, now only a matter of two months or so away. It was actually nearer three months, but it was better for the team's morale to talk in terms of two rather than three months.

Talk of the new season helped to sustain restless spirits during the bleak winter months. Poring over the averages and statistics of the previous season could, of course, alleviate the interval between the close of the season and Christmas. But such activity was well and truly exhausted by the New Year. Mercifully, the winter nets became available about this time.

The winter nets were an indoor facility at the Britannia, the local sports centre. The first nets of the year were to be Frank's formal introduction to the team, and indeed the first chance for the team to see him in action. After the Dean's heroic build up, everyone wanted to see what Frank could do.

Frank was, of course, quite nonchalant about the whole thing. By contrast, Frank had nervy diarrhoea for a week before the event. *Frank* had deliberately played upon his nerves and by now he was in a terrible state. The day before the nets, he wandered around in a daze with his levels permanently tied to his forehead. People around the college made allowances for him, but he came close to getting run over several times as he wandered around the adjoining streets. *Frank*, meanwhile, continued to taunt him.

– Frank, he said, You're gonna have to sort yourself out. At this rate, you're not gonna get to the crease. They're gonna have to wipe you off the street.

– Piss off, *Frank*.

– Just trying to help, old boy.

– If I wanted your help, *Frank*. I wouldn't ask for it.

– Now, now, Frank.

– I don't know why you're so fucking smug, *Frank*. It's not as if you can bat.

– Bat, Frank? My middle name.

– Says you.

– It's true, Frank. I'm good at racquet games. It comes from playing all that tennis. Played for my county, don't you know, Frank.

– Haven't heard that one before, *Frank*, said Frank rather tetchily.

– No good getting sarky, Frank. It'll make you all twisted inside.

– Anyway, this is not like tennis, *Frank*.

– Can't be that different.

– It's played with a bat, *Frank*. A wooden bat, said Frank slowly, trying to get his message across. And a fucking hard red ball that's thrown at you with the deliberate intention of causing you GBH. It comes at you at about ninety miles an hour and if you can't get out of the way quick enough, this fucking hard red ball knocks your teeth out. Try to understand, *Frank*, the game is nothing like tennis.

– Details, Frank, details, said *Frank* airily. The principle's the same. Eh? Hand eye co-ordination?

– I remember you saying much the same thing about table-football, *Frank*. Hand eye co-ordination?

– That's not the same, said *Frank* defensively. That's a much harder game to play.

– Ah, piss off, you cretin, said Frank with a final vehemence that suggested that *Frank* really had outstayed his welcome.

Clearly, Frank was in no mood to listen. *Frank* shrugged his shoulders and told him to get on with it.

Left to his misgivings, Frank wandered aimlessly around the streets. Late in the afternoon, guided only by his levels, he found himself in a branch of W.H. Smiths. He must have walked six or seven miles since that morning. He was exhausted. His feet ached and his head hurt. But none of that mattered. For there, in front of him, appeared to be the answer to his prayers: a slim DIY volume on cricket technique: *How to Bat and Survive*, subtitled, *In Ten Easy Lessons*. Frank ripped off the levels from his head and, with the book clutched tightly to his chest, headed for the cashier. *Frank* watched him pitifully. He hadn't even bothered to open the book. He shook his head as Frank paid for the book and headed for the door.

Spurred on by the euphoria of finding the book, Frank had spent the return journey home on top of a bus trying to read the manual. However, by the time he returned, the euphoria had vanished as easily as it had arrived. He had concluded that the book might as well have been written in Chinese. Most of it was totally incomprehensible to him. He realised he simply didn't have the vocabulary to assimilate the text.

Back home, he pulled his trusty levels out again. Old friends, he thought, gently stroking his troubled brow. Best friends. He held the levels up straight. They were as true as a die. They had never let him down. They were the straightest things he had ever known. As he stared at the levels with renewed faith, he suddenly caught a resonance of something that had been mentioned in the cricket manual. He casually flipped the book open again. It opened on the last page. The author's final paragraph caught his eye:

'Remember, that as a batsman, the most important thing you should endeavour to do – at all times – is to hold the bat straight. If you can do that, the game will hold no fears for you.'

Frank experienced a sudden thrill down his spine. Here was a writer who obviously knew what he was talking about. He put the levels to one side and picked up the book again. He read the manual for a second time. With the author's final message firmly etched in his mind, he made some sense of the idea of playing straight. It was perhaps only to be expected since a good many people, people who knew about such things, had been impressed by his grasp of the concept. At any rate, with the book propped up as a guide on the dressing table, he spent the best part of the evening trying to hold a straight broom. It had seemed impossible, until he realised with a start, that if he tied his spirit level to the back of the broom, it was easy. In effect, the broom became a large spirit level. From then on, everything seemed like second nature. Frank had subsequently devoured the manual.

Having spent most of the night repeatedly reading the manual, Frank lost no time in getting down to the college workshops the following morning. He installed some miniature spirit levels on the top and back of an old bat that he scrounged from the Art School cricket bag. Armed with this bat, he made an impressive debut at the first winter nets.

Frank's hard concentration at the first few deliveries quickly gave way to effortless style as he realised that this really was easy. In fact, he couldn't understand what all the fuss had been about. He paused only to roll up his sleeves before getting stuck in to the bowling. For fully twenty allotted minutes, and twenty more besides, he defied everything the Art School's best bowlers could throw at him. Not that the Art School's bowlers were necessarily the stiffest of tests, but they were all that was available on the night and Frank had despatched them all.

He seemed to have every shot in his armoury: the high straight block to the short ball; a forward defensive block with a straight bat; a pull to leg with wrists rolling over to keep the ball low; the short clip to despatch a late in-swinging ball off the legs. The spinners, too, were given a pasting. Frank advanced to everything and drove the ball at will from mid-off through to mid-on; likewise, the short ball was swept in an arc from mid-wicket through to fine leg. All textbook stuff. But there were unorthodox shots too: the reverse sweep; a swat over gully, and an angled flip shot to a short, pitched ball, seemingly a viable alternative to the hook. The shot lifted the ball clear over where the wicket keeper's head would have been. It would force the fielding side to post a roving longstop to cover the gap between deep third man and fine leg.

Frank's confidence rubbed off on the rest of the team. The recognised batsmen in particular were much invigorated. The Dean was quietly ecstatic: he had been fully vindicated in his find.

*

The winter nets were the first harbingers of the new season. The Challenge Cup match was another. Unlike the nets, however, the Challenge Cup was an immediate precursor to the new season. It was a pre-season game played towards the end of term. This match was an annual fixture between the Art School and a near neighbour: Whitehammel School of Art. Both sides traditionally opened their season with this contest. This tradition had its roots in the Dean's own student days. He was an old boy of the Art School and, as fixtures secretary in his day, had organised the first game against Whitehammel, some thirty-odd years before.

Apart from the fact that the Challenge Cup was the season's first fixture, and was therefore keenly anticipated by both sides, there was a second reason which made the event rather special. This was the scrumptious tea provided at the interval.

Since the Challenge Cup match was played on the field adjacent to the college, the refectory staff provided the catering for the tea. The catering staff always got into the spirit of the game – much to the annoyance of Frost. And probably because the catering demands made upon them in their normal working day were so predictable and undemanding, the catering staff always produced magnificent spreads.

Because the authorities were always pleading poverty, and on the lookout for money-making ventures, the provision of a cricket tea for the Challenge Cup had opened the eyes of the accountants to the possibility of providing catering facilities for the benefit of the college's coffers. And now, the college offered a variety of catering functions to outside parties: conferences, lunches and so on. But also, for the first time this year, the college had booked its first wedding reception. Admittedly, it was for two former students. Nevertheless, it was a first, and it opened new possibilities for generating funds.

As it happened, the wedding party booked its reception for the same day as the Challenge Cup. Not a problem in itself since the wedding reception was a buffet affair and would be held in the refectory garden. However, because of the aeroplane incident, Frost had been difficult. He made excuses about lack of staff and of the difficulty of covering two events on the same afternoon. The wedding reception, being the larger party, consisting of a hundred and eighty guests, was to have priority. It looked very much as though the Art School's tea would be stale rock cakes and lemonade. The Five, meeting at Frank's table in the refectory debated this state of affairs.

"He's just being vindictive," said Gilbert.

"Absolutely," said Barnes.

"Seems to take everything personally," added Hobbs.

"That's obviously his problem," said Hammond.

"Ought to see the funny side of things," said Hutton.

"Would be good for him," said Hobbs.

"We could do it ourselves?" ventured Gilbert, trying to cheer everyone up.

"Pigs could fly," replied Barnes.

"There's something in that," said a thoughtful Hammond.

"What do you think, Frank?" said Gilbert.

Frank was engrossed in a bitter dispute with *Frank* about the exhibition and didn't hear the question. *Frank* prodded him for a reply.

"What?" said Frank, removing the spirit level from his eyes.

"I said, what do you think about the idea of us making our own tea for the match, Frank? Didn't you mention you'd once worked in Butlin's kitchens? You must have picked up a thing or two about catering for large groups."

"That was a long time ago. And I didn't do any cooking. We just used to dish out the food. They cooked it somewhere else."

"Oh, right," said Gilbert, as Frank got back into his tête-à-tête with *Frank*.

Prudence, who had stopped for some tea, as she usually did at this time of day, and who, for the last two years, been trying unsuccessfully to get The Five to pose for her, sensed an opportunity and offered to negotiate with Frost. She was, in any case, rather intrigued as to the kind of underpants this rather frenetic, would-be entrepreneur, might be wearing.

"Leave it to me," she said, as she strolled off to track down the refectory manager.

Since he never ventured far from the refectory, Frost wasn't hard to locate. Prudence found him going over some figures with his one of his kitchen staff.

"Excuse me, Mr Frost?" said Prudence in her most innocent voice.

"Yes," said Frost hoarsely, taking in Prudence's cleavage.

"I wonder if I could have a word?"

"A word?"

"I need some help," said Prudence in a helpless sort

of way.

Put like that, Prudence was hard to resist. Frost shooed away his minion and gestured Prudence into his office.

"It's about my work," said Prudence, wandering over to the plants in the corner and bending over to have a good look at them. "Aren't these cute?"

"Er, yes," said Frost, cleaning his glasses.

"I need some help to move my work," said Prudence, coming to the point. "From home to college. And I just wondered if you could help."

Though Frost had the title of refectory manager, he was technically also responsible for deploying a small task force of brown-overalled porters. His first impression was that Prudence wanted a porter to help her.

"Oh, I see. You want to borrow a porter," said a disappointed Frost.

"Or, whatever," said Prudence, being rather open-ended about the whole thing. "It doesn't have to be a porter. I know how busy they can be."

"Actually, they are all rather busy at the moment," said Frost in a manner that suggested that if they weren't busy, he would jolly well make sure they were suitably occupied. "What sort of work is you need to move?" said Frost expansively as he motioned for Prudence to take a seat.

"Just some paintings on underpants. They're quite small pieces of work, but they're mounted on wooden frames. which makes them a little heavier to carry. And I have got rather a lot of them."

"Paintings on underpants?" said Frost, taking the bait.

"Er, yes," said Prudence, slipping effortlessly into a well-honed sales pitch.

Chapter 15

Frank had to work extremely hard to show any interest in the discussions over the Challenge Match tea. That and *Frank* carping on about his exhibition pieces persuaded him to leave the refectory and head for his factory studio.

Frank was still burbling on about his Mystery Art, but at least he was preoccupied with something concrete. That gave Frank an opportunity to reflect on his own response to the impending degree show. What to do? He looked around the studio. It was a large space with little in it apart from a growing stack of *Frank's* take-away cartons and a few objects wrapped up in brown paper. It looked as though *Frank* had already started his Mystery Art wheeze.

He wandered over to the window and found, to his surprise, quite a pleasant view of the river. Pushing open the window revealed a small balcony. Frank stepped out into hazy sunshine.

There's room here, he thought, for an easy chair. Moments later, he was ensconced on the balcony looking out over the river. He breathed in the sun and the water. It felt good. He brought out his levels to complete his sense of being and began levelling the gentle swell of the river.

Little by little, he lost himself in his task. Somewhere in the distance, he could hear an engine chugging away with blessed regularity. The river, and his sense of unease over his lack of work for the degree show, floated away over the distant blue horizon.

He slipped easily into a reverie and found himself astride a bicycle in unfamiliar, watery surroundings.

I'm going to be able to get away, he thought. But then he heard a noise, which suggested he wasn't far from familiar places. *Must try harder*. He tried to concentrate on pushing the noise away. It seemed an obvious enough thing, but he couldn't seem to manage it very well. Also, the bicycle that he was astride wouldn't move. Frank looked around for an explanation. He got off the machine, only to sink fast. As he went down, he realised with a smile that the reason for the bicycle's lack of momentum was the fact that it had square wheels. Not that they were completely inefficient, but they were clearly the reason for the lack of forward motion. He pushed at the tyres and found them to be made of plaster of Paris.

Not very comfortable, he thought. *I wouldn't want to be riding this bike for long: certainly not on a hard surface.* He imagined, however, that it might be ideal on a soft lunar landscape.

He smiled as he then imagined himself back at the crease at the indoor nets. They were trying desperately to get him out.

"Well Frank, I don't think that we can do any more to test you here," the Dean had said, "but I wonder what you're going to be like against a really fierce seam attack."

"Haven't you got any fast bowlers in the Art School?"

"We've got some medium pacers, but they're nothing

like the Aussie twins that bowl for Whitehammel. Or the other dozen or so Asian and West Indians seamers we seem to come up against every year."

"Are they quick?"

"Ninety miles an hour plus. That's been our problem over the years. We've always been undone by pace. There are a lot of big lads around here. Unfortunately, none of them play for the Art School."

"What you need," Frank had said in an inspired off-the-cuff remark, "is an AI driven bowling machine."

"What's that?"

"A bowling machine that can chuck a cricket bowl at high speed, but one, which is controlled by Artificial Intelligence software that can learn and adapt to a batsman's technique. It'd be just the job here in the nets. Not only would it be good for bowling out people, but it could also train someone to overcome defective technique."

"Would that such things existed," said a thoughtful Dean.

Frank began ruminating on the mechanics of a really fierce AI driven bowling machine.

Some curves, he thought. *A long cylinder, of course; some straight edges; some cams to simulate the action of the bowler's arm; a rotating shaft; a feeder mechanism for holding the balls: you'd need to hold at least a dozen balls. What about the mechanism for throwing the ball? Hmm, some hydraulics and a spring or a catapult mechanism; or maybe even a small explosive charge. The circuit boards and video cameras for the recordings and the screen for the playback. Where would they go? And the software. What to program it in? Python? C++? A neural net?* The machine seemed to long to take form.

The next day, Frank strolled down to the college stationery shop. He picked up some large sheets of paper and various drawing tools. Back at the studio, he sketched out his really fierce AI driven bowling machine. The sheets of paper soon proved to be inadequate for his explorations: he needed something longer.

He attempted to resolve the problem by getting some cheap lining paper from the local hardware shop. However, this too proved to be inadequate: he needed something wider and longer. He solved the problem by getting hold of some industrial strength hoarding paper. Back at base, he went to with a vengeance. But contrary to expectations, the image of the machine seemed harder to pin down than he had expected.

He rethought his approach to the drawing. What he really needed to do was to think top downwards. He would begin at the beginning with some broad views and would then refine his drawings as he zoomed in on the working detail. This seemed much better. He filled large areas of the studio with drawings of monumental images. The broad views resembled architectural drawings for some immense industrial apparatus.

Two weeks later, he sensed he'd just about got the detail sorted. He stood back to find he'd also got a studio full of drawings. They were spread out everywhere. The walls, the floor, and bits of the ceiling were covered in plans and elevations.

"They look jolly complicated, Frank. What are they?"

Frank turned to find a perplexed looking Fairly at his side.

"Oh, hello, Pete," said Frank absent-mindedly.

"I wish I could churn out the stuff like you seem to,

Frank. I'm still struggling with this wretched still life."

"What's the matter with it?" said Frank unenthusiastically.

"It just doesn't look right. I'm wondering if I did the right thing in taking Hendricks's advice about attempting still life instead of carrying on with the life drawing."

Fairly persuaded Frank to pop next door and have a look at the still life that was causing him so much bother.

"There! See what I mean?" lamented Fairly as he flopped moodily into an armchair. Frank looked at the canvas to find it completely bare.

"Where is it then?" said Frank, looking puzzled.

"Well, it's in front of you, Frank," replied Fairly, pointing to the table in the corner.

"But that's the still life, Pete. Where's the painting of it you're working on?"

"That's just it, Frank. I can't get started because I can't seem to get the still life right."

– This bloke's mental, Frank, said *Frank*.

– You're not wrong there, *Frank*.

"Are you saying, Pete, that you can't get started because you're not happy with the organisation of the bits and pieces?"

"That's it. Isn't that right, chaps?" said Fairly to the weary-looking camera crew.

"Dead right," said a chorus of unsympathetic voices.

"How long have you been working on this piece then, Pete?"

"Oh, ever since I stopped going to the life classes: about ten days."

"You've spent ten days in setting up this still life and you're still not happy with it!?"

"Well, no. Not all the time. I've also spent quite a lot of

time cleaning out the studio. Isn't that right, chaps? I've also painted the studio," said Fairly before the camera crew could reply to his question. "I can't think what the previous occupant did in here, but it was in a dreadful state. Anyway," he continued in defensive vein, "I have made several starts. It's just that they weren't great, so I scrubbed them. But I have come to the conclusion," he said with an air of a man who has made a significant discovery, "that it's the set-up of the still life that's causing the problem. Which is why I'd like your help, Frank. Please," he implored, "see if you can do something with it."

Frank looked at the still life. It comprised two bottles and a large bowl of rotting fruit. The whole thing was laid out on a bit of old curtain.

– Can't see the problem, *Frank*, said Frank.

– Nor me, Frank. It looks fairly straightforward. Fairly straightforward! Get it?

– Yes, *Frank*, said Frank laconically. I'm sure he's never heard that before.

– Actually, he is fairly new to this sort of thing. Fairly new, Frank. Hah.

– Get on with it, *Frank*.

– I mean, he's finding it hard because he's new to the scene.

– If you ask me, said Frank, he's finding it hard because he's an idiot. And also, he's wasting our time. I've got a good mind to give him a piece of my mind.

– Hang on, Frank, said *Frank*, somewhat alarmed at Frank's tone. He's the man with the cameras and the connections. I'm gonna need him later on in the year.

– Well then, you help him, said Frank curtly.

– Leave it to me, Frank. I'll set him straight.

"Um," said *Frank*, turning to Fairly, "you know, Pete, the reason you're having such a hard time is because you've not yet developed the perceptual outlook that's necessary to do justice to a classical still life."

"Really," said Fairly with something approaching relief that Frank had made a telling diagnosis regarding his difficulty. That would put the damn camera crew in their place. Really, they had been most unsympathetic in this endeavour. "How does one develop this…, this perceptual outlook, thingy?"

"Well," said *Frank*, warming to his theme, as he flicked through Fairly's folder, "looking at your work, Pete, it seems obvious to me you need to go back to school."

"Back to school? I don't understand."

"You need to return to a younger time and learn again to see the world as a child sees it: with fresh eyes at the wonder of it all. With eyes that aren't yet tainted by the need to say something interesting and perhaps controversial."

"I say, that sounds awfully good," said Fairly. He motioned to the camera crew to make sure they were getting this down. The crew sprang into life like the well-honed professionals they were. And thankful they were too, for something useful to record. After Fairly's snivelling, they were in a ready state to appreciate richer fare.

"You must unlearn some of the perceptual habits you've developed on the journey to becoming an adult," said *Frank* with just a hint of a smile as he caught a glance of the scampering crew behind him. "Only then can you hope to stand in front of a still life and see it as it really is: a series of angles and planes; as blocks of intersecting forms; as juxtapositions of pure colour in a sea of bounded edges."

By now, *Frank* was in full flow. He would happily have continued, but Fairly appeared to have got the message.

"That's it!" he exclaimed. "That's what I want to see."

"That's all very well, Pete," said *Frank* tantalisingly, "but seeing's one thing; putting it down's something else. There are actually two problems to solve."

"Yes, I see what you mean, *Frank*. Yes, obviously they're quite different things. And in fact, even if I learn to see, I suppose I may never have the skill to render what I see accurately?"

"Got it in one, Pete."

"Thank you, *Frank*. Thank you," said Fairly with one eye on the camera. He shook Frank's hand with exaggerated gusto. "I'm awfully grateful to you, *Frank*. You've opened my eyes to the immensity of what I've yet to achieve. But at least I know now, not only the direction I've got to take, but I've also got an idea of some signposts to look out for."

Frank brushed his hair back for the benefit of the camera before taking his leave. He left it to Fairly to arrange a visit to a local primary school with a view to enrolling there for a week or two. Frank quizzed him as soon as he got back to his own studio.

– What was that stuff you were handing out to Fairly, *Frank?* said Frank, somewhat surprised at *Frank's* sudden artistic volubility.

– I'm not sure I know myself, Frank. Fact is, I heard the Dean giving that speech to some of the foundation students last week. It sounded the part. Didn't it? That's the key thing. And now I've got a friend for life. He'll be bloody useful come the degree shows when I need some advice on making a video of my pieces. He's also going to be out of your hair for a while,

Frank. So, you should be pleased about that.

– A good result all round, in fact, *Frank*.

– I should cocoa, Frank.

Chapter 16

There was little in the way of scheduled formal monitoring or assessment of students' work at St Sigeberht's. It was left very much up to individual tutors how they approached this subject. There was often tacit agreement between tutor and tutee that assessment would get done when the student was ready to talk about his or her work. In practice, this sometimes meant never. Students could always maintain that they didn't want to talk about their work, or they weren't ready or whatever and, tutors could of course maintain that the students hadn't requested a meeting and they didn't want to intrude on the creative process.

However, St Sigeberht's had an interesting mechanism which allowed for an informal means of assessment of selected students' work. This was the open seminar.

The open seminar was a gathering of students and lecturers at which one or more students submitted their work for general discussion. In keeping with the spirit of assessment, this was a voluntary affair. No one was obliged to submit his or her work, and there wasn't a formal means of ensuring that everyone participated. It was a forum that operated on the basis of invitation. Its character was perhaps closer to TV chat show where a different guest or guests are invited each week to talk about themselves.

The seminars were organised by the Art History department. They were the only things organised by the department, which were genuinely popular. They were popular, no doubt, because they gave everyone a chance to indulge in some lean and mean sounding discourse at somebody else's expense. Of course, the informality helped too. In fact, the seminars were so informal the student or students whose work was being discussed didn't have to be participate or attend.

Frank, not unnaturally, found himself the target for a seminar. And not unnaturally, he found himself in two minds about taking part.

– No way, said Frank.

– But Frank, said *Frank* remonstrating, just think. It's a good idea because it'll force us to produce some work by a set deadline and that'll help with the degree show.

– They don't want to see new stuff, dummy, said Frank in rather a superior tone of voice. They'll want to see the stuff we've been doing in the refectory over the last term. Stuff that lots of people have already seen and commented on. They're for people who appear to, I repeat, appear to have done some interesting work.

– Oh!

– Exactly. And they'll want an explanation about the mirrors and all the scribbling.

– Hmm, said *Frank*, musing on the situation. I suppose you're right. It could get embarrassing.

That would have been the end of the affair, but before Frank could definitely reject the proposal, the tutor came back and asked if he would mind sharing a seminar with Peter Fairley. Apparently, Fairly had heard that Frank would be the subject of a seminar and had specifically asked to share the platform with him. The prospect of getting in front of television cameras provided *Frank* with the incentive to think of a way round Frank's decision not to get involved. Frank was not too pleased.

    – No way, said Frank.

    – We've had this conversation before, replied *Frank*.

    – True, *Frank*, and I can distinctively remember that we decided not to do it.

    – Yes, but that was before I realised Fairly would be involved.

    – That's even more of a reason not to take part. I mean to say, *Frank*, if you don't want to make a fool of yourself in front of a couple of dozen people, you certainly won't want to do it in front of a few million.

    – But that's just the point, Frank. There'll be millions of people watching when Fairly's programme goes out. It's a great opportunity to get our work in front of all those people.

    – *Frank*, you're an idiot. And I don't want any part of it.

    – You're being terribly negative, Frank.

    – I'm being sensible.

    – Negative's the word that I'd use, Frank.

    – You've already used it twice.

    – And I don't mind using it a few times more.

    – Won't make any difference, *Frank*.

"Er hello, Frank," said Fairly, sidling up to Frank with a cup of tea in his hand and the camera crew in close support.

Frank nearly fell off his chair at this sudden interruption of a private conversation.

"May I join you," said Fairly, having sat down.

"Yes, do, Pete," said *Frank* enthusiastically before Frank could say no.

"I hope you don't mind," continued Fairly, "but I've taken the liberty of saying to Miles Baker that I'd like to share the next seminar with you. I'm quite keen to get some feedback on the work I've been doing for the past two months. Not that I'm expecting anyone to jump up and down, you understand. But it would be nice to see what one's peers think of one's work."

Frank, conscious of the camera crew focusing on him, and conscious also of the fact that Frank was rather twitchy, tried to make some enthusiastic noises while trying to sound laid back about the whole affair. It didn't quite seem to do the business and both Fairly and Frank were unsure of what *Frank* had actually said.

"I take it then," said Fairly in a hopeful tone, "that you don't mind, in principle? That you're just not sure about the format?"

"Em, yes," said *Frank,* caught in two minds.

Fairly was also in two minds. He had been sure Frank would be keen to get involved. He tried the obvious explanation. "It's the camera, isn't it?" he said, trying to get a lead.

"What?"

"You're worried about being in front of the camera. That's it, isn't it?"

"No. Not at all," said Frank, before *Frank* had a chance to say anything. "I'm just not sure how, um, how er…" Frank thought frantically for a second or two before discovering the get out. "I'm just not sure how we could re-create my work in the studios."

"I see what you mean," said Fairly, looking around. "You mean all these mirrors?"

"Exactly," said Frank with something approaching relief. Let *Frank* try to think of a way out of that.

"Well," said Fairly, "you know, there's no real reason we couldn't have the seminar in the refectory. In fact," he said, becoming visibly exited at the idea, "it would be rather fun. I'd be happy to bring my work in here. There's nothing much to speak of, anyway. It would only be half-a-van-load."

"Oh," was all Frank could say. *Frank,* on the other hand, had plenty to say. But he settled for saying that it sounded like a good idea.

"But what about the refectory?" said Frank, recovering somewhat. "I mean, the refectory has to function normally. We won't be very popular if people can't use the facilities."

"Yes, you've got a point there, Frank," said Fairly, "but it's nothing to worry about. I've got firm assurances from the Warden about being able to film anywhere in the college."

"Ah, right," said Frank quietly as he reached for his levels.

Fairly wandered off in a chipper mood, followed by his entourage. *Frank,* in turn, started chirping on about exposure and how he would make the most of it.

    – You'll get exposure alright, said Frank.

    – There's no need to be sarcastic.

    – *Frank*, I wouldn't want to be in your shoes when everybody starts asking you what it all means.

    – Listen, Frank, said *Frank* reassuringly. It'll be all right on the night. Trust me.

Frank knew better than to pursue matters when *Frank* was in this kind of mood. He left him wittering at the table while he wandered over to the pavilion for some sympathetic company. He found The Five sipping tea and in pleasant form. They were playing snap with a set of old cricketing greats.

"What-ho, Frank," said Gilbert.

"Pull up a chair, old boy," said Hammond.

"Spare cups in the kitchen, old boy," added Barnes. "You know the way."

"Have some cards," said Hobbs generously. "Plenty to go round."

"Have some of mine," added Hutton. "I've got tons."

"Er, thanks, chaps," said Frank, trying to sound cheerful. "I'll just watch for a minute."

Frank pulled up a chair and heaved himself into position. It wasn't long before his long face drew comment, and he declared his reticence at having got involved with Fairly and the forthcoming seminar.

"I take it then, Frank," said Gilbert, "that you wouldn't be upset if said seminar got, um, disrupted, shall we say?"

"I wouldn't be in the least concerned if a herd of stampeding rhinos ran through the seminar."

"Leave it to us, old boy," said Gilbert. "There's a new piece that we've been developing. I think you'll find it should stop any business in the refectory on the day of said seminar."

"Really," said Frank hopefully. "What are you planning on doing?"

"Can't go into that, old boy. None of our pieces are discussed in public before they're performed. Isn't that right, chaps?"

"Absolutely," said a chorus of four.

"Oh, I see. But you think it'll disrupt the proceedings?"

"No question, old boy. Dead in its tracks."

"Dead as a dodo," confirmed Hutton.

"Really?"

"Trust us."

Frank wandered off still not quite convinced. But then he remembered the incident of the imaginary aeroplane in the refectory and cheered up. The change of mood brought *Frank* out of his musings.

> – What's happening, Frank?
>
> – Oh. Er, nothing in particular, *Frank*, replied Frank with a knowing smile.
>
> – You seem chirpy, Frank, said *Frank* thoughtfully.

*

Despite Fairly's confident assurances to Frank regarding his access to the refectory via the good offices of the Warden, Fairly in fact had to work hard at securing the refectory as a venue for this particular seminar. Frost had been very disagreeable about the whole affair. However, he had been seen off in the end and in fact, Fairly was left with quite a bit of artistic licence to pursue his idea.

For the week prior to the seminar, Fairly was in a high state of excitement. In between his bouts of pacing up and down, Frank could hear him mumbling on about his work to the camera. The camera crew was obviously bored out of its collective mind. The crew members kept nipping out for lots of lengthy tea breaks. Still, that gave Fairly a chance to practise his asides to the camera.

Because of all the commotion next door, Frank was spending rather a lot of time with his spirit level glued to his face. As the day for the seminar drew closer, he became increasingly nervous at the prospect of finding himself in front of an audience. *Frank* on the other hand, was looking forward to the event. He kept popping in and out of Fairly's studio to check on camera technique to be sure of presenting himself properly. Frank tried to reason with him, but *Frank* wasn't listening.

– You're gonna come a cropper, *Frank*.

– No way, Frank. I've got the whole thing sussed. All you've gotta do is look the camera straight in the eye. That's what Fairly does.

– And then what? What are you actually gonna say, *Frank?*

– Ah ha, replied *Frank* mysteriously.

– And what about answering questions? It's not just a case of giving a monologue to the camera you know. You'll be expected to answer questions.

– Questions, smestions. They're all the same to me, Frank, said *Frank* with a flourish as he disappeared into Fairly's studio again.

Fairly was putting the finishing touches to his little group of paintings. He congratulated himself on the fact that despite his initial problems, he had accumulated over a dozen canvases in just over six weeks. His prolonged visit to the local primary school had been just the ticket to get him started.

"Ah, Frank," said Fairly in an expansive mood. "Come in, old boy. Just putting the finishing touches to my *Untitled Piece*."

"Don't want to overdo it, Pete," said Frank, sensing an opportunity.

"No danger of that, Frank. Surely? There's hardly anything on the canvas."

"Oh, yes, Pete. Easy to do," said Frank casually.

– Frank! interjected *Frank*. Leave the poor bloke alone.

– He's asking for it, *Frank*, retorted Frank.

"Really?" said Fairly in alarm, pulling his brush away from the canvas.

"Done it many a time myself," said Frank continuing in his bogeyman vein. "Got to learn to leave well alone. When a piece is done, you've got to walk away from it. No other way."

"How does one know, exactly? I mean when a piece is finished. How does one know when to stop?"

– Frank, I'm warning you.

"The piece will tell you, Pete."

– Frank. Stop!

"How's that, Frank?" said Fairly quizzically.

"If you can see, Pete," said Frank meaningfully, "if you can really see, the piece will tell you when it's time to stop." Suddenly Fairly felt rather more unsettled than he had done for a while.

– That's it, Frank, said *Frank* categorically. Another word and I'll pull the plug on you.

– Keep your shirt on, *Frank*. I'm going.

"I've got to dash, Pete," said Frank, making for the door. "See you soon."

Fairly looked forlornly at the disappearing figure. "You'll have to explain that to me again sometime, Frank," said Fairly, following him to the door. "I didn't quite understand the last bit." His voice trailed off as he turned back to look forlornly at his painting.

*

The seminar was due to be held the following Tuesday.

Fairly and his crew spent most of Monday in the refectory. There was no way there would be any technical hiccups. Fairly fussed around any and everything. This would be his day. His chipper mood was in marked contrast to Frank's.

Frank had tried to get him motivated, but he'd washed his hands of the affair and was determined not to get involved. Fairly too had tried to elicit a response from him, but it wasn't easy, especially as Frank insisted on holding his levels to his eyes throughout any conversation. Moreover, he insisted in speaking only in monosyllables.

But of course, there wasn't anything to be worried about. Fairly with his newly found sensibilities could attribute Frank's mood to artistic temperament.

"Probably thinking up a new piece," he said confidently to the crew.

"Looks pissed off to me," said Wally the cameraman, but Fairly didn't seem to hear.

"Probably be okay tomorrow," concluded Fairly. "Yep. Let's go, gang. We're all finished here."

*

The next day saw the refectory fuller than usual. It promised to be a jolly affair. The chairman was about to get the seminar started when Fairly interrupted him. Being a seasoned professional, he knew this moment to be important, and wanted to acknowledge it. Not least of all for the benefit of discerning viewers.

"Er, If I may, Mr Chairman," he said modestly as he rose to his feet. "I would just like to say a few words before the proceedings get under way."

He turned to the camera and with obvious emotion in his voice related his feelings at securing what was in effect his first exhibition.

"I little realised, when I started on this adventure some two months ago, what I'd let myself in for. The experience has not been without a degree of anguish, and yes, even a certain amount of pain. The act of creation is not something that comes easily – certainly not to this reporter stroke artist. There were moments when I really wondered what I was doing here. But now, with this work you see before you," he waved in the general direction of his pieces, "I feel that I have at least made a modest start on the road to becoming an artist. The pieces represent a struggle to release, to release some of the, the...," he paused to collect his thoughts.

Unfortunately, he wasn't destined to get any further. He caught a flash of white out of the corner of his eye. Turning, he saw a group of players in cricket whites. Two of them were padded up. A third player was tossing a ball up and down in a casual manner – suggesting there really wasn't much point in the batsmen being there. There were two others wearing white coats. Obviously, the umpires.

To some extent Fairly took this in his stride. Part of his briefing had covered the refectory. However, he wasn't prepared for what was about to befall him and his seminar. As he looked at the players, he noted they appeared to be looking upwards. As they did so, the lighting in the refectory became noticeably darker. The players were by now walking nonchalantly around the refectory – while continuing to point to the four corners of the ceiling. Most of the refectory crowd was also looking up at the ceiling. Many of them remembered the fiasco of the incident with the aeroplane last term and were looking for something equally entertaining. It was bound to be better than the dry seminar that had stalled over in the corner.

Fairly looked around apprehensively. He hadn't been around for the aeroplane performance, but he had read the report the refectory manager had written. He hadn't quite believed it. He wondered now if there hadn't been something in it. Surely not? Not during the seminar? He'd cleared it with everybody. He turned to look around him with more than a touch of consternation. The camera crew too had lost interest in what he had been saying and were now also looking up at the ceiling with an air of expectation.

Fairly shivered and then realised there was a bit of a wind blowing through the refectory. It was coming from the back entrance, and it appeared to be getting stronger. Instinctively, he checked his beret to make sure it was secure. His notes rustled and then floated off the table onto someone's lap. It wasn't an especially strong wind, but it seemed to get noticeably colder. With this observation came the realisation that a fine mist was descending from above. Fairly muttered something about telling him it wasn't a dream to no one in particular. He looked at Frank and found him engrossed in a pair of spirit levels. Perhaps he was dreaming the whole thing after all. His cameraman came to his rescue.

"I don't know what's going on, Pete, but I can't operate the camera in this. I thought we were filming indoors; I didn't bring any wet-weather kit."

On the field of play, the players had come together in a huddle and were talking about the possibility of rain stopping play. Their voices clearly audible thanks to some strategically placed radio mikes. The sound of their voices brought Fairly back to some sense of reality. However, like the rest of the refectory crowd, he found himself listening to the dialogue of the players.

The square leg umpire waddled over to the bowler's end.

"It doesn't look good," he said to his colleague while shielding his face from the mist.

"No."

"Shall we offer it to the players?"

"Yes, I think so."

They motioned for the striking batsman to join them. The batsman walked over slowly. En route, he stopped several times to prod the ground. He seemed quite unperturbed by the fine spray falling across the imaginary pitch. A sizeable minority of the refectory crowd was also taking things in its stride. They were seasoned Five watchers. They felt as much a part of this piece as the performers. The same could not be said of others. In fact, some people were definitely stirring in their seats. However, thanks to the artistic minority, there was a reluctance to make too much of a fuss. This, despite the fact that fine mist was the sort of atmospheric veil that one might expect to find on open moorland but would be hard pressed to find in a college refectory. In fact, there was remarkably little fuss made, even though the mist had by now turned to gentle rain.

Meanwhile, the striking batsman had joined the others in the middle of the refectory.

"Do you want to come off, batsman?" enquired the umpire.

"Come off?" said the batsman in obvious surprise. "On what grounds?"

"Rain stopped play?" suggested the umpire in a very congenial tone.

"Rain? What rain?" said the batsman curtly before

starting back to his own crease. He made sure of the remaining bumps as he walked back. Upon reaching his crease, he looked around himself – no doubt making sure the fielders hadn't moved. Then, with a flourish of his bat, he took guard. As he did so, a sudden flash of light lit up the whole refectory. It was followed closely by the sound of distant, booming thunder. The refectory's clientele was now in an extremely nervous state. There was still the sizeable minority who had taken the situation in their stride, but the majority were now attempting to leave. Frost heard the thundering in his office and realised immediately that something was amiss. He tried to shoot out of his office, but found the door locked. Apparently, whatever was happening was going to happen in his absence. Frost wasn't alone in his predicament. Those in the refectory who were trying to leave found the entrances locked. It seemed they were a captive audience.

By this stage, the rain had become quite heavy. It appeared to prompt a second consultation in the game. Once again, the striking batsman and the square leg umpire conferred at the bowler's end. This time, the striking batsman acknowledged the rain but declared himself willing to carry on.

"Probably just a passing shower. Can't let this hold up the game. Hmm. I'm keen to press on. What about you, old man?" he said to his companion.

"Absolutely."

"That's settled then."

With that, he ambled back to his crease.

By now, the refectory was awash. Students that were inclined to move were trying to find some sort of shelter. The balcony overhang provided respite for a quite a number, but it was inadequate for the whole refectory. Several students tried to climb over the counters to get into the serving and kitchen areas. This wasn't easy because the kitchen staff did their best to repel boarders. They certainly didn't want a lot of students trampling all over the fresh food. The only other obvious place of shelter was under the tables and within a short space of time, most people who wanted to find shelter had found a spot. A few people tried to remonstrate about the rain, but there seemed little point in arguing under a downpour.

Fairly and his camera crew had lost out on this brand of musical chairs. The crew's equipment had militated against them finding a place to shelter. Fairly had got stuck because of his canvases. He had tried vainly to gather them up. An impossible task. Several of them had been trampled in the rush. One or two had a foot pass through. They were certainly sodden. Fairly looked around in anguish and broke into tears. All that angst and hard work; all that pacing up and down. It looked for a moment as though he was going to stand there blubbing. The camera crew half-persuaded, half-dragged him over to the food counter, where there was a little space to shelter.

The removal of Fairly and his crew left the refectory with just the players and the genuine aficionados still in situ. The bowler took the opportunity to adjust his field. He waved some instructions to fine tune his field and then started back towards his marker. By now, the rain was a deluge. It was bucketing down. The whole of the refectory was awash in several inches of water. Not that it seemed to bother the players. They were unaware of anything except the game. As the bowler reached his marker, he turned immediately and started his long run-up to bowl. However, just as he was approaching the crease, the batsman stood up from his guard, causing the bowler to slide to a halt. The batsman signalled to his companion at the other end of the wicket. They both walked slowly towards the middle, prodding the wicket as they went.

"Looking a bit damp, old man," said the first batsman.

"Yes. And frankly, I'm a bit worried about the wicket now."

"It could get very cut up. We ought to save something for the cup match."

"My thinking exactly."

"Shall we call it a day, then?"

"I think so."

With that, they motioned to the umpires they were retiring and made their way slowly to the pavilion. A polite round of applause followed The Five as they left the field. The rain too appeared to have run itself dry and stopped as suddenly as it had started.

Frank peered out from under his levels. The light was getting visibly brighter. He had sat all through the performance, not daring to breathe a sigh of relief. He had thought at first he would be cornered for an explanation of his work. It had been touch-and-go. As it was, things had turned out far better than he had dared to hope. The seminar had been a total washout. Additionally, Fairly's paintings were a complete mess. There was no way he could resurrect those in a hurry – if at all. And there was no prospect of the seminar being repeated, since there would not now be a vacant slot in the schedule before the end of the year. He was trying to keep a straight face so that *Frank* wouldn't suspect that he had contrived to wreck the seminar.

– What unbelievable luck, said *Frank*.

– Yes, unbelievable, replied Frank.

– I still can't believe it.

– I sympathise, *Frank*. But there it is. Just as well, I suppose.

– What do you mean, Frank?

– I mean about not having to talk about the work.

– I had it all worked out.

– What?

– What I was going to say about the work and everything.

– Oh well, *Frank*. It doesn't matter now.

– No, I suppose not, said *Frank* philosophically.

– I suppose we'd better see how they're doing in the pavilion.

Frank wandered over to the pavilion and climbed the steps. He was surprised to find The Five were already dry and drinking tea and eating buttered scones. He himself was soaking wet.

"Ah, Frank," said Gilbert. "Pull up a chair and have some tea. I hope the performance was as useful for you as it was for us?"

"What? Oh yes. Very useful."

– What does he mean useful for you, Frank? said *Frank*.

– Oh, nothing. It's just a figure of speech.

"You chaps seem to have got changed quickly," said Frank, changing the subject.

"Had everything laid out before we took the field, old boy," said Hobbs. "By the way, I hope our timing didn't put you in any bother with Fairly. Only we were late in getting started. Had some problems in getting the tea-urn set up."

"Er, no. No bother," stammered Frank.

– What's he mean by that, Frank? said *Frank* with a growing suspicion at the back of his mind.

– What?

– Don't give me what, Frank, said *Frank* in an aggressive tone of voice. You knew about this little performance. Didn't you?

– I may have done, replied Frank defensively. What about it?

– What about it? You knew the whole thing was going to be a washout, and you didn't give me so much as a nudge or a wink. You let me spend all that time in making up stuff to say when all the time you knew I wouldn't get a chance to say anything.

– And what about you, *Frank*? It didn't seem to bother you that I didn't want to have anything to do with this sodding seminar.

"More tea, Frank," said Gilbert, interrupting the tête-à-tête.

– I'll see you about this later, Frank, said *Frank*.

– Not if I see you first, said Frank, getting in the last word, for now.

Chapter 17

The last week of the spring term. For some it seemed to herald an agreeable conclusion; for others, it had a sickening feel to it. It was another week closer to the degree shows, with little to show to prospective examiners and external assessors. *Frank*, very much in the former camp, was becoming more and more ebullient. Frank, on the other hand, thought himself encamped on the Titanic, and was getting more and more desperate. Luckily for him, he was distracted by other considerations. In particular, the preparations for the Challenge Cup match.

On the day of the game, art school students came to college dressed in their gaudiest best. Ladies Day at Ascot would have seemed tame by comparison. The Dean led by example and spent a lot of time and effort in organising the bunting and the flags. He had also been busy working with Fairly's crew to ensure a decent video of the match.

The Five, after umpteen meetings with the authorities, had persuaded them that a pavilion was essential to help create the right atmosphere for the most important fixture for the Art School XI. Given the go-ahead, they spent a happy week building a replica of the refectory pavilion on the edge of the pitch: it seemed sensible to use a tried and tested design. The mechanical monkey, whose task it was to sit atop and fan the flag – a task for which he was now clearly redundant – had also been included in the design. A decision welcomed by everyone.

They completed the structure with barely a day to spare. The Art School turned out en masse to cheer as they hoisted the Art School flag. On a sunny spring morning, there was a hint of a breeze to rustle the flag in harmony with the leaves of the trees encircling the pitch. The tooting of improvised horns contributed to a very emotional ceremony. The monkey too looked pleased: he had been given a mate to help him with his never-ending task of flag waving.

With the flag hoisted, the team repaired inside to finalise the batting order.

"Well, chaps," said Gilbert, "this is what it looks like. See what you think…. Frank and Ivor to open. I'm sure everyone's in agreement with that. And, for the record, that's likely to be the opening partnership for the rest of the season."

"Hear, hear," said a chorus of voices.

"I'll come in at number three. I've got a slight twinge in my back, so I won't be doing any bowling. That means Hobbs and Hammond will open the bowling."

"I'd quite like to come down the slope," said Hammond. "I reckon it'll help with my inswing."

"I'm happy with that," said a generous Hobbs.

"Right. That's okay then. So, Hammond will come in at number nine with Hobbs at number ten. Hutton at number four, Barnes at five and Bunny at six. Bunny, I've moved you up since you didn't get much of a bat in the last match."

"But that was last season," said Bunny, somewhat surprised.

"I know, but still. Must balance the accounts. Albert, you'll come in at number seven."

Albert nodded, "I'm happy with that."

"Good. Jim, I've got you down at number eight. That means you'll come on as the first bowling change. That just leaves the number eleven spot to fill. I hoped Manny would play, but he'll be going for an interview – Royal College, I think. But anyway, I'm sure I can persuade Nigel to play. He's keen to make amends for the duck he made last time he played."

The match was scheduled to start at two; by one, the spectators had ringed the playing field and were enjoying an outdoor lunch prior to the game. And since it was the end of term, everyone was there and determined to enjoy themselves. The bunting said it all for most people. It was a promised intent of gently waving colour; and it was everywhere.

At one-twenty, with no sign of the opposition, Gilbert decided that while they were waiting for Whitehammel, they would put on an exhibition of spirited fielding for the spectators. He led the team on to the pitch to a generous round of applause from the spectators.

The cheers really fired up the Art School. They set to with an infectious enthusiasm. There were dramatic high balls thrown from one end of the field to the other to demonstrate how a high ball should be caught; the players made darting short runs to pick up a ball as it sped towards the boundary rope; the slip fielders made spectacular diving catches to show that nothing was going to get past them, and most dramatic of all, there were fierce shies at the stumps to show what would happen if the opposition dared to steal quick singles.

Unfortunately, in all the excitement, one of the fierce shies missed the stumps by some distance and knocked out several of Nigel's teeth. Gilbert led an inconsolable and bloodstained Nigel off the field. He was promptly dispatched with a companion to look for the nearest dentist. However, the side was now a man short: a not uncommon state of affairs for the Art School. However, as had happened in the past, Prudence stepped into the breach.

"Probably a good omen," opined Gilbert, to a much subdued-looking side to the one that had taken the field ten minutes earlier. "And perhaps even a fortuitous one. Not that I want to take anything away from Nigel, but it is quite possible that Prudence will actually be more valuable to the side for the sympathy runs that she will undoubtedly collect."

Fortunately, from the point of view of the Art School's morale, the opposition suddenly turned up and helped to focus minds.

"Shall we look at the wicket?" said Gilbert to the opposing captain as he led his team out to join the Art School.

"Yes, let's press on. I'm sorry for being late. Some fool's parked a JCB near the car park entrance and we got stuck behind a van trying to navigate a way around it."

"Not to worry," said a smiling Gilbert. "It happens all the time around here."

Gilbert marched up and down the pitch looking for only he knew what. He checked the wicket several times from both ends. He had apparently discovered something amiss on a length at both ends and called for a bat to flatten out the irregularities.

"Well," he said eventually with a sad shake of his head. "At least it looks pretty straight."

This was a fairly orthodox opening gambit by Gilbert to suggest there was something wrong with the pitch, and that he wouldn't bat on it first if there were a choice. As an opening gambit to the first game of the season, it probably wasn't bad. However, his opposite number had been playing against Gilbert for several years and knew his gambits almost as well as Gilbert knew them himself.

"I'm surprised to hear you say that, Gilbert. Very generous of you."

"Oh?"

"Yes, most generous," said the opposing captain, and left it to Gilbert to work out quite what he meant. In the event, it didn't matter since the Art School won the toss. Gilbert elected to bat despite his apparent misgivings about the state of the wicket.

Notwithstanding Nigel's accident, spirits were high in the pavilion. Frank and Ivor padded up in good humour. Frank was in a bullish mood at the prospect of his first innings.

- Are you ready for this, Frank?
- Too right I am, *Frank*.
- Bladder empty, Frank?
- Never been emptier.
- Got your box, Frank?
- Check.
- Thigh pad in position?
- Check.
- Pad straps tucked in? You don't want to be given

out just because a ball clipped your pad strap.

– Say no more, *Frank*. I'm ready. Good and ready. And what about yourself, *Frank?*

– Me? said *Frank* incredulously. Is the sky blue, Frank?

– It's blue, *Frank*.

– Is the grass green?

– 'Tis that.

– Is the ball red, Frank? Just answer me that. Is the ball red or what?

– It's red.

– Damm right it is.

– Say no more, *Frank*.

– So, Frank. Do you reckon you'll make a few runs?

– Half a century – at least. Just watch me.

– A half century? Is that all you're going to make, Frank?

– That's just off the first fifty balls, *Frank*. I'll be doing the same to the second fifty.

– You're gonna take fifty balls to crack a half century?

– That's fifty balls between me and the other opening bat, *Frank*. Can't say fairer than that.

– That sounds more like it, Frank, said *Frank*, breathing a sigh of relief.

Frank picked up his customised bat, and he and Ivor trundled out to the middle. The middle seemed to come out to meet them. In next to no time at all, Frank found himself at the striker's end. He checked the stumps with his bat to see that they were properly vertical. He did both ends just to make absolutely sure. A bemused looking keeper helped him to rearrange the bails as he came back to the striker's end.

"Do you wish to take a guard, batsman?" said the

opposition's umpire in a tetchy sort of voice.

"No, that's all right," said Frank, suddenly remembering he hadn't yet marked his guard. He walked behind the stumps and, with the aid of the levels in his bat, sighted a guard for himself.

– I think that'll do, *Frank*, said Frank.

– Looks about right, Frank. What about the fielders? Better just check to see what they're doing.

Frank raised the bat to eye level once more and did a three-hundred-and-sixty-degree rotation to locate the fielders. Then, with a flourish of the bat, settled into his stance.

The whole rigmarole had taken fully five minutes.

– Head down now, Frank.

– Say no more, *Frank*.

On the edge of the boundary, the other team members looked on with undisguised admiration at Frank's professionalism.

"Frank seems to have got the measure of the opposition," said Barnes.

"They certainly don't seem to know what to make of him," remarked Hutton.

Meanwhile, the umpire – having been unable to get any response out of Frank as regards his readiness to play – signalled to the bowler to start.

The bowler was one of the Australian twins that played for Whitehammel. He was known affectionately as Twin One on account of the fact he had been born two minutes before his brother; he was naturally enough known as Twin Two.

Twin One thundered in off his thirty-yard run up and sent down a ferocious loosener. Frank met it with a bat as straight as a plumb line and with his weight fully behind the ball. A fine example of a classic forward defensive stroke.

– Did you see that ball, *Frank*, said Frank?

– All the way, Frank.

– Hard, *Frank?*

– Piece-of-piss.

– Say no more, *Frank*.

Over at the pavilion, the Dean and the rest of the team heaved a sigh of relief. Despite what Frank had been doing in the nets, he had yet to prove himself in front of a real pace attack. However, if the first ball was anything to go by, Frank wouldn't have any problems.

Twin One looked hard at Frank's follow-through and decided he'd obviously bowled the ball far too slowly. The batsman clearly had plenty of time to sight the ball and get behind it. His next delivery was thrown down even faster. Frank's response was even more assured. He also blocked the next three balls. Twin One glared at Frank. He stopped to mop his brow and get his breath back for the last bowl of the over. With his arms and legs pumping furiously, he stormed to the crease and hurled down an almighty delivery. However, by now, Frank's reactions were as quick as they could be. He sighted the ball early and drove it through where mid-off should have been. The ball cleared the boundary marker before anyone moved.

"Nobody move, man! Nobody move!" yelled a chorus of delighted beer-swilling voices from the boundary's edge. A generous round of applause rippled around the pitch; the pavilion broke into cheers. The Dean did a little jig around the cricket bag. He couldn't remember when he had seen a better shot. He felt as though his prayers had been answered. All those anguished moments of the last few seasons were surely now a thing of the past.

As Whitehammel changed ends, the pavilion settled down to enjoy their cricket. After seeing Frank deal effortlessly with the first over, they watched without really taking much notice. They were more interested in passing the tea around. Twin Two thundered in from the opposite end to bowl to Ivor. The next moment caught everyone by surprise.

"Oh my God! He's gone," croaked someone as Ivor's middle stump went tumbling. "He's gone first ball."

"Oh, dear," mumbled Hobbs, dropping a tray of crockery.

"Better get padded up, Hutton," said a grim-looking Gilbert. He pulled on his batting gloves and started walking towards the middle.

The Dean sat down quietly and watched a disconsolate Ivor lope back from the crease. Gilbert met him halfway to the pavilion.

"What happened, Ivor?"

"Oh, my," said Ivor. "I just didn't see it."

"Must have kept low," said Gilbert, trying to console him.

"Yes, I suppose it must have done."

"Bad luck, Ivor."

"Oh my, oh my," said Ivor as he arrived back at the pavilion.

"Bad luck, Ivor," said a chorus of sympathetic voices.

"I just didn't see it. I think I must get my glasses seen to," he said, reaching for a deck chair.

Barely had he sat down when a great cheer went up from the middle. Apparently, Gilbert had also gone first ball. Suddenly, Ivor didn't feel so bad. An embarrassed silence greeted Gilbert upon his return to the pavilion.

"Sorry, chaps. I just didn't see it."

"Oh, my," said Ivor. "That sounds just like the ball I received."

"Suddenly this has all the makings of a classic Art School collapse," suggested Barnes.

"No, no," protested the Dean. "You mustn't think that way, Barnes. Early days yet. Two lucky balls; I doubt he'll bowl two like that again all season."

They watched apprehensively as Hutton walked out to the middle and took guard. Twin Two was now on a hat trick and naturally enough, the captain brought everyone in to crowd the batsman. Twin Two thundered in again. Fortunately for Hutton, the excitement got the better of the bowler. The ball sailed well wide of the off stump. Everyone breathed a sigh of relief: not least of all the occupants of the pavilion. The relief was short-lived, however, as Hutton only lasted for two more balls before being clean bowled.

"Oh, shit!" was the common exclamation back at the pavilion.

"Looks like a collapse to me, Dean," said Barnes over his shoulder.

The Dean was nothing if not an optimist.

"That's the end of the over and Frank's facing again. The so-called collapse is going to stop right there. I'm absolutely certain."

Frank did his best to calm nerves in the pavilion. He started where he left off in the first over. This time he clipped the first ball off his legs and sent it through mid-wicket for his second four. The second and third balls were blocked straight back to the bowler. The following delivery was rather short: Frank hooked it over square leg for a whopping six.

"That's more like it," said the Dean jumping up and down in the pavilion.

"Much more like it," added Hutton.

"I should say so," said Bunny.

"Collapse? What collapse?" said the defiant Dean.

The answer came in the next over, when Twin Two took two more wickets, bringing his haul from two overs to five for nought.

"Oh my," said Ivor. "It looks as if we could be having tea very shortly."

Ivor's words proved prophetic. Despite Frank's best efforts to protect his partners, Whitehammel took four more wickets extremely cheaply – leaving Frank at the bowler's end as Prudence came in as the last bat. A smug looking opposition clapped her in to the crease. The opposition captain became rather chivalrous and motioned for his bowlers to take things easy. A businesslike Prudence did her best to look competent. She declined the umpire's invitation to take a guard and settled for an unorthodox stance with the bat wrapped around her neck: ready to swat the ball. The fielders, who till now had been extremely alert in their approach to the game, sensed that the end was near and adopted a fairly relaxed looking field.

Twin One came in off a two-yard run up and lobbed a gentle full toss to Prudence. She held her breath while she took an almighty swipe at the ball. To her astonishment, she missed it completely. Luckily, being fairly tall, she also missed the stumps as the force of her stroke carried her around in a full circle. The ball bounced harmlessly wide to the wicketkeeper and was back with the bowler via a bemused looking set of slips before Prudence had recovered her composure. She concluded she must have been temporarily blinded by the sun, and so decided against modifying her approach to the next delivery. With the next bowl, Twin One bowled underarm and allowed the ball to drop in front of Prudence. She repeated her stroke. This time she hit the ball with the middle of the bat. The ball sailed over mid-wicket, and to the cheers of the spectators rolled over the boundary for four runs.

This is more like it, thought Prudence.

Two more fours followed, thanks to further gentle deliveries. Suddenly Prudence found herself as the second highest scorer, second only to Frank.

Time to go for a huge hit, mused Prudence. *A six into the trees.*

Twin One, however, decided that his bowling figures were going to look a mess at this rate. To avoid that embarrassment, he delivered the next ball with some spin. Prudence played exactly the same stroke, missed the ball, and lost her balance. Inevitably, as she fell, she knocked over the stumps.

– Shit, *Frank*, said Frank at the other end. There goes my fifty. Just my luck to run out of partners.

– Still, she did good, Frank.

– That she did, *Frank*. That she did, said Frank, as he put his arm around her and walked her back to the pavilion.

The Art School found themselves all out for forty-nine runs. The score book made sobering reading. Frank carried his bat and ended up with twenty-two. Prudence got twelve as a result of some chivalrous bowling by the opposition. Gilbert's prediction about Prudence getting sympathy runs had been spot on. Extras managed six. That left the rest of the team with nine runs between them. A chastened Art School XI sat down to an unexpectedly early tea.

After tea, the Art School took the field in their normal zealous fashion. There were balls flying everywhere. The team limbered up with a confidence which belied their score, and the fact that they had already lost a man through their enthusiastic pre-match fielding display.

Forty-nine all out by anybody else's standards would have been hopeless to defend, but the Art School XI were optimistic. Their optimism was not entirely groundless. Pritchard, the newly appointed Art School scorer, had taken the trouble to check the figures in the score book and announced to the team at tea that a score of forty-nine would have won the match on no less than four out of the last eleven fixtures. So, there was hope yet.

Whitehammel didn't quite see it that way, of course, and took their time in coming out for their innings.

With only fifty needed to win, they wanted to make sure they at least made the most of the magnificent tea provided by the Art School. The first thing to go had been the scrumptious tiered cake. Whitehammel disposed of the whole three layers in three minutes flat. That just left the rather prosaic chocolate gateau, the raspberry cheesecake, the buttered scones, the mince pies, and the cucumber sandwiches. All washed down with large mugs of tea.

Eventually, with the plates licked clean, and the mugs emptied, Whitehammel sent out their opening pair along with their umpire. Needless to say, after doing justice to the spread, the opening pair looked decidedly lethargic.

The opposition's umpire didn't look too happy either. Of course, it wasn't just the calories that were causing problems. The Whitehammel team was about to become the unfortunate victims of Frost's revenge.

*

Frost had been busy organising things that morning. He had rather more on his plate than most. Apart from the Challenge Match tea, he also had to organise the catering for the wedding reception. All in all, though, he was rather pleased with himself. He had, of course, been coerced into doing the tea. Thanks to Prudence, he had little choice in the matter, but he had ensured it would be a tea to remember – in more ways than one.

On the face of it, the Challenge Match tea the refectory staff produced looked as magnificent as it had done in previous years. But Frost made sure there was enough laxative in the cakes to clean out a herd of elephants.

"That'll fix the fuckers," he muttered to himself while lacing the cake mix the previous day. Driving into work that morning, Frost chuckled at the prospect of the players finding themselves in need of a loo seat during play. It occurred to him that what he really ought to do to consolidate matters was to go around that afternoon, just after lunch, and remove all the paper from the loos in the immediate vicinity of the playing field.

"That'll really fix the fuckers," chortled Frost as he pulled into the college.

*

Out on the field, by contrast to the Whitehammel opening pair, the Art School XI looked to be full of beans. Fortunately for the side, most of them ate little of the spread. The Five were, of course, vegan and had brought their own sandwiches. They eschewed the tea completely. Prudence was on a diet and heroically restrained herself to fruit. Frank chose to bring in fresh samosas from his favourite Indian restaurant. The rest of the team could in theory have tucked into the spread, but because of their miserable performance on the field, hadn't done much except pick at the cucumber sandwiches. Whitehammel, by contrast, had developed a ravenous appetite and devoured their half of the spread. They were now in a very sorry state. The opening pair barely got to the crease before they started clutching at their stomachs. The facing bat seemed to be in some considerable discomfort. As Hammond came up to bowl to him, he suddenly lost control of his stomach and found himself with something sticky trickling down the back of his legs. His concentration wasn't quite one hundred per cent, and he was to be seen scuttling back to the pavilion a fraction of a second after being clean bowled. His companion hesitated only momentarily, before he too dropped his bat and shot off towards the main building: clutching his stomach with one hand and his posterior with the other.

Meanwhile, things were also stirring in the botanical garden. The wedding reception party had arrived at about the same time as the players broke for tea interval. Frost had foreseen that such an eventuality might occur and had taken the precaution of hiring additional staff to serve the wedding guests. However, what he hadn't foreseen was that the refectory staff would try to minimise their workload by combining jobs for the two events. Consequently, the cake mix he laced with laxative, and which had been used to prepare the tea for the match, was also the mixture used to prepare quite a lot of the fare for the wedding reception. Inevitably then, at about the same time as the Whitehammel players came running into the main building in search of toilets, many of the one-hundred-and-eighty odd wedding guests were heading for the same loos.

It wasn't long before the garden emptied as elegant looking ladies in swirling satin gowns and smartish men in Moss Bros suits were pushing past each other in search of somewhere private. Of course, logistically, it was impossible that everyone could be accommodated at once. Once the loos were full and there was no alternative, several people overcame their natural shyness and took to the bushes in the garden. But even these were limited in number and couldn't accommodate the demand. Those that hadn't found a private spot were inevitably overtaken by events: the bride and groom included.

Frost, coming in chuckling at seeing the players running off the pitch, was struck down by a wave of guests running out of the building in search of public conveniences. The awful truth dawned upon him as hysterical looking kitchen staff came running up to tell him what had been happening. Frost took one sniff in the gardens before realising he had to be somewhere else. He shot into his office with strict instructions that he wasn't to be disturbed while he emailed some important papers to the accountants. An anguished looking bride and groom failed to batter down his door but did let him know they would sue him for every 'Fucking penny' he had.

The match resumed three-quarters of an hour later. Whitehammel tried for a postponement, but the Dean, sensing a reprieve, insisted that the challenge game had always concluded before the Easter break. And really, because the Art School had only made forty-nine, they ought to finish the game off.

"Besides," he continued, "as fixtures secretary, I have to say that we really have got a pretty full fixture list. I don't see how we could reschedule this game after Easter. I dare say you've got a fairly tight schedule yourself?"

The Whitehammel team reluctantly agreed and were congratulated by the Dean on showing the right sort of stuff.

Most of the Art School side had, of course, escaped Frost's revenge. Those that were caught weren't particularly badly affected since they had eaten little of the spread. Whitehammel, by contrast, was a different side. They had lost their spring and easy confidence. Gone too was the cockiness. Number two and three batsmen came to the crease, looking like medicated corpses. They lasted about as long as the Art School's first three wickets and managed only a leg bye between them. The next batsman to come in brought a runner in with him because he didn't think that he could run between the wickets. But he needn't have bothered. He only lasted for three balls before he was dismissed leg before wicket. At this stage Whitehammel were down four wickets with only five leg byes on the score board. The Dean, sitting in the pavilion with the scorer, considered offering a prayer of thanks.

The captain came in next, and he played a genuine captain's innings. He held his end down and tried to take as much of the bowling as he could. Slowly, the runs began to mount. The Art School, nervous about giving anything away, brought in a fairly close field. That was a mistake because it suited Whitehammel to go for the boundary: they really didn't feel inclined to do too much running. But they didn't particularly enjoy standing at the crease, either. Play was held up several times as batsman left the field temporarily. Word about the tea incident had got around the spectators and, of course, these little adjournments were the source of some considerable hilarity on the side lines. Not unsurprisingly, batsman lost what little concentration they had and so wickets fell steadily.

With nine wickets down, Whitehammel still needed twenty-four to win. At this point, Gilbert's sense of captaincy intruded into his thinking. He decided that, as they were practically home and dry, he would give Barnes an over. He hadn't been in the game very much and this seemed an opportune time to bring him on. Barnes was an unorthodox, slow left-arm bowler and could usually be relied upon to take one or two wickets in every game. He did sometimes give away the odd boundary, but with nine wickets down and twenty-four runs to spare, Gilbert calculated he could afford to give him at least an over. If nothing else, he thought, it would give the spectators something interesting to watch.

As it happened, Whitehammel's captain had to face Barnes. He peered thoughtfully as the bowler tossed and twirled the ball in his hands. They were still twenty-four short, and having faced the faster stuff, he didn't feel inclined to go out to a spinner. The ball came down, landed in line with middle stump and broke towards leg. Being left-handed, he blocked the shot fairly easily.

This stuff, he thought, *could be a problem if you were right-handed.* But as he wasn't, he decided he'd be pretty safe if he went after the bowling. The opportunity would be unlikely to come his way if the quickies came back.

Anyway, they only had one wicket left. He had to make this over count.

The Dean, watching from the pavilion, reacted with alarm when Gilbert brought on his spinner.

There's surely no need to dilly-dally at this stage, he thought. *Really, they ought to finish off the opposition. There'll be plenty of time to be generous in the bar afterwards.*

However, after the first ball, he relaxed slightly. But he sat bolt upright when the batsman smashed the next ball past cover point for four runs. And when the third ball hit the mid-wicket boundary, he was up on his feet in a cold sweat.

Out on the field, Gilbert tried to put a brave face on it, but he repositioned the field just the same. There was now only one man in to save the single; everyone else retreated to the boundary, but it didn't help. The Whitehammel captain chopped the next ball through where the second slip would have been. The fielder at third man couldn't run round fast enough to cut it off before it crossed the boundary.

Eight runs to win, thought Whitehammel's captain. *Better make the most of the last ball of this over.*

Barnes tried his best to avoid giving away another boundary, but by now, Whitehammel's captain had the proverbial bit between his teeth. He came out and lofted the last delivery over mid-wicket for six. On the edge of the boundary, the Whitehammel team and supporters started chanting:

"Easy! Easy!"

Gilbert called on Hammond to take the next over.

"Two to lose, Hammond. Good time to try your LBW ploy on the umpire."

"Absolutely, skipper," said Hammond, taking the ball.

Hammond had been practising shouting for the LBW appeal for most of the term. It seemed as if fate had given him the ideal opportunity to see if all his practising would pay off. He walked slowly back to his marker and paused for a moment as Gilbert adjusted the field. With practised care, he rolled up his sleeves as the batsman waited nervously for him to start his run up. Then, with a sudden hop, he broke into his stride. He knew he needed to get past the bat in order to justify making an appeal. This bowl had to be straight and delivered as fast as he could manage. The ball hit the pitch with a blur and thudded into the batsman's rear pad. Hammond span around and with his eyes a-popping and foaming spittle shooting from his mouth screamed at the umpire as if possessed by a howling demon.

"HOWWAAAZZZZAATTT!"

He caught the umpire totally by surprise. The poor wretch jerked back and raised his left hand involuntarily to defend himself. His right hand was, of course, in his pocket, keeping track of the pennies he had been using to count the balls. None of that mattered. The fact was, he had raised his hand and appeared to give the batsman out. Naturally, he wasn't given time to reflect on his decision. The Art School players raced to congratulate Hammond. And before Whitehammel or anyone on the side lines knew what was happening, the stumps had been pulled up and Gilbert was shaking his opposite number's hand.

"Bad luck, old man. You nearly had us. Better luck next year."

Summer

Chapter 18

Four weeks after the refectory washout and at the start of a bright new summer term, a bubbling camera crew screeched to a halt outside Fairly's mews. An impatient trio, they jostled each other at the possibility of filming more lovelies in the life studio. The Land Rover shook with laughter as they recounted the highlights of last term. Clearly, there was no time to waste.

"Go and fetch his nibs, Wally, and tell him to get his skates on," was the general refrain. Wally jumped out and rat-a-tatted the door in a crisp manner. He repeated the procedure for good measure to let Fairly know the lads were keen to begin filming. The crew raised their thumbs to show their appreciation at his sense of urgency.

In the event, it took half a dozen series of progressively louder and more impatient knocks to bring a bedraggled looking Fairly to the front door. He blinked in the morning light and peered quizzically in Wally's general direction – without really seeing him. A bemused Wally watched as Fairly slowly got him into focus.

"Hah, Wally!" he exclaimed at the sight of an apparently long-lost friend. "You've come just at the right time," he blurted in relief, reclaiming the step he had lost when he jerked back in recognition. "I've run out of plonk," he explained, with palms outstretched in disbelief. "Be a sport and fetch some more, would you, Wally? And," he motioned for Wally to come closer, "have a couple yourself, Wally" he said, putting his arm around him. "Do you the world of good, Wally. No question about it." Wally moved his head back involuntarily to put some distance between himself and Fairly's odours. Mercifully, Fairly released him and pottered back inside with an uncertain step and an injunction to be as quick as he liked.

With the morning's agenda stalled, Wally heaved a resigned sigh and headed back to the Land Rover. A short explanation later, with a deflated crew in tow, he headed back to the house. Fairly, by now, had disappeared back inside, shutting the door behind him. Further rat-a-tatting without a response from Fairly dampened everyone's mood. Eventually, they forced their way in through a back window and found a morose Fairly slumped in his armchair with several empty bottles of plonk beside him. In fact, there were empty bottles all over the house.

"I'm gonna put a few people straight," muttered Fairly to the assembly.

The crew strolled over to the remainder of the elegant three-piece suite and plonked their posteriors on the forgiving foam. This was likely to take some time.

"I'm damn well gonna put people in their fucking places," he continued, thumping his fist on the side of his armchair.

Wally shrugged his shoulders and went to make strong coffee. Half-an-hour and several cups later, Fairly had sobered up enough to stomp around the living room. And in marked contrast to the tearful inebriate he had been on the doorstep, he was now rather robust.

"Out of my way, Wally" he said, pushing the camera man to one side. He marched over to a side table and punched the college's number on a defenceless handset. In curt and clipped tones, he insisted on an immediate meeting with the Dean and Warden and slammed the phone down before the Warden's PA could respond.

He also insisted on driving to college, despite the crew's protestations that he was well over the limit. In the Warden's office, he lost no time in coming to the point. He had rehearsed his lines whilst careering across London on the way to the college. Every subtle nuance had been weighed; the telling points contrived to coincide with his good side pointing to camera. With the Warden and Dean sitting opposite him and the camera rolling, he launched into a blistering attack on the way they had desecrated his work. He was emotional; he was ironic; he was bitter. He contrived to wring his hands in the best theatrical traditions and followed that up by pressing them to his breast to show exactly where he'd been hurt. He was eloquent; he was passionate; he was magnificent. Had there had been an audience, a standing ovation of considerable duration would have followed, surely.

But it wasn't to be. The Dean gazed at the cup of tea in his hand, swirling the liquid. A heavy silence descended upon the scene. The Warden, who should have been a natural ally, gazed thoughtfully at the floor while stroking his chin. Though he was not unsympathetic, he had lost his ire against the Art School. Notwithstanding his outraged feelings over the affair of the Christmas panto, he had been soothed because, in the publicity's wake, applications to the college had tripled since this time last year. And as a bonus, the quality of the applicants was a considerable improvement over the preceding years. Improbable as it would have seemed a few months ago, the Warden found himself indebted to the Art School for providing a fillip for raising academic standards. He cleared his throat quietly and looked across to the Dean. Fairly suddenly found himself nonplussed and sweating inexplicably. Surely, this couldn't be right. His paintings had been ruined. Two months of anguished pacing up and down thirty feet of studio space. Yet, somehow, he felt like a candidate who had become an embarrassment. He sensed the glare of the spotlight hovering somewhere above him and was acutely aware of the camera still rolling. He looked at the two men. The Dean seemed to have stopped swirling his tea.

"Peter," he said, "I know you've only been here a few months, but I must confess I am surprised. Surprised that you haven't developed a deeper understanding of the role of an artist.... I know you think your work had some significance, but really, it's thoroughly irrelevant. It's gone, and that's all there is to it. You've got to walk away from it."

"Walk away from it!" exclaimed an incredulous Fairly. "Walk away from it! I went through hours and hours of agony to create those paintings. I put my body and soul into that work. I endured physical pain in giving birth – and I don't think that's too strong a metaphor – to a group of paintings and drawings. All that work, destroyed, by a bunch of anarchic students, who incidentally did thousands of pounds worth of damage and who don't appear to have been disciplined by the college. And you tell me to walk away from it!?"

"Only way," replied the Dean.

Fairly shook his head in disbelief. By now, he really had

forgotten the camera's presence.

"The only question worth asking yourself, Peter," continued the Dean, "is whether you're the same person who came through our doors in January. If you are that person, you might have a point, but my thinking is you've developed somewhat from that individual."

"I don't understand."

"Artists," began the Dean in a practiced voice, "have to let go of their work if they're to progress. As an artist, one can't afford to hold on to yesterday's ruminations. That would be folly. One would become a prisoner of one's own creation. To continue to create and grow as an artist, you must walk away from your past accomplishments. The true vocation of artists is to reinvent themselves continuously. The work is merely the excrement of the artistic journey. Its smell is meant to propel you on your way. But you see, Peter," said the Dean, warming to his task and not unaware of the need to preserve a decent camera angle, "some artists, not unlike those struck by Medusa's gaze, are perpetually seduced by the smell of their own excrement. They spend the rest of their lives playing with it. It's a sorry sight to see," said the Dean in a reflective voice – as though he had someone specific in mind. "A woman gives birth; a man merely excretes. Such is life."

"There's a song there somewhere, Dean," said the Warden.

"You've said so before, Warden."

"It's worth repeating, Dean."

"How kind you are, Warden."

"Well, what is the damn point of it all," interjected Fairly, feeling somewhat excluded from this chummy conversation. "Hmm. What is the point of the artistic struggle if not to create beautiful works of art?"

"The point, Peter, is to make yourself," said the Dean, waving his hand as he wandered nonchalantly towards the door. "Never mind about anything else. Artist, make thyself. You, Peter, are the artefact."

"Oh!" said Fairly in a sudden flash of illumination. Then, turning to the camera, with genuine insight, said, "So, what you see is what you get. I'm a WYSIWYG and I didn't know it! Oh, well," he said with an understandable twinge of resignation, "back to the studio, chaps."

*

Frank was back in the refectory at his favourite table. And since the students had returned from their school placements, the atmosphere was blissfully reminiscent of the autumn term. Indeed, upon reflection, it seemed better than he remembered. Probably because everyone was glad to be back in college. The consensus was that it was rather nicer to be in a friendly college environment than out in unsympathetic surroundings. And of course, summer had almost arrived. It was a short term and the prospect of sunny holidays beckoned in the not-too-distant future. The only dark cloud on the horizon was the degree show; that could conveniently be ignored for the time being. There would be time enough to fret about the lack of artistic oeuvre. For now, *Frank talk* was very much the order of the day.

> – The light's brighter, *Frank*, said Frank with the authority of a man who knows a thing or two about light and doesn't expect to be contradicted by any Thomas, Richard or Harold.
> – I'll say, Frank, said *Frank*.

Frank removed the levels from his eyes to better confirm

his observation.

    – And all that flowing hair, *Frank*?

    – Seems shinier.

    – My thinking exactly, old boy. And the ponytails seem to have more bob in them than I recall.

    – I have to concur. And the sweaters?

    – They seem to be brighter.

    – And tighter.

    – Couldn't have put it better myself.

    – And what about the jeans now, Frank?

    – Arresting, *Frank*. Arresting.

    – They seem tighter to me.

    – That as well, *Frank*.

    – And what about the bounce now, Frank?

    – Seems to be all there.

    – Check, Frank.

    – It's good to be back, *Frank*.

    – It's good to be a chap, Frank.

    – In England, *Frank*.

    – In a college refectory.

    – In summer, *Frank*. In summer.

    – De didde di de di de.

    – My favourite tune, *Frank*.

    – Really?

    – Really.

    – Great minds, Frank.

    – Say no more, *Frank*.

    – No more, Frank!

Periodically, he got up to fetch tea and polish the odd mirror or two. It seemed to be appreciated. He had acquired the status of an artist at work. And people seemed genuinely helpful when he needed to get to an inaccessible mirror. He continued to scribble, of course. It was an integral part of the performance and couldn't be avoided. However, he had become used to doing it and it now seemed a natural part of him. Thus, he no longer felt anyone was being compromised, least of all himself.

As the week wore on, Frank forgot about the good intentions he had devised for himself over the holidays regarding his degree exhibition. There were important things to do: posteriors needed to be remeasured, for one; there were also ponytails to admire and lovely smiles to behold; a gentle ocean of femininity in which to swim.

Frank, too, was engrossed in things feminine. Gone was the rather materialistic attitude that had been prevalent of late. He was, in fact, quite agreeable company at the moment. Frank wished he were like this more often.

– Did you ever think you'd died, *Frank*, and gone to heaven?

– Just once or twice, Frank.

– Like when?

– Like now, Frank.

– Great minds, *Frank*.

– Say that again, Frank.

– Great minds, *Frank*.

– I like it when you're playful, Frank.

– My very nature, *Frank*.

– Tell me now, Frank. What takes your fancy the most?

– A hard question, *Frank*. There's so much a man would be happy to die for.

– I know what you mean, Frank.

– Listen, *Frank*.

– Mmm.

– I vote we amend our will so that when the day comes—

– Heaven forbid, Frank.

– When the day comes, we get to be buried here.

– What? In the refectory, Frank?

– Under this very table, *Frank*.

– I like the way you think, Frank.

– You like the idea then?

– I've heard none better today.

– That's settled then. I'll get someone or other to draw up the papers.

– What's that mean then, Frank? said *Frank*, somewhat puzzled.

– I don't know, *Frank*. But it's what they say in all the movies.

– Ah, right. A bit of realism. Eh, Frank? I'm all for that.

Chapter 19

On the Friday, Frank was in the refectory shortly after it opened. At the table, tea and levels in place: waiting, with an ache in his heart. He told *Frank* it was indigestion, but he hadn't sounded terribly convincing. He got up to ease the tension, but it only made matters worse. Back at the table, he nose-dived into his chair and drew a blanket over his feelings. *Frank*, too, seemed to be preoccupied. He peered out through the levels and waited for the moment to arrive. What else was there to do? Time had no meaning for him, then.

Zoe was due back today after her three-month exchange visit. Though he hadn't mentioned it to *Frank*, he had been thinking about her almost constantly that last week.

– She'll be making an artist's entrance, I expect, said *Frank*, rubbing the levels gently against his brow.

– Who? said Frank.

– Don't give me that, Frank.

– You know?

– Course I know, Frank. Do you think I've missed her any less than you?

– Oh!

Like the consummate artist she was, she blew into

college like a fiery dancer. The approach to the main entrance had gone unnoticed and unannounced. So, when the entourage suddenly appeared, it was full of presence. It had been an extremely difficult three months, but she was back now: back with things to do, people to see and scores to settle. Through the swing doors with a swirling swagger; with barely a casual glance at the porter's desk; Miles in close support and in some danger of losing his neck as the doors swung back with a worn vengeance; then down the corridor: arms outstretched to reclaim the dingy magnolia walls. Her hair longer now and full of curls. Lots and lots of welcoming faces and also the ladies in the college shop to say hello to. Miles given a chance to catch his breath and wipe the lens clean. A quick stop to say hello, then past the back entrance to the bar, past the union noticeboard – still selling desperate belongings. Past the black and white easy chairs and matching floor tiles. A left turn, and then to stand in the refectory entrance. A fantastic feeling. As full as ever. A sea of faces, but only one that mattered. Easy to pick out: over in the corner, way past the salad bar, past the staircase, near the back entrance.

"Hello, Frank," she said, putting her bag down on the table. He smelt the new black leather. She reached out to touch him, gently.

Frank looked up to see, yet again, a realm of unfamiliar faces.

     – Not yet, *Frank*, he whispered.

     – No, Frank.

     – Must be soon now.

     – Must be, he said, without belief.

     – Plane could have been delayed.

– Possibly.

– Traffic maybe.

– Maybe.

– She may stay on.

– Maybe.

– Frank looked at him disconsolately. Don't say that, *Frank*.

– Wouldn't you be tempted?

– I don't want to hear it, *Frank*.

– Well, wouldn't you be?

– Don't say it, *Frank*. You might make it true.

– Got to be a chance she'd stay, Frank. Maybe more than a fair chance. Have to face facts maestro.

– No, *Frank*. I don't, he said with desolation in his voice.

Round the one-way system, past the swimming pool, accelerating now to overcome the additional incline as the car drifted into the bend. Stopping now at the rear entrance. Waving goodbye to the lift and hello to Mac on the back gate. Dashing up the concrete steps two at a time and in through the side entrance. Turning to look in passing at the notice boards. Stopping to look in at the gloomy scene leftwards. Dragged in by lots of hellos and hugs and kisses. Into the dim light of the union bar; making apologies for rushing and promising to come back in a while. Out trippingly into the corridor, blinking briefly in the cross-light. Past the toilets and then hesitating briefly about which entrance to use. Turning left in the event, then right again, pausing in the doorway; wonderful to stand there and see the bustle. The briefest of pauses; making her way through the crowded room with difficulty; heading now for the main table.

– Where?

– Here. Right here. Here right now. Look up, Frank. She's here, now.

– You look, *Frank*. I couldn't bear it again.

– Yeah, but she's here this time.

– How come you're talking to me then?

– Just wanted to see you right, Frank. I know you've missed her.

– No more than you, *Frank*.

– No more than me, Frank?

Just a peep from behind the levels with heart raised half-a-beat. Looking and looking and looking. Finally, picking up the emptiness and then gulping back inside. That old blanket was more than comfortable.

– That blanket, *Frank*?

– This blanket, Frank?

– The very same, *Frank*.

– It's yours, Frank.

– Thanks, *Frank*.

Frank had hoped for a discreet homecoming, but Zoe had other plans. Her ideas about performance art had undergone radical changes, and she was making these public for the benefit of anyone who happened to be around when she returned.

The primary change which Zoe had undergone during her exchange visit to America was to consider performance art as part of a group activity rather than as a solo act – a transformation stimulated by exposure to American cheerleaders and majorettes. What had impressed her about these institutions was the energy that cheerleaders and majorettes generated. That and the suppressed energy of the early silent black and white movies had moulded her thinking about the direction of her work. Her thoughts had coalesced in a flurry of activity and had been made manifest in the creation of a performing troupe: the Trophettes.

The troupe now alighted outside the college and immediately formed a menacing looking ring in front of the college's main entrance. The ring undulated with a disciplined energy as Zoe passed – sergeant majorette like – back and forth along its perimeter.

Zoe's troupe might have lacked something in an obscure setting. Say, in the middle of a field, in Derbyshire, on a moonless night, but here, in the heart of London, in the middle of the day, in front of the college, they lacked nothing, least of all presence. Bemused passers-by skirted around the group as Zoe marched the ten-strong leather-clad troupe towards the college. Two lines of them burst through the door carrying a very severe-looking Zoe dressed as a silent and writhing drum majorette.

The lodge porter jumped out of his gate. He, too, had elected to be seen wearing his most severe expression. He was intent on setting the troupe to rights, but he was no match for the severity of the expressions worn by Zoe and her Trophettes. One good look was enough to send him scuttling back behind his desk. But like the proverbial Jack-in-the-box, no sooner had he ducked behind his desk, then his head popped up again. Prompted, no doubt, by the afterimage of the taut, thrusting bosoms in black, silhouetted against the off-white walls of the corridor.

He wasn't the only one to be mesmerised by the taut images of Zoe and her Trophettes. A lot of the college's male students also found themselves rather taut as Zoe and her entourage snaked their way down the corridor

– commando style. Not that the Trophettes would have expected any trouble. Their average height being five eleven; they could all punch like pro-boxers and kick like mules. One person, however, was privileged enough to get close to the troupe without endangering life or limb. Certainly, close enough to be envied: good old Miles, of course.

Miles, faithful as ever, had been at the airport to meet the flight complete with his video equipment. Initially disappointed at the prospect of having to share Zoe with a retinue, Miles had quickly adapted himself to being closeted with so many voluptuous females. He had been truly spoiled on the way from the airport. He was now showing a spirited enthusiasm in recording Zoe's homecoming. It had been a lean three months for Miles, but happy days were here again.

Round the college's corridors wound the entourage with no obvious aim except apparently to acquaint their writhing forms with every inch of the college's corridors. Round and round they went. And when they had covered the ground floor, the procession wound its way up the stairs to the higher levels.

The Trophettes fanned out in pairs as if looking for some hidden menace which might threaten the integrity of their leader. They wrapped themselves around pillars, posts and protruding bits of architecture to secure the college in a way that any self-respecting feline would do to secure its domain. They left nothing untouched.

For most people, the entourage passed by like a fleeting dream, which they didn't have to take too seriously. The lack of sound added to the surreal experience of those who witnessed the procession. Students, tutors and administrators alike did double-takes as the Trophettes sped by.

The group finally descended back to the ground floor, sweeping everything before them. Finally, they turned and swept through the refectory doors and hurtled through the tables, scattering students in all directions. They came to a stop beside Frank's table. Frank, like everyone else, was rather surprised and retreated behind his levels. However, given the physiques of the Trophettes, he wasn't so surprised that he didn't keep both eyes and a level head on the proceedings. The Trophettes paused momentarily as if getting their bearings against a night-time sky and then assembled themselves in a secure ten-pin formation. It was a futile gesture because they were then almost immediately bowled over by Zoe as she rolled across the refectory floor.

"A strike, Frank?" she said with a slight hesitation in her voice, sitting down in front of him. She, too, was uncertain.

"A strike, lovely," he echoed quietly, as he reached out to take her hand.

Chapter 20

With Zoe's return, Frank surprised himself by concentrating rather less on the ogling and more on drawing. He spent his days in the refectory, drawing, seemingly without aim or effort. Drawings sprouted from his table like wild flowers hurrying to catch the retreating warmth of the sun. What surprised him even more was the fact that he was actually enjoying the experience and focused discipline of life drawing. Hendricks would have been proud of him.

Frank, too, seemed to have quietened down somewhat of late. He resisted the temptation to score cheap points over Frank's latest preoccupation. Frank wondered if he was all right but didn't want to raise the question directly: sleeping dogs and all that.

As regards the quality of the drawings, he couldn't say if they were any good, but that didn't seem to worry him unduly. What was perhaps more important at this stage, though he wouldn't have admitted it to himself, was the fact that he was producing a quantity of work to put towards his degree show. He occasionally fancied he half-caught sight of a bemused *Frank*, but thought it best to pretend he hadn't noticed him.

People dropped onto his table from time to time. Drawing apart, there was always plenty to chat about. Not that they discussed a wide range of topics because cricket, and in particular the weekly fixture, dominated the conversation.

They played games on Wednesday afternoons, and these inevitably provided more than enough incidents to keep a half-decent conversation going till the weekend. Frank had yet to lose his wicket and was feeling rather messianic as regards his batting.

The Dean visited regularly. He was never less than ebullient on account of the fact that the Art School XI had yet to lose a game this season. Not without reason, therefore, he wore a rather paternalistic expression whenever he encountered team members.

The early part of the week was, of course, spent in assessing the forthcoming match and poring over the score book at last year's equivalent fixture. They carried out this exercise in the pavilion where Gilbert & Co. would present an analysis of last year's game. Gilbert, in particular, had a phenomenal memory and was rather prone to illustrate his analyses with a ball-by-ball commentary of the fixture in question. Esoteric stuff, but luckily, his concomitant thoughts regarding this year's equivalent fixture tended to be not much more than an exhortation to turn up for practice. As it happened, a spell of fine weather had settled over the region. And so, the Art School XI – plus sundry auxiliaries who had wandered in off the streets – spent the early part of the evenings on the playing field in vigorous pursuit of a place in the team for next Wednesday's game.

Although Frank's place wasn't in any doubt, he, like the others, looked forward to the daily practice sessions.

Not least of all because it made a welcome change and forced some fresh air into his lungs after a focused day of drawing. A mandatory session at the Buoy followed the practice sessions. And then, of course, the curry supper. Frank couldn't imagine a more perfect existence. The days passed by in blissful measure.

*

A month into the summer term and with the degree shows looming large on the horizon, the conversation began to stray ever so slightly. Nothing immediately obvious, but Frank, being the sensitive soul that he was, sensed nervousness amongst kindred spirits. A further two weeks on revealed a very anxious attitude compared to the carefree atmosphere of the early part of the term. With the degree shows now two weeks nearer, most students were definitely getting distracted. Gone was the one-track conversation and the easy banter; gone too was the sense of united purpose.

It was no longer tenable to be in two minds about one's contribution to the degree shows. Which probably explained why Frank woke one morning to find himself at loggerheads with *Frank*.

Frank tried to insist he should have priority over the space in the studio for his *Mystery Pieces* (as he called them). Frank, of course, had been vigorous in repudiating any such claim. A very fractious attitude developed on both sides.

They had spent a week in this state of affairs and things had been getting steadily worse. Concomitantly, the studio developed a look comparable to the bedroom of an angst-ridden teenager. Sheets of drawings and brown paper parcels lay scattered all over the studio – both fighting for the same space. *Frank* insisted the parcels needed a clean environment in which to be seen. Frank insisted his drawings could only be viewed in a room free of clutter. Fairly popped in and out but retreated each time because of the tension in the room. There was something about how Frank was stumbling about the studio with levels tied permanently to his head and seeming to yell at the walls, which sent a chill down the collective spine of the reporter and his hardy crew. The slanging was very unnerving.

Fascinated as he was by Frank's antics, Fairly was torn between picking up tips on the creative process and preparing his own work under increasingly difficult circumstances. In the event, he took to wearing ear mufflers and left it to Wally and the crew to split their time between himself and Frank.

Zoe looked in occasionally but she herself wasn't quite on the same plane and inevitably conversation in the factory became rather elliptical. She tried to mediate, but there wasn't the cohesion there should have been. And anyway, she had her own show to prepare and the Trophettes to keep amused.

Frank found himself in a grim situation. *Frank* was being more difficult than usual and no longer negotiating. Either way, nothing much got done. There was simply too much bile swirling around the studio. Clearly, there wasn't room for two of them in that space.

Viscously, as though through a thick liquid, he saw himself trying to see himself. Listening to an orchestra, he imagined himself being made, but perhaps not very well. Sluggishly, and without sharp definition, with sleep encroaching upon his consciousness, he saw himself trying to make himself. The edges became fuzzier when his gaze tried to focus on the corners. A part of him wanted to hide in the foggy, amorphous feelings. A distinct part sensed the crispness underneath the amorphous form. Though not as crisp as it might have been, he could recognise the sharpness when it arose. It commanded immediate attention. So focused that it stopped everything in sight. Somehow, he had to escape from this fog of possibilities. There was so much to do. So many wrongs to settle. So many people to put right. Not least of all *Frank*.

In a quiet, exhausted moment, in the early hours of a tough night, he managed to string together several coherent thoughts without *Frank* interrupting and persuaded him that his *Brown Mysteries* would be better displayed somewhere rather more public than the third floor of the factory. *Frank* must have been totally exhausted because he simply nodded his assent. Frank looked hard to make sure that he wasn't asleep and that he really had nodded. He wasn't, and he had. Frank offered a small prayer of thanks as he slipped into unconsciousness. *Frank* watched him go with a ghost of a smile on his lips.

The following morning, they agreed to take stock and divide the space for the degree show. It was agreed that Frank should look after the mirrors in the refectory. After all, they were his idea. These had to remain in situ, together with associated equipment. He would take responsibility for the studio space. The drawings would be mounted there. He would also prepare the maquettes for the *AI Driven Bowling Machine*. These models would be the sole concrete expression of the machine. Frank had briefly thought about constructing the machine for real, but realised it would impossible, given the crude facilities of the Art School workshop. He would have to be content with small-scale maquettes.

Frank, meanwhile, would show his *Brown Mysteries*, the take-away cartons, and anything else he fancied in the refectory garden area. Frank shuddered to think what other drivel *Frank* might dream up, but at least he'd be out of his space. *Frank* also offered to take responsibility for the five-thousand-word essay required by the Art History department as part of the course work. One more headache he could do without, and he was quite pleased that *Frank* had offered to write the essay. Though quite how *Frank* would do everything and write a longish essay, he couldn't work out.

Still, thought Frank, *it'll keep him out of my way.*

Frank also appeared to have forgotten about the quiz show he had threatened to create as part of his contribution to the degree show. Perhaps it would all work out.

Chapter 21

– **By the way,** *Frank*, said Frank with the mildest sense of curiosity. What are you going to write about?

– Eh?

– The essay, *Frank*. What's the title of the essay?

– Ah, well now, Frank, said *Frank* coyly. It's not an essay, exactly.

– Oh? What is it then?

– You'll have to wait and see, Frank, replied a smirking *Frank*.

An alarm bell rang somewhere in the recesses of Frank's subconscious, but *Frank* wouldn't reveal any more. He insisted Frank would only interfere if they started discussing it.

– Just let me press on with it, Frank. I know what I'm doing.

– You could at least tell me the title, *Frank*. Would that be too much to ask?

– Look, Frank, said *Frank*, playing his trump card. Do you want to do it? I don't mind you taking over. I've got loads I could be doing.

Frank declined. But he didn't have to wait long to discover what *Frank* was planning to write. The following morning there were posters all around the college proclaiming the death of Cretinous Art and the rebirth of an ancient art form: Mysterious Art (*Art Mystérieux*). He'd metaphorically scratched his head as he passed the garish things in the main corridor but had been none the wiser.

At morning break, on a crowded table, in the midst of a packed refectory, he'd only just sat down when loud strains of Chopin's funeral march hushed the babbling throng. The sound was coming from a nearby public address speaker. But it wasn't the only source. Up and down the refectory, he could see students turning in different direction to locate the music.

The Five's refectory washout was still fresh in everyone's mind. Students looked around rather nervously. Many of them had thought things out beforehand and were determined not to be caught out again. They scooped up their belongings and bolted for the rear exit. Given the history of past refectory performances, it was the safest route out of the place.

> "The art of the fart is finally dead," announced a familiar booming voice over the music. "Its lingering odours had been with us since 1917. But no more. And no more will we need to say politely, *plus de thé, Marcel* ?"

Frank wondered how something could take so long to die. But this perhaps wasn't the time for wondering about lingering odours. He fumbled anxiously for his levels, sensing an imperative to get them into position. He locked them to his head just in time. In the next instant, the rear entrance of the refectory opened to reveal a funeral procession in waiting.

A scuttling group of students found themselves confronted by an energetic group of Trophettes. As the obituarist came on again, the procession began a slow march through the refectory: Zoe preceded four pallbearers and half-a-dozen frenzied Trophettes.

An open coffin containing a urinal was passed between them. They danced, they twirled, they writhed forward in silence and drove all before them. In the middle of the refectory, with students retreating like an ebb tide, the procession turned sharp left and headed for the refectory garden.

The tide followed in the Trophettes wake. They flowed through to see the Trophettes giving the last rites to the coffin. It only seemed appropriate, then, to cheer loudly, and to join in giving the heave-ho to the coffin. On an orchestrated count of three, they hurled the coffin through the air and into the ornamental pond. The loudest of cheers accompanied the urinal's bubbling descent.

That looked to be the end of the affair, and indeed the funereal music had stopped, but back in the refectory, the students found the public address orator had a lot more to say....

"Farty art has been sent to meet its architect,"
continued the booming voice.

Frank thought he should have been able to place the voice, but recognition eluded him....

"That particular order of art has followed
its maker, Dead-end-Duchamp, into the
evolutionary cul-de-sac that was its inevitable destiny."

He removed the levels and looked around for an
explanation. There appeared to be bemused expressions
all over the refectory. He caught someone's eye on the next
table and got a grinning thumbs up.

The refectory staff were still going about their business.
They were ignoring the whole affair. Frank focused once
again on the content of the tinny message....

"Art is no longer anything you can get away
with," continued the booming voice. "Farty
art has finally been wafted clear by the opening of our collective windows."

He heard one or two approving sniggers at this tack....

"Farty sinecures are to be removed. People
who claim to be artists of the old school are
no better than benefit fraudsters."

This prompted one student to shout, "Hear! Hear!"
The narrator continued:

"There is an older art form. An art as old as
mankind. The art of the mysterious. The only
art form in touch with the human condition."

– Strong stuff this, *Frank*, he said. The Five have gone

to town on this one.

– Impressive. Eh? said *Frank*.

– What?

– Not bad is it, Frank?

– Has this got something to do with you, *Frank*?

– Don't you recognise the voice?

– You, *Frank*!? exclaimed Frank in genuine surprise. I thought it was one of The Five's pieces.

– I don't know what gave you that impression, Frank? You see any sign of them?

He listened again to the compelling monologue....

"Farty attempts to create art were always doomed to ephemerality. Mysterious art is not based on the ephemeral but on the eternal. Mysterious art requires us to embrace the universe. True mystery lies in the self. In being able to live a life without succumbing to the gaseous pronouncements of mischievous wannabe artists."

– What the hell's going on, *Frank*, said Frank in growing alarm.

– Just a little manifesto, Frank, replied *Frank*. And as they say, a little thing but mine own.

– A manifesto?

– Yep, Frank. A manifesto and an art history essay in one go.

– I don't understand, *Frank*. What manifesto? And what's it got to do with the art history essay we're supposed to do?

– It's quite simple, Frank, said *Frank* patronisingly

as the message continued to bellow out of the PA system. Listen to this bit, he said, getting side-tracked. It's really good....

"Mystery nourishes and sustains man and woman and has done so for countless millennia…"

– *Frank*, this is absurd, said Frank remonstrating.

– I know, said *Frank* with a smirk.

– Listen, you bloody moron. It's not just absurd. It's absolute bloody drivel. You won't be able to get away with it.

– Says who?

– Me for one and I'll lay money on being in the majority.

– Don't count on spending your money just yet, Frank, retorted *Frank*.

– I'm gonna take you to the cleaners, *Frank*.

– You wish, Frank. You wish, he repeated, to emphasise his point.

– Well, what is the bloody point of the whole thing, said Frank, switching tack.

– The point, Frank, is that this manifesto that I've written—

– Dreamt up, you mean.

– Written, Frank, said *Frank* emphatically. Written. Like with my own fair hand.

– Yeah, and pigs can fly.

– As I was saying, said *Frank*, getting rather irritated with Frank's attitude. The point of the manifesto is that it'll provide the theoretical framework for the work I'm knocking out for the degree shows. And, he said, pausing for effect. Since the manifesto is five thousand words long, it'll also do for the Art History essay.

– They'll never wear it, *Frank*.

– Who won't wear what?

– This, this drivel you've churning out.

– I repeat, Frank. Who won't wear it?

– The Art History department for one. There's no way they're gonna accept this drivel as an essay. And there's definitely no way you're gonna be able to pass your parcels off as anything but a con trick. *Brown Mysteries*, my arse.

– You're wrong, Frank.

– Don't think so

– Dead wrong.

– Don't think so, matey.

– Actually, Frank, said *Frank* with the kind of flourish that only genuine poker players can muster, Miles couldn't get enough of it.

– What!? I don't believe it. In fact, I've just twigged. Now I know you're telling porkies.

– What d'you mean, Frank?

– I mean, how could Miles possibly know about this manifesto? We only agreed last night that you'd write the art history essay. And there's no way you wrote five thousand words overnight. Even if you did, he continued, brushing aside any thought *Frank* might have had about raising valid objections, even if you wrote five thousand words in one night, and I still don't believe you did, how could Miles read it before we got into college this morning? And how could you organise the posters and the public address for today? Not to mention that funeral performance with Zoe. Tell me that, *Frank*? Go on, why don't you?

– Fact is, Frank, I didn't write it last night.

– Ha! I knew it wasn't yours, said Frank in triumph.

– I wrote it, Frank, continued *Frank*, choosing to ignore Frank's interjection, last term.

– Last term? When?

– Just before that seminar with Fairly in the refectory. Remember? The one that got washed out. When you didn't bother to tell me, you'd arranged it with The Five. The one that was gonna be televised nationwide. Audience of umpteen million.

– You wrote this stuff for that seminar? And you never let on?

– Why are you acting so hurt, Frank? I don't remember you saying much about the weather forecast for the refectory.

– And you've been keeping this under wraps all this time? That's devious, *Frank*. That's bloody devious. And I suppose you've already been to see Miles with it in your hot little hand?

– Check, Frank.

– And he liked it?

– Understatement of the year, Frank. In fact, he insisted on helping financially.

– How?

– Miles insisted on helping to finance this morning's affair. He also coughed up for the publication of the manifesto: "The Manifesto of Mysterious Art" Hot stuff, eh, Frank?

Miles's apparent generosity wasn't entirely altruistic.

And as *Frank* had intimated, he was certainly happy about the whole situation. In fact, he was more than happy. No longer the despondent and desolate figure seen in the New Year, alone in a barren archive in the Art History block. This was a vibrant and fully throttled Miles, firing meaningfully on all four cylinders. As an art historian, there wasn't any other place he wanted to be. This was where it was happening. And he was in the enviable position to record a new and dynamic art form as it emerged and developed in perhaps the most avant-garde institution in the country, perhaps even in the world. He didn't want to be too presumptuous, but this was surely going to be a significant factor in his appointment to a professorial chair.

Meanwhile, the narrator concluded his manifesto:

> "Artists must be given every opportunity to explore their mysterious inner self."

Frank shook his head. Clearly, Frank had got him into something of a corner. He made a half-hearted appeal to his better nature.

– *Frank*, said a despondent Frank. This isn't what my work's about. You're just hijacking aspects of my work to fit your ideas.

– They fit pretty well, though. Don't they, Frank?

– That isn't the point, *Frank*.

– Well, what is the point then?

– My work isn't about *Mysterious Art* or whatever you want to call it.

– Well, what is it to do with then?

Frank became decidedly uncomfortable and found

himself hard pressed to provide *Frank* with any kind of answer. He rubbed his levels gently against his forehead. He needed time to think.

Chapter 22

Of course, not everyone was neurotic about the impending degree shows. There were others who had nothing to fear from a close inspection of their work. Prudence certainly had as strong a body of work as anyone at the college. The Five, too, had a solid portfolio to draw upon. But like Zoe, they were essentially performing artists and could only show photographs or videos of their work. Notwithstanding this strong body of work, they were apparently planning a rather ambitious piece for the shows. However, as usual, they were secretive about the project.

Prudence also had performance ambitions. Like everyone else, her mind was on the final piece for the degree shows. She went through her work in the studio, deciding how to mount the pieces. Each was a rich kaleidoscope of colour. Each brought up a fresh memory for her. It had been a good haul. She counted up her collection of underpants pieces. It amounted to a grand total of 920 pieces. A formidable body of work by any standards, but Prudence knew there should be something else. Something was missing from this collection, and, like every collector, she was acutely aware of the missing gap in her portfolio.

She had tried for years to get the missing bits, but The Five – these it was she coveted – had resisted all her advances. In fact, apart from when they wanted her to bat for the Art School XI, they took little notice of her. She had originally speculated that perhaps The Five were gay, but that wasn't it at all; they always seemed to have regular girlfriends.

An odd, ritualistic bunch, she reflected. Not that she minded especially. The team had always had six other rotating players, and over the past three years, she had bagged a fair number of these. But the lesser players were no longer enough. She realised now they had all been too easy. She wanted to work harder for her final piece. After all, this would be the highlight of her show.

Prudence shook off her reflective mood. Time was running short. She only had a little more before the opening of the shows. If she was going to top her degree show with a pentaptych of The Five's underpants, she had to sort something out quickly.

*

Preparations for the degree shows were fairly minimal. No one had the time to do any more, even if they felt so inclined. Most studios, with one or two exceptions, were painted white. These were simply touched up with a roller just before the shows. The debris and the detritus of daily activity were swept out of sight. By the time the degree shows opened to the public, the studios would look presentable.

The shows were marked by an external assessor, together with the college's own tutors. The format required an assessor and tutor to go round with their clip boards to look at student's work. They would then compare notes

269

and arrive at a consensus about the merits or otherwise of the student's work. After the formal assessment, the work was shown at a private viewing. The following day, the degree shows were opened to the public.

The marking was supposed to take only a day. However, in practice, things were never that straightforward. Invariably, problems arose because a lot of the work that students produced didn't lend itself to this kind of assessment. Performance artists were difficult to mark because they inevitably required an audience. So too were pieces that involved any element of time to appreciate. Garden sculpture, such as cabbage patches and tables of cress, suffered from this kind of handicap.

The tutors did their best to get external assessors to appreciate such pieces, but with the best will in the world, it was hard to get an assessor to stare at a bed of floating water cress for long enough to appreciate its artistic content. What the student typically specified for this kind of piece was an unbroken two-week stare. What they got was a minute or two of sullen lip biting. And it was, of course, debatable whether this kind of arm twisting by the tutors did any favours for the students. External assessors (particularly those arriving in middle-of-the-range cars) had little patience for such pieces.

Examinations aside, the degree shows were also the college's chance to show its students to the outside world (or not as the case might be). For the students, it was a chance to show their talents to potential collectors (or not as the case might be) and, of course, to wangle some kind of regular employment. It was a very sobering time for most students, and for fine art students in particular. After several years of insulated existence, they now faced the prospect of having to earn a living in a world where their *artistic training* would prove less than useful.

An alternative was to apply for a post-graduate place. One or two of the *lucky ones* managed to land a place, thus securing another three years of the same and putting off the day of reckoning.

Most of the other students, the fine artists that is, stuck plaintive little notices alongside their degree shows asking for part-time work – so they might carry on with their *art*. Inevitably, the majority were left with the prospect of working in jobs where they were *over qualified*. All desperate stuff.

The private viewing of the degree shows was an odd sort of affair. Predictable disparate bits of flotsam-art decorated the walls and floors of the studios. The only thing that held the show together was the meagre hospitality. Cheap white wine with a few bottles of red thrown in for the oddballs. The wine glasses of yesteryear were replaced with disposable plastic cups. Cheese straws, crisps and salty peanuts were the staple fare. The salt always creeping around one's fingers, while bits of crisps found their way into the various forms of strident facial growth that seemed to emerge for the private viewing.

The shows were an event for which different groups had very different expectations. Freshers and the second years derived considerable amusement from seeing their supposed elders and betters on show. Established artists always turned up to pose in uniform: clean jeans with corduroy jackets in deep brown; or perhaps an olive green, with soft warm coloured shirts and trekkers. These were safe, comfortable things, but occasionally, one might spot a sharper cut. A bold check perhaps, or a crisp collar. Such items were invariably worn by someone with more money than sense. Longish hair was of course de rigueur, along with a well-worn face, which had clearly been witness to a thousand sleepless nights – nights which had been spent pacing around a paint-splattered studio, somewhere in Kensington – trying to get the thing to work through a haze of alcohol after closing time. And next morning tired, but pious in the knowledge of having spent some forty odd minutes trying to do something worthwhile against considerable odds.

For a good many of the final-year students, the private view was an ordeal. It was, after all, the first time their work was put on public display.

It was also a public summation of three years of endeavour. That wasn't the worst of it: there were proud parents or obscure relatives to escort around the show. Many an embarrassed student could be seen leading anxious parents around the studios. For them, the shows offered a chance to see what their offspring had been getting up to over these last three or four years. It was always a sad sight to see students who had been socialised in the mores of an art school, trying to help their parents bridge the gap so they night understand what it was the dear chap had been doing for the past three years. Most parents took it hard. The mothers would nod uncomprehendingly while the fathers would find a quiet corner in which to shake their heads in bewilderment. *Thirty-thousand pounds in fees. For this?*

Of course, there were those who were visually able to appreciate the work at face value. Such aficionados proved a godsend to less certain carriages. A train of such anxious parents was often pulled along in the wake of a brisk and voluble conversation:

"Yes, I like that. You know?"

"Mmm," would say a companion for no apparent reason.

"It seems so right."

"Yes, I know exactly what you mean."

"And yet, it's not without a certain... a certain amount of risk, shall we say."

"I see that."

"In fact, it's pretty close to saying something embarrassing. It's a wonder he can hold himself back from going over the edge. But of course, that's what makes it such an exciting piece. You know?"

"I do."

"I find the piece..."

"Invigorating?"

"Well, I wasn't thinking that, exactly."

"Colourful? Striking?"

"Well yes. It is that, but..."

"Difficult?"

"Yes, Difficult. I think you've put your finger on it."

"It isn't, really."

"No?"

"No. Not in the slightest. Look. What do you see?"

"An amorphous sea of colour?"

"Really?"

"Well, yes, actually. I do."

"Yes, but there's much more to it. Look at the tonal scales; look at the balance; look at the proportions. Use any of the classical canons and you'll see that it's quite a conservative piece. In fact, I'd go as far as to say it is a classical piece. You can trace its roots back to Cezanne and through him to the great masters of the Italian Renaissance."

"I see. I just read it as a study of amorphous colour. How wrong can one be?"

Chapter 23

After a neurotic half-term or so, most of the art students managed to focus themselves to prepare for the degree shows. And then began a fortnight of frenetic activity. For many students, it meant breaking the habits of the last few years. Knocked out of their somnambulant state, they were swept along with the tide of excitement and activity. Not an uninteresting state of affairs – for a while.

Fairly too had become infected by the atmosphere in the Art School community. The impending degree shows had a gravitational pull that was irresistible. Not that Fairly was going to be examined like an art student. Nevertheless, he had his own examination to worry about: the one in front of several million viewers who were expecting to see him produce the goods. He'd already had one washout; he didn't much fancy the prospect of another dampener.

One morning, Fairly overheard a conversation between one of the fine art tutors and his tutee to the effect that you couldn't really call yourself a painter until you'd done a hundred-foot canvas. Apparently, it didn't matter about the other dimension. Just so long as the canvas was at least a hundred-foot in length. Since a hundred-foot canvas would need umpteen litres of paint and therefore cost a small fortune in pigments, his challenge to the student was unlikely to be taken up. However, a hundred-foot canvas was just the sort of reasonable budget item that an intrepid reporter could have underwritten in the name of art. Consequently, Fairly found himself with a suitably macho project to wipe out the memory of a sodden event and one that would guarantee his social acceptance amongst the fine art fraternity.

He lost no time in getting down to practicalities. With a clear objective in mind, he was at his best. Everyone said so. And so, he mobilised his back-up team to prepare the canvas. It was only after he had given instructions regarding said canvas that he realised he'd overlooked a couple of major obstacles. How could he have been so stupid? Where on earth would he put a hundred-foot canvas? None of the studios was more than thirty feet long. And what on earth was he going to paint?

As he had become accustomed to doing, whenever he had a problem, he wandered into Frank's studio for some advice.

– Here you go, *Frank*, said Frank, cheering up. Here comes today's entertainment.

– Quiet, Frank, said *Frank*.

"It's fairly simple, Pete, said *Frank*."

– I see you've picked up the habit, *Frank*.

– Quiet, Frank, said *Frank* in a tetchy voice.

"Em, you don't put it up in your studio, Pete. You put it up in situ."

"In situ? But where's that?" said Fairly.

"Well, wherever you're going to display the painting."

"Well, I, er," said Fairly, humming and hawing.

"Oh, I see," said *Frank* with a wink.

"Eh," said Fairly, catching something of *Frank's* intonation. Though he wasn't quite sure what.

"You haven't actually got anything by the way of content, have you, Pete?"

"Not with you, old boy," said Fairly, genuinely puzzled.

"You want to make a hundred-foot statement, but you haven't worked out what it is you want to paint. Is that about right?"

"Er, well um," said Fairly, and then after an embarrassed pause admitted there was something in what Frank had said.

"Don't let it worry you. It's how most people work around here. You've actually arrived!"

"Don't follow you, *Frank*."

"It's quite simple, Pete. Most people here struggle to produce interesting art, but they're obliged to produce something every once in a while. Bit like a parlour game. Eventually the game gets round to you and if you don't chip in you get thrown out the game."

"You don't mean that, *Frank*," said Fairly, feeling distinctly uneasy. "You're just being cynical?"

"Not a bit."

"But surely the tutors ensure that sort of thing doesn't happen."

"They're in the same boat. In fact, they're under more pressure than the students to produce regularly."

"Yes, but I imagine their work is examined critically by their own peer group. They simply couldn't get away with anything less than a totally honest approach. I mean, that's what it's all about. Isn't it?"

"That's the theory. Doesn't mean it's what happens. Stands to reason. Hmm? Not everyone can produce *ART* to order. It's easier just to knock out something spurious or challenging and then invent the artistic theory afterwards."

"Oh!" said Fairly.

"If I were you, Pete," said *Frank*, "I'd put it up somewhere busy."

> – Yeah, like on the main road, said Frank, interjecting after a quiet spell.

Frank did his best to ignore him and attend to Fairly. He was obviously going through a difficult patch.

"Don't follow you, old boy."

"Somewhere where you're likely to be in the way."

"Really?"

"Somewhere like a busy corridor. It's the only way to get noticed."

"Wouldn't I be in the way?"

"Of course. That's the whole point. You've got to let people know you're producing interesting stuff."

"Yes, but a *corridor*," said Fairly, revealing his anxiety. "It's such a public place. People will stare."

"Wouldn't have thought that would be a problem for you?"

"It isn't normally, but one feels self-conscious about..., being creative, in public."

"You'll get used to it. Come on, I'll give you a hand to put the thing together. The best place, the only place that's covered, is the main corridor. Everyone passes along there. Several times a day, in fact. And it's the main route to the refectory for staff and students from the rear part of the college. You're bound to be an obstruction. And it'll be a fire hazard as well."

"Oh!"

"No, that's okay," said *Frank*, trying his best to reassure him. "It'll be just the job. I almost wish I were doing it myself."

"Yes, but if it's going to be a fire hazard...."

"You don't understand, Pete. It'll be an excuse to have a fire engine standing by. Just think of the publicity. Not to mention the nuisance value."

Frank chortled at the prospect.

"But what should I paint? What can I possibly use for a subject that will cover a hundred-foot canvas?"

"Two words, Pete."

"Two words? What words?"

"Spots and splodges. Cover the canvas in spots and splodges."

"Spots and splodges?"

"Yep. The bigger the better. They'll cover larger areas."

"Large spots and splodges?"

"Actually, add a few smaller ones as well. Just to get a range of values. That'll make the painting look more considered."

"Really? I'm not at all sure about this approach, *Frank*." It doesn't sound very artistic."

"Just think of it as a flower meadow. It'll help you to visualise the piece."

"Oh, right. A flower meadow. Yes, I think I can do that."

"Good. Just make sure you don't use small brushes. Otherwise, you'll never get it finished. Nothing smaller than six-inch brushes. You can get huge brushes from any DIY store."

"Got it."

Fairly broke into a sheepish grin. His imagination caught hold of the idea and he was swept along with *Frank's* enthusiasm.

The two of them headed off to the corridor to prepare the fixings for the canvas. Frank was left shaking his head.

– It'll end in tears, *Frank*, he called after the pair.

Frank pretended not to hear him.

Chapter 24

The last day of assessment for the degree shows coincided with the private viewing. In the morning, the third-year fine art students were gathered in the refectory – talking in very subdued tones. Frank appeared to be more than usually preoccupied with his levels and was given even more latitude than normal. Prudence likewise seemed to be not altogether there. Altogether missing from the scene were The Five. Several students queried their absence, but they didn't have to wait long for an answer. The refectory PA system unexpectedly crackled into life and Gilbert's distinctive delivery came floating over the airwaves:

"Good morning listeners and welcome to the fifth and final test match between England and a fine Australian side, which has been touring here this summer. I needn't remind listeners that this is the deciding test between two very contrasting teams. You join us here at Victoria Park on a sunny morning. The report from the weather centre suggests we're going to enjoy fine weather for the rest of the week. Just a slight question mark, apparently, over the early part of next week, but let's hope that won't come to anything."

The bemused reaction at Frank's table was echoed

around the refectory. People more or less stopped what they were doing and focused on the words coming out of the speakers.

"The pitch looks to me to be in first-rate condition," continued Gilbert. "Fred Partridge, the groundsman, has done an excellent job in preparing the field. I can't remember the last time that the Victoria Park ground looked as well as it does today.... I'm joined now by Bill Sutton. William will provide us with expert summary over the course of the game. It's a pleasure to see you here this morning, Bill. I trust you had a pleasant journey?"

"Yes indeed, Brian," replied an authoritative sounding Bill, whose voice everyone recognised as that of Hammond. "Good morning, listeners," he said, not forgetting his manners. "Yes, I drove up from London this morning. There were no signs of the road works that seem to plague so much of the motorway traffic these days. Just to pick up on your comments about the pitch, Brian, I recall the last time we were here. There was some problem with water at the Saffron Lane end. Do you remember?"

"Yes, I do, Bill. As a matter of fact, we went down there after the game with Fred. Apparently, it had something to do with the canal being so close. But I understand they've sorted the problem out now. So, we shan't be seeing anything in the way of a waterlogged out-field. That's good news for all concerned."

"Where do you think they're broadcasting from?" asked someone at the table.

"Must be in the pavilion."

"No. Can't be. The flag's down. It's normally hoisted whenever they're in."

"That's right. They're not in there. I looked in there ten

minutes ago. They might be in the backfield pavilion. I saw them there early this morning. They were carrying in a load of stuff."

"Maybe they'll tell us where they're holed up if we listen...."

"The news from the dressing rooms is that both sides are fully fit. Metcalf's little niggle seems to have cleared up. I was speaking to the England physio earlier this morning, and he seemed pretty confident he'd be able to bowl without restraint. So, that's good news for England."

Good news it might have been for England, but it wasn't something that made Prudence want to jump up and down. After a common bemused reaction at hearing Gilbert's voice and a further common realisation that The Five's showpiece was to be a commentary on an imaginary game of cricket, and that said commentary would be broadcast from the back field pavilion, she realised that it was now going to be extremely difficult – if not downright impossible – for her to paint The Five's underpants for her pentaptych. She had been hoping to get them during the early part of the day, but that was going to be impossible since, clearly, they would spend most of the day in the pavilion. She tried to ask if anyone knew whether they'd be coming out for lunch, but she got shushed down as the group around the table got drawn in to the commentary....

"The two captains were out earlier, looking at the pitch. They tossed a coin; Clive Pringle called correctly for England, and they've elected to take the field. A slight question mark over that decision, Bill?"

The table held its breath and waited for Bill's reply....

"There would be if this was an ordinary match, Brian, but in this case, I believe one can understand Clive's thinking. I suspect he's anxious to ensure his batsmen don't get exposed early in the game."

"Ah! Yes, of course," chorused a nodding table.

"Well, they should certainly avoid that," said Brian. "But actually, the pitch looks to be pretty true. And given the weather forecast, there's not likely to be much help for the bowlers. So, I do wonder about Clive's decision. Anyway, we shall just have to wait and see."

"Oh! incidentally," exclaimed Bill as he remembered a bit of good news. "I bumped into Tubby Hayes the other day. He sends his regards."

"Oh, good old Tubby. How is he?"

"He's very well, actually. He told me he no longer needs to take the drops now. His little problem cleared up after a visit to a herbalist."

"Well, that is welcome news. We must ask him to come up next week."

The table – except for Prudence – again nodded in agreement. One or two got rather in to the spirit of things and gave a little cheer (*Muppet-like*) at this unexpected, good news.

"It'll be nice to see the old boy again. Is he mobile now?"

"Oh, yes indeed. In fact, he's become rather sprightly."

"That's marvellous, Bill. Best bit of news we've had for some time.... Well, the players have taken the field. Let's give the listeners the field placings. Do you want to get the ball rolling, William?"

Prudence wondered off disgruntledly as Bill began his analysis of the fielding positions.

"Well, Pringle's set a slightly unorthodox attacking field. He has two slips and a gully; cover; mid-off; mid-wicket; a man at deep square leg; third man. That's not really unexpected since there's a long boundary at the gas works end. There's just one surprise for me, and that's the man at longstop. What do you think, Brian? Is that perhaps something of a luxury?"

"Yes, I think you've got a point there, Bill. Now that's either saying something about the keeper or the bowler. Well, we shall just have to wait and see which. Although now that I look closely at third man, he does look to be shifted slightly towards deep backward point. Interesting.... Well, It's going to be Holford from the Saffron Lane end. He's just going through his warm up routine now. A pretty thorough routine, Bill?"

"Indeed, Brian. There's no doubt about the fact that Holford has probably the most complex warm up routine in the business."

"He never used to do much in the way of a warm up routine. Just toss the odd ball to a couple of outfielders before launching into his spell. But I understand about three years ago he pulled a muscle in his shoulder. Ever since then, he's become quite meticulous about warming up. It's a wonder he has any energy left to bowl after his routine. But he does. So, there you are. It's horses, for course, I suppose.... Well, it looks as if they're ready to make a start. The umpires have signalled to the batsmen that they're ready for them. They're making their way down the pavilion steps. They turn now past the members' enclosure and approach the gate. One of the older members holds the gate open and they step onto the turf. A generous round of applause from an exceptionally jolly crowd."

The table took that as a cue to break into applause, too. Others in the refectory were taking a lead from Frank's table and joined in. Meanwhile, there was a bit of admin.

news...

"Incidentally listeners," said a very reasonable sounding Brian, "I've just been informed by the club secretary that there are still plenty of seats left if any of our listeners are thinking of coming down. We shall be very glad to see you."

The table didn't quite know what to make of that, but when Brian gave directions to the back playing-field, everyone decided they had nothing better to do today than to listen to some cricket commentary in the sun. The table got up in a jovial mood and headed off for a day of cricket commentary. Suddenly, the refectory emptied as others too got excited at the prospect of some first-rate commentary and followed Brian's voice along the corridor speakers....

"He comes in now and bowls. A good length ball just outside the off stump and keeping uppish. The batsman lifts his bat out of the way and lets it go through to the keeper. He takes the ball waist high with a little backward hop, and then casually slips it sideways to first slip. The ball then gets thrown from first to second slip then onto gully. All in a gentle arc. Gully throws it to mid-off and then it gets back to the bowler just as he gets to the end of his run up. The whole affair is marvellous to see. Real economy of action. I suppose it keeps everyone on their toes and keeps them engaged with the game."

"Yes, you can always tell the character of a team by the way they pass the ball while the bowler's walking back to his marker. Now this seems to me to be an especially chummy side."

"I think you've got something there, Bill. This is the first time that I've seen deep square leg and mid-wicket involved in returning the ball to the bowler."

*

While the commentary progressed, Prudence was pacing thoughtfully up and down her studio. She had done everything she could do in terms of preparation, but it looked as though her sketches and maquette for the pentaptych were unlikely to be realised as an actual piece. She sat and tried to think how she could get into the pavilion. But even if she could get in, how to persuade them to drop their trousers and consent to having their underpants painted in the confines of the pavilion? That was never going to happen. She toyed with the idea of perhaps being able to get each of them alone in the pavilion long enough to do the business. But really, she eventually decided, that was a fruitless line of thinking. The alternative was to get them out of the pavilion. But how? They'd got everything they needed in there, and from talking to others, it had become clear they planned on remaining inside for five days. And even if she did somehow get them out of there, how to persuade them to co-operate? They'd made it clear enough in the past that they weren't interested in being 'Done'.

"Come on, Prudence," she muttered to herself. "Think it through. There're two separate problems here: number one getting them out; number two, getting them to drop their pants. Keep them separate."

Musing thus on her problem, she wondered back to the college. By now the back playing-field was packed with students in determined good humour. A loudspeaker over the pavilion kept them abreast of things, and in between balls, the commentators were doing their best to keep the crowd informed and entertained....

"You can tell a lot about a man by his run up, Bill," said Brian as a typical opening line.

"Absolutely, Brian."

"I mean, take Parker, for instance. He's all over the place as he runs in; arms flapping and feet going in different directions, but when he gets to the crease, the whole thing comes together. You can't fault his line or length. Yet to look at him, you'd think he was a regular carthorse. Extraordinary. And I believe he's like that normally."

"There's true, Brian. I've known him all my life, and he is just like that. Never looks like he's going to make it at anything. But when it comes to the crunch, he's always there. Right on the spot. Holford told me he was like that with his homework at school. He'd always be the last one to hand it in. Often, he'd just be finishing as the beak called his name. Yet, often as not, he'd get top marks. Beats me how he did it, but apparently, he did."

"Well, at least he's remained consistent, Bill."

"True."

*

Prudence wandered back into the refectory in search of inspiration and some refreshment. Coincidentally, the commentary turned briefly to the subject of listeners sending in things to commentators and, in particular, sending in cake for the tea interval. Nibbling on her favoured pastry, Prudence suddenly had the germ of an idea for tackling her problem. Moments later, she was sitting in Frost's office and putting to him the suggestion that he could do her a big favour – if he felt so inclined. Frost nodded without hesitation; he recalled the last time that Prudence had asked him for help and declared himself willing to help again.

A couple of hours later, with the water to the pavilion firmly turned off, courtesy of Frost, and a clutch of cakes on a large plate, Prudence presented herself at the pavilion door. Although they wouldn't let her in – she hadn't expected them to – they took the cakes from her with obvious relish.

"Prudence, old girl," said Hammond. "This is most kind of you. And look chaps, she's made named cakes for each of us."

"They're made to a vegan recipe," said Prudence, thus reassuring them that there wouldn't be an issue with their vegan principles.

Phase one complete, thought Prudence as she wandered back to the building to await developments – and in particular, phase two. Half an hour later, a stricken Hammond emerged from the pavilion clutching his stomach. Prudence smiled to herself as she saw him make for the nearest loo. Thanks to Frost and the lack of water in the pavilion, the consensus in the pavilion was that the toilet should not be used until the water had been restored. Since this was unlikely to be till the morrow, Hammond now headed for the nearest convenience to relieve himself. This was an isolated cubicle, which the college had installed for the benefit of disabled students. Moments later, a desperate Hammond arrived at the toilet in dire straits. He found Prudence standing in his way.

"Out of the way, Prudence," he yelled as he pushed past her. He tried to yank open the door, but it was locked.

"Jesus!" he groaned, clutching his stomach and dropping to his knees. For a moment Prudence had a pang of remorse, but she let it pass. With one hand on her hip, she held the key up in her other hand.

"The key to all your problems, Hammond," said a smiling Prudence. "I just need you to pose for a painting."

He tried to lunge for the key, but she backed away.

"Fair exchange, Hamond," she said, while holding the key above a convenient drain.

"That's blackmail, Prudence," he groaned again. "You can't do that."

"I'm not asking for much, Hammond. It'll only take a few minutes of your time."

"I won't do it. There are plenty of other toilets in the college."

"Suit yourself," said Prudence, without betraying her anxiety that Frost's mixture may not have been strong enough. But she needn't have worried. A fresh wave of contractions persuaded Hammond that he hadn't any alternative if he didn't want to make a spectacle of himself in front of the adjacent crowd of enthusiastic listeners. A triumphant Prudence opened the door for a desperate would-be commentator. He dashed in and hurled himself into the inner cubicle. Prudence followed him into the outer chamber and locked the door behind her.

No sense in being disturbed, she thought as she waited for Hammond to emerge from the cubicle. Ten minutes later, a victorious Prudence emerged into the sunlight, followed by a strangely quiet Hammond. He headed off back towards the pavilion. Prudence watched him go with a touch of sympathy. She smiled, knowing that wouldn't be the last she saw of him.

Back in the pavilion, the others barely had time to ask him if he was okay. The commentary had to resume again after a short interval, and it was his turn to take the mike. He couldn't say anything to the others, even if he had wanted to, because Prudence had made him promise he wouldn't. She, meanwhile, was busy getting ready for her next visitor. Add if Frost's calculations were correct, that should be Gilbert. And right on cue, he emerged from the pavilion with a delightful look of anguish on his face. She had to hand it to Frost. He had varied the mixture in the cakes so they would fall victim at roughly thirty-minute intervals.

Just time before the end of the day's play, she thought, to get all five of them hung drawn and painted. She allowed herself a slight smile as she welcomed a distraught Gilbert.

Chapter 25

The broadcasting by The Five of their cricket commentary engendered a feel-good factor which touched almost everyone in the college. Everyone except for Frank.

Frank had spent most of the day in a trance. With the ending of the day's commentary, he had been left in a state of high tension. There had been moments when he had forgotten about the impending evening, but with the passing of each sheltered moment, *Frank* had re-emerged to remind him he was planning on making a complete spectacle of himself at the evening's private viewing of the degree shows. It really was too much for him. He couldn't face the prospect of being associated with *Frank's* artistic endeavours. And so, by late afternoon, he was huddled up in a foetal position in a quiet corner of his flat. But even with both levels lashed against his head, he still felt vulnerable. And of course, *Frank* wasn't averse to having a go at him in this state.

Almost as an involuntary reaction, he started shaking his head to clear *Frank's* taunts from his mind. It seemed to help, but pretty soon he had the most awful headache. In desperation, he picked up his cricket bat to focus on something else. The contact with his trusted bat brought immediate relief. He was then inspired to pick up a cricket ball and started to knock and keep the ball up in the air. The rhythmic knocking of the ball against the willow gave way to focused counting as Frank tried to see if he could keep the ball aloft for a hundred knocks. And when he got to a hundred – and it had proved fairly easy – he refocused and went for a thousand. An arbitrarily large target and one that he didn't expect to achieve. He simply set it to that figure to give himself an excuse to keep his mind occupied on the ball. However, as the rhythmic count progressed, Frank lost his sense of fragility and persecution. By the time he got to a thousand, he was positively upbeat. Fifteen hundred came and went just as easily. At two thousand, he put down the bat and ball and decided he ought to get going.

There were places to go, people to see and people to put in their places. He held both levels to his eyes like a pair of blinkers and cantered swiftly over the cobbles towards the college. There was a place for everything, and everything was in its place. There was surely a time for everything and surely it was *Frank's* time, this time. This way and that-a-way. Quickly now. Through the arched terrace way and dancing down the shallow steps, three at a time.

Ahead of him, ten minutes or so, he saw a zombie quiz show host going through his frenetic paces. *So soon, Frank? So soon?* There'll be plenty of time for that in a minute. When I catch up with you.

Although *Frank* had disguised his intentions about the mystery quiz show he was going to present at the private viewing, he was nervous about Frank suddenly turning up at the wrong moment to put his oar in. He also wasn't too sure if he could actually pull it off. All in all, he wasn't in a confident mood. Not surprisingly, then, a strange sense of foreboding took hold of him. It wasn't something he could put his finger on. He sensed an immediate presence somewhere behind him, and just to the right. He turned to look behind every so often. Inevitably, it began to affect his quiz master's technique. He dropped his cue cards and started mumbling his lines. The suave, easy manner and the ready banter gave way to an emerging imbecile.

Frank sensed his discomfort and quickened his pace. This was no time to empathise. Too much had been said. The time for cutting understatements had passed long ago. Professionalism was a million miles from his thoughts. Direct action was now his preferred option. Something told him he would regret his anger, but it was too late for rational thought. A terrible burning sensation, somewhere deep inside, seemed to help him focus his thoughts. His chest was taut and breathing became difficult. He rubbed his breast to ease the tension.

His discomfort gave *Frank* a chance to make something of a recovery. He was helped by chancing upon a contestant who appeared to be a reincarnation of Dr Johnson. No matter what *Frank* threw at him, he took it in his stride. His rapid-fire responses to *Frank's* probing and the audience's appreciative noises, conjoined to slow down, if not actually halt his jerking. With each correct answer fired by this hyperactive encyclopaedist, the tension and excitement of the audience rose towards a crescendo of sound and movement. And with it rose *Frank's* sense of control and wellbeing. By the time this perky little contestant had worked his way towards the final question, *Frank* had managed an almost complete recovery. With the final question in hand, he did a little jig in the manner that quiz show hosts are prone to do. With a great show of silly me, he returned to the contestant and got his attractive assistant to lead him towards the soundproof booth. A quiet drum roll continued to play throughout this rigmarole and continued to rumble in the background. *Frank* made a great show of testing to see that the contestant couldn't hear anything save via the microphone. With a final flourish, he brought out the question card from a sealed envelope. Amid an expectant hush, he cleared his throat and posed the jackpot question to his brave little punter. There was an audible gasp from the obviously knowledgeable crowd at this impossibly difficult question. *Frank* posed theatrically and half-turned to the audience. He then turned back to face the contestant to confirm he had heard the question.

It was now Frank's turn to sense that the situation had become challenging. No time for discretion now. He shook his head and re-positioned the levels. He seemed to come into focus. As he did so, *Frank* sensed him approaching. His concentration wavered for a second; only for a second, but it was enough. A moment later, Frank was upon him.

– No, you don't, *Frank*. Not this time.

– Up yours, Frank, he said, neatly side-stepping Frank's lunge.

– You're not gonna get away this time. You fucking parasite.

– Look who's talking, taunted *Frank*, swerving to avoid a retreating camera man.

He missed the camera man, but unfortunately clattered instead into the auto-cue. The poor producer didn't know whether to look bemused, upset, or plain angry. In the event, he didn't have to spend long worrying about that problem, because in the next instant, a swinging boom microphone knocked him over. A sympathetic researcher attempting to help put him out of his misery by falling over him, knocking him senseless.

By now, the audience had become seriously restless. It must have been obvious to even the dimmest amongst them that this was not a scripted part of the proceedings. *Frank* tried to put a brave face on things as he shimmied his way through and around a collapsing set. However, with a grim-faced nemesis chasing him, it was hard to convince anyone, let alone a disenchanted audience, that this was all an act and that any minute now they were all to going to go, *ha ha,* and slap their thighs at the hilarity of it all.

A resourceful *Frank* tried to slow Frank down by throwing missiles in his path. He sacrificed a mobile monitor without a second thought. A second camera man followed in a similar disconcerting fashion. But it was no use. Frank had the levels and could steer a clear course through all the obstacles in his path. Panting his way around a crumbling set, *Frank* realised how unfit he'd become cooped up in this television studio these last few weeks. He resolved to insist that the next contract he signed would ensure there was some exercise equipment provided en suite.

This was likely to prove academic, however, as he found Frank bearing down hard upon him. In desperation, he veered off the set and into the back-room area, gaining just enough of a head start to prevent Frank from seeing him slip into a make-up room. Frank shot past the room a moment later. In the time it took him to realise he'd lost his quarry and hence to double back, *Frank* had disguised himself. He emerged from the make-up room dressed as a work of modern art – there hadn't been time to do anything more elaborate. Frank barely gave him a second glance as he strode past him in a purposeful frame of mind.

Twenty yards down the road, however, his frame of mind must have slipped because he twigged what must have happened. He swung around and gave chase. He came up to him pretty quickly, but *Frank* always put on a spurt the moment that he was about to be caught. It was like trying to catch a forward reference. Just as he got to where *Frank* should have been, he found an indirection pointing to some other place. Still, he kept moving. Confident in the knowledge, his levels would pick *Frank* out no matter where the snivelling wretch was hiding.

Frank stopped momentarily to get his breath back and found himself outside the studios. He looked up to see a vast cavern of silvery stars. They held him entranced. Set deep against a mauve-black sky, they beckoned to him. Or at least they seemed to offer the prospect of unlimited space. They danced for him then and lifted him effortlessly into the breathless heavens. His mind paused, and he realised then that time was standing still for him. With nothing moving, he could miss nothing. He looked inside and found a lack of desire. Reassured, he stopped then to look at everything. As he did so, he saw himself dissolving and spreading in all directions.

The rising smell of a newly dug sculpture brought him back to earth. The piece revealed the possibility of there being no gap between heaven and earth. He stood astride the ditch to confirm his feelings. The gap was bridged. Could he make it count?

He retraced his steps back to the studio and saw *Frank* back on stage. It looked as if he had never left. *Frank* really was in his element as the jolly quiz show host. Frank glared at him from the other side of the quad with a growing sense of loathing. Leaning against the plate glass, he was filled with a sense of conviction, his head dead level. Zoe kept filling his glass at regular intervals. He kept his end up by knocking the stuff back and nodding genially and half consciously to various bodies about sundry items. One had to be civil, after all.

Frank was now playing with the audience and building up to a climax. He trotted back and forth across the make-shift stage like some latter-day TV chat show host at his most excruciatingly banal. Frank found himself focused on his accoutrements. The winkle-pickers of yesteryear were perhaps the only thing that seemed sane in a medley of banal props.

He had found a hapless punter – obviously the wealthy pater of some Nigel or other and was busy giving him the opportunity to make an utter wally of himself. The pater smiled obligingly through the whole ghastly proceedings and landed a startlingly small prize: one of Frank's lesser *Mystery Pieces*.

With most of his attention required to juggle the mechanics of the quiz show, *Frank* was kept pretty busy. But he kept half an eye on Frank over at the sidelines. At first, he had been slightly nervous about Frank's brooding presence, but as the show progressed, he became more relaxed. Till now, he couldn't give a shit about Frank and his brooding manner. What was more, he hadn't been backward in letting Frank know about it. Frank had gradually retreated behind his levels. It was the only way he knew of keeping him at bay.

– Not this time, you fucker, shouted *Frank* in a very objectionable sort of voice. It's no good you sneaking behind those fucking things.

– You're nothing but a bloody peasant.

– And you're nothing but an effing Bo Peep.

– You're not gonna get away with this, *Frank*.

– Just watch me.

– You didn't manage it last time, and you won't this time.

– Screw you, Frank. You're nothing but hot air.

Frank resorted to some very crude language. Frank found himself unable to compete in such a public situation. *Frank* sensed his discomfort and piled on the expletives. Despite his resolve, he retreated under the onslaught. *Frank* grinned at his discomfort. From almost being out for the count, he was on the point of making Frank look small. Very small indeed.

A sea of embarrassment surrounded him. Engulfed by the pain, he realised he was naked. Naked and observed. It couldn't be. It felt so painful. Like a bubble of air under water, he had to rise to escape from the observation and oppression.

He stumbled out of the refectory garden, shrugging off Zoe's sympathetic arm. With all the composure of a drowning man, he attempted to buckle his levels tight against his eyes. Somehow, his instincts carried the moment, and he stumbled out into the quad. He leant against the brick work, gasping for some elusive air. Slowly and painfully, he composed himself to clear his mind. And it did clear, and surprisingly quickly in the event.

With the clarity came a sense of finality. A sense that

the time had come to put an end to this affair. *Frank* really had done it this time. He made his way swiftly and surreptitiously to the Factory.

– There comes a time, *Frank*, when a man's gotta do what a man's gotta do.

– Eh, said a puzzled *Frank*.

– Jesus Christ! exclaimed Frank under his breath. Nearly let it slip.

– What's that, Frank, enquired *Frank*.

– Er, nothing, *Frank*, said Frank, lying with an ease that surprised him. Just mumbling out loud.

– Oh? said a quizzical *Frank*.

In his studio, he slid out his old trunk from the cupboard. He had willingly shared everything else with *Frank* – except this. This was the one piece of kit he had kept from him. He'd often wondered how he'd managed it in such a small space, but he had. *Frank* seemed to have a real blind spot for the cupboard. Everything was as he had packed it a year ago. It wasn't even locked. He took out the covering blankets to reveal the weed killer mixture. It was potent stuff – as he knew only too well; but it was harmless in its current state. He poured the mixture into a shiny new container and packed it tight. He had to be careful to keep his mind clear lest he give the game away. If it worked, it would undoubtedly Guy Fawkes *Frank* into a new dimension. He suppressed a tremendous sense of anticipation with great effort and headed back to the college. The Last Supper was definitely not on his mind.

*

Supper for *Frank* was a closely observed daily ritual. Ever since he could remember, he had eaten nothing but Indian take-aways every night. It wasn't something that he questioned. Nor was it something that raised any particular eyebrows since most of the students ate take-aways regularly – particularly Indian take-aways. The college's surroundings boasted a multitude of Indian restaurants. Indian food was therefore cheap, plentiful and tailored to the pocket of the local students.

Frank differed in his affinity to the food of the sub-continent in two ways compared to other students. First, where they might occasionally go for a Chinese or fish and chips or would actually cook something at home, *Frank* ate nothing but Indian food at night: every night. Frank had sometimes raised the matter with him, but inevitably it caused a row and he always ended up giving in. After all, as *Frank* put it, it was hot stuff, and he could always satisfy his hankering for other food during the day. It was a line of argument he hadn't been able to counter, but perhaps he didn't really want to.

Where *Frank* was open and vociferous in his attitude towards Indian food, he was subliminal about the eventual fate of the meal he ate each evening. Frank was totally unaware of the motions that *Frank* went through each morning to preserve the memory of the meal of the night before. Probably just as well, because his fastidious nature would have been mortified if it had been privy to *Frank's* morning ritual.

Frank was not unaware of the embarrassment that was likely to result if Frank ever became aware of his early morning routine. To cover his activities, he had contrived to get Frank to meditate first thing in the morning. It took about ten minutes to get Frank into the swing of things. By this time, he would normally be well entranced. This gave *Frank* the opportunity to slip away and use the aluminium cartons that had housed the take-away the night before to accommodate the morning motion. The contents were then sealed post-haste with a cellophane wrapping machine. Given the source material, it was usually all over in a couple of minutes, and *Frank* was always back before Frank had come out of his trance. It was a good start to the morning for both of them: Frank attained a deep state of relaxation; *Frank* attained a deep sense of relief in a satisfying motion. By the time the degree shows arrived, *Frank* had accumulated over two hundred cartons. The recycling of the containers appealed to *Frank's* conservationist frame of mind and hence he had rather aptly named his growing collection of cartons his *Green Piece*.

He began by keeping the cartons in the flat. However, they soon took over all available space. It was clearly unsatisfactory. Not least because he couldn't view them properly. In the round, so to speak. There was also the problem of keeping them away from Frank. After he'd moved them into the Factory, he played around with them to show them to their best advantage. The discovery that the piece as a whole could actually cut space in sympathetic surroundings had come as a revelation, and he'd spent many an happy hour experimenting with different permutations of the cartons. Frank had repeatedly chided him on his preoccupation with the spatial characteristics of what were no more than empty Indian take-away cartons. He did his best to ignore him. What did he know about it? He was just a scribbler, while he was a *Spatialist*. He eventually arrived at a synthesis of space and volume, which he believed was his best piece to date.

The *Green Piece* had been given pride of place by *Frank*

in the middle of the refectory garden. It was the only non-mystery piece in the whole show. Not unnaturally, it had drawn a fair bit of attention. One or two people had been tempted to open a carton or two but had been shooed off by the gorilla impersonator *Frank* had hired to guard his work for the duration of the degree shows. He had proved effective against all comers. However, he proved to be no match for Frank.

On his way back from the studio, Frank armed himself with a large bunch of bananas. A simple ploy, but it proved effective. Not unsurprisingly, he got through to the piece without any problems from the gorilla impersonator. *Frank* glanced over to see what he was up to. He'd sensed something suspicious, but as he was still on stage and going through his routine, he'd been unable to come over. Frank nonchalantly dropped his explosive device right in the middle of the piece and retired to a safe distance. Alarm bells jangled in *Frank's* head, but it was too late. Frank had used a very short length of fuse. Moments later, a latter-day Krakatoa exploded on an unsuspecting gathering of students, tutors, self-confessed piss artists, assorted auxiliaries and honest to goodness guests.

The blast took away the air for a moment, but the stench of a year's excrement, fully revived by the searing heat, followed closely in the wake of the explosion.

"My God! What was that?" was one reaction; but there were others:

"Fucking hell!"

"Shit!"

"My God! It's shit!"

"Shit! I'm covered in shit. Shit from Indian take-aways."

"Jesus Christ! I don't believe it."

Fogg, recently returned from his overseas assignment, and still trying to get the goods on Frank, experienced a certain déjà vu. "Uh My God!" he exclaimed as he trod on something unspeakable.

The refectory garden emptied quickly as people scrambled to get away from the stench. Not unsurprisingly, many of them headed for the toilets. Frost, always bemoaning the fact that students waited till his back was turned before committing their outrages, was, for once, on hand to experience for himself the excitement of an *event*. He tried in vain to avoid being trampled over by a wave of excrement-induced hysteria. But it was not to be. He too had come to terms with the college's lack of facilities as he tried to jostle his way towards the communal showers in the sports hall.

Frost wasn't the only one having to come to terms with a fast-flowing tide. Out in the corridor, next to the refectory garden, a dumbstruck Fairly struggled helplessly as a demented horde tried to rush past his entourage in search of hot water and plenty of it. He watched in horror as many of them mistook his lengthy canvas as a gigantic Kleenex. By the time the crush had passed, his masterpiece had been transformed from a multi-coloured melange into an unambiguous, scented brown statement.

Frank, looking on from the safety of the far corridor, managed a wry smile. He took off his levels and shouted across to *Frank*.

> – I always said your work was shit, *Frank*! How right can one be!

Frank seemed not to hear him. He stared at the devastation before him. There was nothing left. Absolutely nothing. His face was burning. His stomach felt as though it had been ripped open. There was just a dumb ache where there should have been no sensation. He turned his shell-shocked brain and headed for the exit. He made his way through the college, down the main corridor, looking neither left nor right. Down the slight incline, out of the gate, past the lights, over the one-way system and through the half-concealed door. He climbed the steps to the flat and vaguely saw the colour of the carpet for the first time. The distraction only lasted a moment but made him feel his anguish all the more. Within the narrowness of the flat he looked in vain for some other way to rid himself of the discovered pain. He turned to a discarded novel and buried himself in its lines: for a minute or two; for a while; for the time being for a day or so. He surfaced once in a while, only to find, the stifling presence of his pain. Through the while; through the anguish; through the long hours, he said nothing. Zoe appeared, but he seemed not to hear or see her. He read and read, trying to lose himself in the lines of the text. She made tea periodically; he seemed not to need it.

Three days later, in the small quiet hour before dawn, with Zoe still wrapped tightly around him, Frank reappeared unexpectedly.

– Every possibility of rear entry, *Frank*, he said hoarsely.

– Every possibility, Frank, replied *Frank*.

He knelt behind her, mesmerised at the wonder of it all.

– Jesus, *Frank*, he said in something of a panic.

For a moment he had forgotten who he was, but he remembered now. Instinctively he shouted for his crutch:

– Get the level, *Frank*! Get the level!

He tried desperately to hold on to Zoe's posterior while

Frank fumbled around for the level. A moment later he had it. Had it sighted and levelled, and not a moment too soon, as everything came together for all concerned.

> – Jesus, *Frank*, said Frank looking around him. Where are you?

He was surprised to find no response. *Frank* seemed to have disappeared off the face of the earth. He tore the level from his eyes. It clattered against the bed-side table, and in that moment, he found a big hole where *Frank* should have been. But it didn't seem to matter. Zoe was there now. He felt an overwhelming need to hold her tightly to him. She was wearing his red socks. *Frank* would have approved, he was sure.

> – *Frank*! exclaimed Frank with some surprise at *Frank's* sudden reappearance. Where did you disappear to?
> – Me disappear? What are you talking about Frank? You're one to talk. You're the one who's been AWOL.
> – What d'ya mean? *Frank*, said Frank in surprise.
> – I mean you disappeared just as things were getting interesting. Hot around the nether regions. No less.
> – No, *Frank*, said Frank with a finality that surprised *Frank*.
> – *Frank* looked at him as if seeing him for the first time in a long while.
> – Are you awake now, Frank?
> – You know I am, *Frank*. They looked at each other.

There didn't seem to be too much more to say. Except maybe, goodbye.

> – You're gonna miss me, Frank, said *Frank* sotto voce.
> – I know.
> – Don't forget though, Frank. I'll always be here if you need me.

– I'm counting on you always being here, *Frank*.

– You know I've been here these past ten years, Frank?

– I do now.

– Do you know where you've been staying, Frank?

– I'm gonna make it my job to find out.

– That's got to be a promise, Frank.

– I know.

– When did you find out?

– This morning.

– Say good bye, Frank.

– Good bye, *Frank*. Say good bye, *Frank*.

– Good bye, Frank.

*

One would normally expect an explosion in a major capital city to create something of a security issue. Especially one that had occurred in the middle of a crowded, formal college gathering. It should have landed Frank in jail for years. However, Frank's defence at his hearing had been impregnable. He maintained that the eruption was simply a part of his *Green Piece*. Its intent – literally and metaphorically – had been to cover the landscape of *Babblistic Art* with the necessary fertiliser for its renewal. It was clearly an act of self-sacrifice, since in the explosion, he had destroyed his own work for the greater good. It shouldn't have washed. But unexpectedly, events conspired to help Frank.

This particular chain of events began when Fairly received a phone call from Nolly La Valle, the acquisitions director of the East Hamling Museum of Modern Art. Nolly, a man renowned for having a nose that could sniff out an opportunity for publicity, offered Fairly a five-figure sum for his 'Flower Meadow'.

Fairly was dumbfounded. But only for an instant. Being the savvy media person he was, he quickly realised that the *Art World* was claiming the event as one of its own. Clearly, the explosion and the subsequent fallout, was going to be a godsend for his career. Not only that! He was going to make a small fortune from what he thought had been an absolute calamity. Not only that!! Surely!? He was bound to emerge from this as an artist of some significance. He hummed a little ditty as he contemplated a shopping spree and a prolonged holiday exploring the vineyards of Bordeaux: "O, happy day."

Fairly wasn't the only one who realised that 'where there's muck, there's brass'. Many of the guests who attended the private viewing had, of course, binned their clothes and initiated angry demands for compensation. But those attendees with a better understanding of the *Art World* realised straight away that they had been an intimate part of an event where an emerging major artist had expressed himself. Consequently, these *enlightened attendees,* carrying excrement-impregnated items of clothing, made a beeline for the major art auction houses. Needless to say, these vendors were able to follow in Fairly's musical musings.

As for Frank, with the *Art World* acknowledging him and with the support of the Dean and Miles, Frank not only avoided the fate of lesser mortals but was awarded a first-class honours degree. A post-graduate place was then a mere formality. Thus, the Dean secured the future of the Art School XI for the next three years, and Miles started looking for another PhD student. He would obviously need someone to research Frank's work. No sense in waiting twenty years to write up this important work…

*

As he walked out of the college after the hearing *Frank* stopped him with a nudge.

    – You still here, *Frank*? said Frank, somewhat surprised.

    – Jesus, Frank, will you look at that now, said *Frank*, pointing to a magnificent posterior in motion. That's a big girl, Frank.

    – That's my lovely, *Frank*, said Frank proudly.

    – She's still a big girl, Frank.

    – Some days, *Frank*, only a big girl will do.

    – Can I quote you on that, Frank?

    – I thought you were going, *Frank*?

    – Bye, Frank.

    – Bye, *Frank*.

Printed in Great Britain
by Amazon